PRAISE FOR

Once again Sara L. Jameson has dropped the readers into a twisting, high-stakes story that will have them flipping the pages to find out what happens next.

— PATRICIA BRADLEY, WINNER OF THE
INSPIRATIONAL READERS AWARD

Death
IN HIGH PLACES

SARA L. JAMESON

Scrivenings
PRESS
Quench your thirst for story.
www.ScriveningsPress.com

Published by Scrivenings Press LLC
15 Lucky Lane
Morrilton, Arkansas 72110
https://ScriveningsPress.com

Printed in the United States of America

Paperback ISBN 978-1-64917-270-9

eBook ISBN 978-1-64917-271-6

Editors: Elena Hill and Linda Fulkerson

Cover design by Linda Fulkerson - www.bookmarketinggraphics.com

1

Antwerp, Belgium, Day 1

In twenty-seven hours, she could be dead.

Glancing over her shoulder, Riley Williams scoped the pedestrians on the sidewalk in front of Antwerp's Opera House. Her breath whooshed out. No fisted daggers, no eyes riveted on her. A brisk September breeze fluttered the newspaper clutched in her hand.

At least they hadn't run her picture with the article.

American soprano who foiled terrorists in Antwerp in June debuts with *Vlaamse Oper* tomorrow evening.

All she needed was more publicity putting her on terrorists' radar. Terrorists who might decide to attend the performance. Finish the job they'd tried to do three months ago. Shudders rippled across her shoulders as she tucked the copies of the *Antwerp Gazette* into her tote bag. She'd need them for her press kit and scrapbook.

If she lived long enough to fill a scrapbook.

No. God had protected her last summer. He would be with

her now. Heels pounding the sidewalk, she strode toward the backstage entrance of the palatial opera house. Beaux Arts architecture, narrow medieval and renaissance gabled buildings —tucked between contemporary steel-and-glass structures. Modern-day Antwerp. She loved every bit of it.

Riley flicked a piece of lint from her navy pantsuit. She had too much riding on these performances to dwell on faceless terrorists. If she aced this gig, maybe the house would offer her a regular contract and she could work close to Brussels, to Jacob. Then, maybe—just maybe—they could set a wedding date. Unless Interpol sent him on another international assignment. She squared her shoulders and entered the opera house.

Curls spilling over her shoulders, she leaned over the porter's desk and scrawled her name in the register. A cacophony of scales and arpeggios floated down the hall as soloists and choristers warmed up their voices. Adrenaline pulsed through her veins. All her life she'd dreamed of singing on operatic stages. And now, here she was, a small-town girl from Cuero, Texas, living her dream.

If only Lacy were here to share it with her.

God had been so good to Riley. At twenty-eight, and only five years as a professional singer, her guest contracts were increasing. Thanks to God and her agent's efforts on her behalf. So many operas had roles for mezzo-sopranos and a coloratura. Riley swallowed the knot in her throat. But leukemia had stolen her twin Lacy's dreams, her life. Some sweet sixteen.

"Mrs. Schoonhoven is expecting you for a costume fitting in room three." The porter slipped the pen in his blue lab-coat pocket.

"*Dank U,* thank-you." The last Queen of the Night she'd replaced had been four sizes larger. Better that than four sizes smaller.

How much would this gown weigh? Pounds of boning and beading on heavy fabrics and hips panniered out the wazoo made her Mozartian-era costumes cumbersome. Not to mention a ginormous headpiece jabbed into her wig.

Inside the dressing room, Mrs. Schoonhoven waited beside a rolling clothes rack. "*Dag*, hello," she said, her voice crisp as a pair of shears. "Let's see now ..." Eyes narrowed like a mental tape measure, she raked Riley's body shoulder to heels. "You're taller than I expected." The seamstress turned to the rack, leafed through the black leotards and tights, and snatched a set. "Try these."

"Uh ... this isn't my costume, is it?"

"Didn't you know this is an avant-garde staging?"

"Nope." Contracts didn't spell out production details. Just the number of rehearsals, her pay, the performances dates. Penalties for cancellation.

Riley shed her pantsuit and blouse. Thank goodness she worked out and kept in shape. Stifling huffs and grunts, she squeezed her body into the spandex tights and leotard. On her five-foot-nine frame, the tights hit her calves like kiddie pedal pushers. Good thing she'd remembered to shave her legs. "What about shoes?"

"These are the director's choice." Lips pursed, Mrs. Schoonhoven dangled a pair of black combat boots from her fingertips.

If directors kept up this insanity, the woman would be out of a job. Wearing a pair of ped shoe-liners, Riley laced up the boots. As she strode across the room, the coarse plastic chafed her heels and mashed her toes. Ten more steps and she'd have bleeding blisters.

But the other boots on the shelf were perfect for Cinderella or too big for Goliath. Sighing, she sat at the dressing table. Mrs. Schoonhoven brought over the Queen of the Night's headpiece.

The contraption looked like they'd stolen it from Elsa Lanchester in the *Bride of Frankenstein*. Two-foot-tall spikes of silver-and-black metal poked from every orifice in the skullcap. Mrs. Schoonhoven slipped it over Riley's curls and pinned it in place. She winced as the underside of the metal tips scraped her scalp. Maybe she ought to rethink another contract here.

"What about makeup?" Riley was almost afraid to ask.

"*Ja.*" Mrs. Schoonhoven whipped a photograph from her lab-coat pocket and laid it on the dressing table. The model wore silver and black eye shadow winged like cat's eyes, extended to her temples. Red lips, glittered eyebrows, and red Fu Manchu talons that would shame a dragon.

"Hmm."

A knock on the door, and a perky teenager practically pirouetted into the room. "Let's get you ready, *Ja?*"

"I can hardly wait."

Muttering a Belgian hard-rock song under her breath, the young woman plunked her makeup tray on the dressing table and set to work. Four songs later, she tossed her pots and brushes on the tray. "*Voilà*, there you are."

"Right. Thank you." *I think.* While the four-inch talons dried on her nails, Riley stared at her reflection in the mirror. The rhinestoned glue itched and tugged on every hair of her eyebrows. All she needed was a diamond-studded leather jacket and a motorcycle for her entrance. A regular crime boss-lady. Don't. Give them. Ideas.

DRESSED, made-up, and voice freshly warmed up, Riley walked backstage. Heart pattering a little too fast. She snugged *The Magic Flute* score beneath her armpit and blew out a couple of breaths. The blocking should be easy to remember. All she had to do was walk on, sing two arias, speak a few lines, add her two bits in the finale. No wonder her contract stipulated a single rehearsal and thirteen performances. Time-saving, money-saving.

But potentially hazardous, since European dress rehearsals invited key people she and every other singer needed to impress. Journalists, agents, patrons, music critics. Writing up the production before the audience took their seats. She squelched the horror stories of botched stage entrances through the wrong piece of the set. Or worse. Nope. Nope. Wasn't going to happen.

A mere slip of a young woman in jeans and a sweater paced behind the side curtain in chic high-heeled boots. She pivoted toward Riley and raked her gaze over her headpiece down to the combat boots.

"*Dag.*" Riley stuck out her hand.

The young woman flicked her long braid over her shoulder, shoved her fists inside her elbows. "I'm your understudy." Her eye daggers said it all—you'd better be great, because I'm ready and waiting to take your place.

Swallowing, Riley forced a smile. She'd have to watch her step. This woman's sting could be as bad as a Texas cave scorpion. "Nice to meet you." Riley glanced at the stagehands waiting in the wings.

A scrawny man in shabby jeans stood against the back wall, a toolbox gripped in his hand. Black hair plastered to his head made his sharp-edged nose more prominent. Eyes beaded on her, he shifted his weight from foot to foot.

Why was he watching her? Stifling a shiver, she walked over to the lady tending the prop table. "I believe you have a dagger for me to give Pamina. And the locket the ladies give Tamino."

"No locket." The prop mistress handed her a cell phone. "You'll give him the cell with a photo of Pamina saved on it."

"Right."

The director must not have read the libretto and studied the music. How could Mozart's text and music work if Tamino and the three ladies sing about a locket/cell phone prop they should already have in hand ten minutes before the Queen made her entrance onstage? And now she arrives and gives him the prop five minutes after he's sung his love song to a portrait/cell phone he's never seen. If this was the director's idea of deconstructing an opera, she'd call it the destruction of a masterpiece.

Sucking a calming breath, Riley walked onstage. She squinted beyond the proscenium arch. A sea of dark heads among the stalls and seats. Focus. Focus. Not on journalists and music critics.

"Ah, I see our evil Queen of the Night has arrived." The orchestra conductor waved his baton in a salaam.

"Maestro." She leaned over the edge of the stage and shook his hand.

Not all the singers were Belgian. Thankfully, her fluency in German, French, and Italian should make communication easier. Probably no chance to use Romanian today. She turned and greeted the Bulgarian soprano playing Pamina, the lead soprano.

Thank heavens for singers' names on the posters outside the opera house. Guest contracts, tight budgets, and minimal rehearsals made bonding with her colleagues almost impossible. And dressing the huge cast in leotards and tights made recognizing a singer's role next to impossible.

Stroking her Rapunzel-length blonde wig, Pamina swept Riley from head to toe with her gaze, flashed a fleeting smile. Mrs. Schoonhoven had layered the soprano's generous girth with a gauze cape and skirt over her expose-all white leotard and tights. The poor woman still probably felt naked onstage. Then again, maybe not.

The tenor singing Prince Tamino grasped Riley's hand and kissed it. Somehow, he merited turquoise tights with white side stripes, a matching tank top that accentuated well- developed pecs, and a pair of snakeskin cowboy boots.

Riley glanced around the stage. No backdrops. A throne that looked more like a decrepit La-Z-Boy stood stage right. Probably for her alter-ego, Sarastro, Pamina's father. At the back of the stage stood metal scaffolding about ten feet high. A set of steps led to center stage.

A gulp knotted Riley's throat. No railing. Ten feet. Only ten feet. She could do this.

"Miss Williams, you look smashing." Slicking back his gelled hair, the director trotted up the house stairs to the stage. "Lars

Smitten." She shook his outstretched hand. With his Van Dyck beard, skintight black jeans, and turtleneck, he could pass for one of the cast.

"You'll sing your arias from the lift as it carries you around the stage." Lars pointed above. "First visible from the rafters."

"Lift?" Riley's voice squeaked. A motor whirred behind her. She spun and stared at a hydraulic lift lumbering downstage. The convulsing platform extended forty feet above the stage. Every inch of her lungs seized. *Dear God, no.* No way could she do this. "I—I don't do heights." The view from a high window invaded her thoughts. She shuddered. How long would that memory haunt her?

"I beg your pardon?"

"I'll puke. Or faint. I'll never be able to sing up there."

"But ..." Lars raked a hand through his hair. "Surely you know the Queen often appears onstage on a platform. Or sings from a catwalk."

"A stable catwalk, yes—but not from a *moving* contraption."

Wheezing like a convict on death row, the lift shuddered to a stop beside her. To her right offstage, the stagehand stabbed the buttons on the control panel. Nothing happened. Then the platform shuddered down to stage level. A backdrop, painted to look like a graffitied wall, had been weighted to the back of the platform. At least the lift had a railing.

"As you sing the roulades, the lift will move over the orchestra pit—"

"You want to do *what?*"

"It will be sensational. You'll be the talk of all Antwerp." His voice rose in near ecstasy. "Of all Belgium. Europe."

So would Lars and his staging. What choices did she have? Hand fluttering on her opera score, she gripped the music to her chest. If she refused, she'd be dubbed a temperamental artist. She'd destroy any hope of building her career beyond a smattering of house auditions and fewer guest contracts.

Acoustics in European opera houses were kinder to small

voices like hers. Most American opera companies hired only as guest contracts, and their venues had lousy acoustics, making it difficult for small voices to project.

Or she could marry Jacob. But right now, their relationship was about as stable as this lift, with his international assignments and her performances scattered across Europe.

Operatic roles she longed to sing flitted before her eyes. She could do this. All she had to do was make it through the runs, the high notes without cracking, no puking. Easy, right?

Heart in her throat, she climbed aboard. She braced her feet wide, gripped the handrail. Don't look down. Isn't that what they told mountain climbers? But with the delay hearing the orchestra from the stratosphere, she'd have to watch the conductor. Could she even see his baton from the next galaxy?

Offstage left, the stagehand jabbed a button and the motor hummed to life. As the platform swooped upward, a scream clawed up her throat. Jaws clenched, she clamped it off. *God, please help me through this.*

Shimmying left and right, the lift jerked to a stop, inches shy of the rafter's floodlights.

Within seconds, their searing heat scorched her skin through her black leotard. Sweat trickled into her eye makeup, stinging her eyes. Soon, she'd look like Alice Cooper. Then again, Lars would probably love it. After all, she was playing an evil queen.

Six miles below her, the maestro lifted his baton, and the Queen of the Night's ominous music wafted toward her.

Drawing a breath, she launched into her aria. What a laugh. Here she was, telling Prince Tamino not to be afraid. Manipulating him with her version of Pamina's abduction, pleading with him to rescue her daughter.

The lift's railing wobbled beneath her white-knuckled grip as the platform dropped her to ten feet above Tamino. What was she supposed to do—throw him the cell? Not missing a note, she leaned over the railing and extended the phone toward him like an imitation of Michelangelo's fresco, The Creation of Adam, God's finger reaching out, almost touching Adam's finger.

Upstage arm stretched toward her, Tamino leapt for the cell with the balletic grace of Nijinsky, but the chasm between their hands seemed twenty phones apart. Not her problem if her three sidekicks hadn't given him the cell for his aria minutes ago as he extolled Pamina's beauty. If they used their own phones, she could text him Pamina's picture. Or tomorrow night, she'd just toss him the phone. Either way, it'd fit with this ludicrous staging.

Seconds later, the orchestra launched into the aria's allegro section. The lift squealed to life, zigzagging left and right, as the stagehand mimicked the ascent and descent of her lightning-fast runs. Nausea churned Riley's stomach, threatened to spurt up her throat.

The phone fell from her hand and clattered on the stage.

Tamino darted forward and retrieved the cell. He stroked the edge of the phone, eyes tender as a lovesick lad.

Without warning, the lift lurched the other direction. Her ab muscles loosened, and her high F cracked. Heat flamed her face. No, no, no. She'd done the unpardonable.

Never mind the terrorists who might threaten her life—she wanted to sink through the stage floor trapdoor and die. She'd cracked on a high C.

2

Brussels, Belgium, Day 1

Urgent need to expose European terrorist financing and channels of distribution. Priority No. 1 assessment. Internet chatter suggests looming coordinated terrorist attacks.

Seated at his desk inside Brussels' Interpol Headquarters, Jacob Coulter reread the page. No mention of where they might attack. Or when. Or how. *Face it, Coulter. This isn't just about catching terrorists.* Ever since his best friend had died in Jacob's arms, trying to warn him and Riles had helped Interpol uncover terrorist cells on the riverboat cruise in June, Jacob had taken these assignments personally.

Sighing, he topped the towering memos in his inbox with this latest warning. Most were top-priority assessments. He yanked at the knot in his necktie. Intel analysts weren't magicians.

Two jiggles of his computer mouse, and his monitor screen sprang to life. These days, too many leads morphed into red herrings. Wasted time and manpower searching to the left, while the enemy took the castle on the right.

"Coulter." His new boss, Helga von Bingen, stood behind his chair. On the carpeted floor, her stilettos were as stealthy as an F-35.

Good thing he still wore his suit jacket. He rose to face her. Usually when she roamed the area, his colleagues tongue-clicked a warning then ducked their heads beneath cubicle walls.

"You've read the latest communique?"

"Yes, ma'am." Up this close, the mid-fiftyish bags beneath her eyes were hard to miss.

"Good." Her cool gray eyes raked him from his head to his well-polished shoes. "I'm changing your assignment." With the practiced touch of a wife, she adjusted the knot in his red silk tie, her breaths warming his lips.

Dealing with her was like crossing Niagara Falls blindfolded on a tightrope. Fist unclenched, he reached for his tie and tweaked the knot loose. Newly divorced von Bingen just didn't get it. He was engaged to Riles. "So—I'm to stop tracking terrorist cells?"

"For the time being." She fingered the strand of pearls circling the neckline of her gray sharkskin suit. "Your success uncovering the riverboat cruise plots was impressive. I'm assigning you to head an international team to find these financiers."

Inadvertently, his shoulders squared. Riles, with all her derring-do antics, had been equally responsible for the terrorists' apprehension. "Do we have any leads?"

"Precious little. Other than references to someone connected to sources in Vienna, Austria."

Why this leap in authority?

Von Bingen's eyes hooded like spring-trapped security doors. "We need to hit the terrorists at their source. Arrest these financiers, shut down their money-making operations. And that, my friend." She poked a well-polished nail in his pec. "Is your job."

"Yes ma'am." Perspiration pooled in his armpits. Maybe she'd set him up to fail. After all, he'd already spurned her squeezes on his shoulder, her fingernail trailing his temple.

Riles' ringtone broke the silence. He reached inside his pants' pocket, stilling the raging aria she'd chosen.

"A personal phone call?" Von Bingen's lips thinned to a gash.

"My fiancée."

"Tell her you're going to be working around the clock. We need a breakthrough on this case. Fast."

"Yes, ma'am." Riles wasn't going to like this. More nights apart. No weekends together. How much more separation could their relationship withstand, with him living in the office and her traveling around Europe, singing?

"I want the names of your team members before lunch today, and your first team meeting onsite tomorrow."

"Will do." And three solid leads on the identity of the financiers, no doubt. Problem was, American and European Union agreements prevented data storage on a person for more than five years. If they were hunting terrorists not in the current database, he'd have no names to give her. With terrorist attacks in the works, massive funding could be fueling their recruitment and training camps, logistics, purchase of weapons.

Von Bingen headed for the conference room where department chiefs were filing inside, coffee mugs in hand.

Back at his desk, the photo of Noel, Christine, and their infant son, pinned to his cubicle wall mocked him. Another self-promise he was failing to keep. Looking after Noel's widow and the baby. He'd envisioned helping her two or three times a week, to take care of little Noel. But Jacob's job kept him deskbound more hours than he was off each week.

God, help me find a way.

Tracy's snapshot was also pinned in the corner, dressed in her boarding-school uniform. Seventeen years between them—his parents' "surprise" baby. They'd been so eager to return to the foreign mission field, they'd plopped her in a British boarding

SARA L. JAMESON

school at the age of six. The poor kid had never known family life. But then, neither had he.

Shaking his head, he pulled out a legal pad, jotted the names of key financier-traffic analysts for France, Austria, Belgium, Germany, Spain, and the UK. Not that terrorist activities were limited to those nations, but their cities were known targets. While he waited for their response to his emailed invites to the group, he dialed Riles, twirling the pencil in his hand.

On the third ring, she answered. "Did I catch you in a meeting?" Her question mumbled around a mouthful.

"Yes." Keeping his voice low, he filled her in on von Bingen's kibosh on his free time.

"Bummer. I was hoping you'd come to Antwerp tomorrow night." More garbling he could barely interpret. "For my premiere."

"Are you eating lunch?"

"No. Burie's chocolates."

Ever since he laid eyes on Riles' press picture on the riverboat, he'd been smitten. How could he have believed she was working with the terrorists? The past three months had been like opening tiny windows on an Advent calendar and finding a sweet surprise inside.

"Is chocolate good for the voice?"

"Not exactly. But it's great for the soul. And dastardly for my hips. You don't mind if I sprout big hips, do you?" Licking sounds bled into the phone. "I really need your support." Shrilling up to one of her high *Cs*, she told him about the death-defying staging.

He jerked forward in his seat. Snatched a pencil from his desk. "That's insane." He needed to be there for her. Three months ago, he'd nearly lost her to the terrorists. "What are they doing to keep you safe on that lift?"

"They're going to oil it before tomorrow night. But the stagehand, Frans, must think he's playing with a joystick."

14

Chomping and lips smacking drifted through the mic. "Maybe I should buy a parachute."

"That'd work about as well as a pair of wings." He tossed the pencil on his desk. "Play the prima donna. Demand some sort of safety harness. A net." Heads peeked at him over the cubicle wall. Huddled over his phone, he lowered his voice. "Anything to keep you safe from harm."

"Right. Better get on that." Phone kisses smooched into his ear. "Love you."

Before he could respond, she'd disconnected the call. Would she take his advice or decide she could ace this gig on her own? Shoving aside his now-cold coffee, he sent up quick prayers. Thanks to all the press coverage after the river-boat cruise, Riles' face was now known to terrorists everywhere.

Terrorists focused on revenge.

Antwerp, Day 1

NO NEED FEAR THE TERRORISTS—FRÉNIE would kill Riley if she didn't mail her a box of chocolates. After all, what were best friends for? Who'd have thought their two years as graduate-level voice students at the National University of Music in Bucharest would stand the test of time and separation?

Riley stepped inside Burie's Chocolatier, famous for elaborate shop window scenes concocted of the confection for every holiday. Soccer matches, even a white chocolate replica of the White House. Whatever appealed to Mr. Burie.

Shelves of gifts and navy-blue boxes, hundreds of chocolates inside the glass counter, waiting to be devoured. She drew a breath and let the scent invade every molecule in her lungs. A dark chocolate on her tongue and she could cope with anything.

"Ah, you're back. And so soon." Wiping her hands on a towel, the clerk smiled at her.

"Half-empty, already." Riley jiggled her blue Burie's bag.

"I see." The clerk tapped the corner of her lip, the universal signal for food on your face.

"Oh, *Dank U*." Riley licked the corners of her lips, and the rich chocolate truffle melted on her tongue. "I want to buy a box for my friend." Then she'd take the next train back to Brussels and chill out in her apartment the rest of the afternoon. Cell in hand, she dialed Frénie.

"Only for your friend?" The woman's eyes twinkled.

"Uh, no. I need more emotional support."

"What size box?"

"A kilo. For each of us."

"A kilo. That is serious emotional support." Smiling, the woman poised her tongs over the trays of pralines and truffles.

Riley pointed to three of Frénie's favorites, then raised four fingers for the amount.

"*Allo, ma chérie.*" Frénie's French accent lilted into the phone, conjuring images of her friend's gamin face, her pixie haircut. So perfect for her career as a musical theater chanteuse. "Where are you?"

"In Antwerp, at Burie's. Buying us kilos of chocolate."

"A kilo? What's happened? Did you break up with Jacob?"

"No, no, nothing like that." At least, not yet. Bringing Frénie up to date on the rehearsal, Riley pointed to three more chocolates and held up five fingers.

"*Chérie,* my advice is—finish these performances, come to London and we'll see the sights. And you absolutely must meet Armand." Giggles erupted on the phone. "He is so—*oo-là-là.*"

"He must be wonderful if you'd give up your job on the cruise boat after we worked so hard to keep it." Subbing for Frénie and dancing with terrorists had been more than Riley had bargained for. "I thought you loved being an entertainer."

"I'm taking a sabbatical." Scuffling sounded in the background. Frénie whispered, "He's fabulously wealthy. Has his own private jet. Last month he bought me a red Lamborghini. Oh *chérie,* he treats me like Queen Cleopatra."

"Yeah, well. Things didn't turn out so well for her." Riley snarfed a truffle from her bag. If she'd learned one thing from her own dating disasters, wealth and looks could be deceiving.

"I tell you, *chérie,* Armand dotes on me. He's even promised to buy me a diamond necklace."

With a plethora of stones and twice Frénie's weight in carats, no doubt. "How did you meet him?"

"He was a passenger on the riverboat cruise six weeks ago. Oh, *chérie,* we danced together all night. Spent every spare moment together. When he invited me to come to London, how could I refuse?"

"Uh-huh." Riley restrained an eye roll. Simple, really. Just. Say. No. "What's he like?"

"He's so gentle, so kind. And very respectful of me."

"Well ... that's good." She wasn't so sure love was actually blind, but infatuation certainly was. The last thing she wanted for Frénie was a disastrous marriage. Stuffing another praline in her mouth, Riley stifled a shudder. They'd endured too much together. Arrests. Romanian Police interrogation. No-good boyfriends.

3

Brussels, Day 2

H is career could rest on not blowing this assignment. Jacob set his mug and laptop on the rectangular table. Outside the wall of windows flanking the conference room, architecture spanning centuries of styles spread to the horizon. The coffee soured in his stomach. Many of the neighborhoods were now home to terrorists.

Dear God, help us uncover these financiers.

Although he knew his team only by email correspondence, von Bingen hadn't blocked his choices. All top-drawer experts, each could light bonfires around his experience. Pushing aside his mug, Jacob opened his laptop. Hopefully he hadn't chosen any prima donnas.

Soft murmurs of conversation filtered down the hall. He straightened his tie, adjusted his cuffs as he moved to the doorway. His team filed in, laptops in shoulder bags and mugs in hand. Ian Harper, from the UK Interpol Headquarters in Manchester. Jean-Pierre Aubert from the Lyons office. Gunter Kraus from Munich. Margot Müller from Vienna. If any leads pointed to America, he'd liaise with national security organizations in Washington. One benefit of being an American posted in Belgium.

"*Guten Tag*, good day." Model-slender, Margot wore her black suit with panache, her dark hair in a bun that heightened her resemblance to the Duchess of Cambridge.

Of the teams' emailed lists of possible financiers, only she named a viable suspect.

Jacob took his seat, Margot across from him. "We're all fluent in French, English, and German. Any preference?"

"How about English. My German's a bit rusty." Redheaded Ian Harper, the first to accept the team appointment, plopped into the chair beside Jacob, then nudged his elbow. "How can we lure you to the UK office?"

"It's tempting. However, my fiancée works here."

"A pity. We could use a good man like you on our side of the Channel."

Navy sweater and rumpled cords suggesting a French college professor on sabbatical, Jean-Pierre slouched in the chair on Jacob's right.

Pulling a pair of half-lens readers from his coat pocket, Gunter sat next to Margot.

When he'd reviewed their creds, Jacob had taken a chance on Gunter Kraus. A gray-haired sixty to his own thirty. But Kraus brought decades of experience and wisdom to the group, whereas the other team members had only a handful more years than Jacob.

The team had divided into native linguistic groups. Next time he'd find a round table for their meeting. "While you're on site today, let's compile lists of bank transfers that might indicate money laundering, bitcoin transactions—"

"*Ja*, their new preferred method of laundering." Gunter chuckled.

"Any known cash couriers, narcotics smugglers, sex traffickers. Even charities. And individuals sympathetic to terrorists." Jacob waited while they tapped in notes.

"We're looking for half-inch needles in haystacks." Ian cracked his knuckles. "By the time we find one, Interpol will be too late."

"Not much prep time, but let's share what we have. We'll start with you, Margot."

"*Ja.*" She brought up a document on her laptop. "We've received numerous reports of a man called the Priest, whom rumors say, is a chief financier of terrorist cells and activities throughout Europe."

"*Oui?*" Jean-Pierre's bushy brows arched. "An actual priest?"

"Or it's a moniker." Gunter cleared his gravelly bass voice.

"Has anyone seen this priest?" Ian drummed a finger on the table. "Do we have any descriptions of him?"

"Our tip came from a street informant." Margot sighed. "But when we show up, there's no one dressed like a priest or anyone connected to terrorists or financiers."

"Perhaps there's an infiltrator inside your ranks." Jacob bounced his pencil's eraser-end on the table. Uneasy glances darted between his team. "Since we occasionally manage to penetrate a terrorist cell, we should assume they can do the same to Interpol." Swallowing, he tried to squelch the images of Noel dying in his arms, murdered by terrorists from the cell he'd infiltrated.

Phlegm rumbled in Gunter's throat. "So how do we flush out this Priest?"

"We try to track him down through his lieutenants." Jacob laid his pencil on the table. "The henchmen who do his dirty work for him, the fixers and facilitators."

"Are we assuming he's based in Austria?" Ian said.

"Possibly." Jean-Pierre shifted in his chair.

"I propose we focus on London." Ian's cheeks flushed. "Sadly, we're the European capital of money laundering ops, offshore unnumbered bank accounts, foreign oligarchs. Factors appealing to terrorist financiers."

"The Priest might not be someone on our radar," Jacob said.

"He may have fingers in multiple worldwide ops. In this age of jetsetters, he might not even live in Europe."

Groans rose around the table.

"Don't you Yanks have a jigsaw puzzle called, Where's Waldo?" Ian said.

Snickers rounded the table, but worried eyes locked with Jacob's.

"Yes. Based on the British book series, *Where's Willie.*" Jacob tugged at his necktie. The last thing they needed was a Where's-Waldo search across the continent. "Let's focus on money laundering ops in Europe. See if we can build on Margot's thread."

"Why not set up a sting operation and see if we can flush him out?" Ian continued his finger-drum.

Jacob turned to him. "What did you have in mind?"

"Do we have time to do this?" Margot, the practical one. "Mounting a sting requires finesse."

"Or should we concentrate on uncovering the terrorist cells they're funding?" Gunter rotated his mug in half circles. "Track a lead through them to the financiers."

"If we can eliminate much of their income ..." Jean-Pierre leaned forward in his chair. "These cells can't buy weapons, fund training camps, and live the high life."

A computer bell dinged. Margot clicked her touchpad, scanned the screen. "We're in luck. One of our more reliable snitches says the Priest will be in Vienna for a lunch meeting with a client at the Sacher Hotel."

"When?" Jacob's pulse quickened.

"Tomorrow."

FIGHTING the urge to loosen his tie, Jacob stood in front of von Bingen's desk. A schoolboy waiting for the principal to cane his knuckles. Apart from her white reveal-nothing coffee mug, there were no family photos, not even a potted plant. Only a broad desk, a chair for her victim's inquisition, and a credenza whose secrets remained hidden. And an impressive view of Brussels rooftops from the broad plate-glass windows. The décor of a transient, not expecting to stay long.

"Bring me up to date, Coulter." Von Bingen tossed a manila folder in her outbox.

In a few terse sentences, he filled her in on the team meeting. "We'll be doing daily Zoom meetings." Given the Machiavellian curve of her lips, she'd probably bugged the conference room. "The team is working from cubicles now, gathering intel. Researching shell corporations and creating lists of possible suspects for money laundering in core countries. And collating lists of known sympathizers to jihad."

"Think outside the box, Coulter. Look at wealthy hotshots not suspected of being jihadist sympathizers."

"Yes ma'am, we're already on that track."

Gaze zeroed on him, she leaned back in her gray leather chair, fingers working the padded armrests. "Well done." Her tone sounded as if the compliment pained her.

"Thank you." The woman made grown men feel like ten-year-olds earning gold stars for household chores. No wonder her husband ended things.

"I want you on a flight to Vienna tonight."

"But—" Tonight was Riley's debut in Antwerp. No way could he miss that.

"Get on it, Coulter." Von Bingen whipped open her laptop. "Now."

AT HIS DESK, Jacob scrolled through available flights from Brussels to Vienna. The latest one left Zaventem at eight. He flexed the knots in his fingers. Riley's performance wouldn't end before nine-thirty or ten. Then it would be nearly an hour back from Antwerp.

The train ride to Brussels was only forty minutes, but she'd be exhausted, and he didn't want her taking a night train without him. After dark, Brussels train stations were dangerous. She wouldn't reach her apartment before one in the morning. He opened a second tab and searched for hotels near the Antwerp opera house.

The opening bars of the Queen of the Night aria "*Der Hölle Rache*," "Hell's Wrath," tinkled from his phone. Riley. "Hey, thought you might be napping."

"Nope. I slept in until noon. I'm good to go."

"That's great." Images of her rented room in Claudette DeBeer's spacious apartment filled his mind as he pulled up a website for florists in Antwerp. The eighty-year-old opera lover had been ecstatic to have Riles move in. He chose a floral shop near the opera house. "Wish I could drive you to Antwerp, but I have team meetings all day."

"No problem. The train's fine. I reserved you a comp ticket on the second row. You can pick it up at the box office." The singsong lilt in her voice sounded like a kid about to blow out her birthday candles.

"Thanks, hon." He selected three baskets of roses, a dozen in each, and entered his credit card information. Tried not to flinch at the bill. Riles was worth every euro of it.

"You seem glum. What's up?"

"Hon, I can't make it tonight."

The silence on her end knifed his heart in two. Would their marriage be like this—choosing the life-and-death call of his job, missing milestone moments with Riles and their children?

"Oh. I see."

"Sweetie, I'm so sorry, but I have to catch a flight to Vienna."

"Couldn't you fly out tomorrow morning?" The wistfulness in her tone made him want to hop in his car and dash to her apartment.

"Tried that. I'd miss the meeting."

More silence on her end.

"Look, it's not the kind of meeting one can schedule."

"Oh." He could almost hear her sit up straight. "One of those." Her voice wobbled. "Can you text me and let me know you're safe?"

"Sure. No problem." He sagged in his chair. This was her debut in a leading role. He ought to be there tonight, cheering her on. That's what good fiancés did. But if he compromised the success of his assignment, people could die.

Von Bingen's office door swung open. Phone in hand, she headed for his cubicle.

"Gotta go." He smooched into the phone and closed the florist and Antwerp hotel websites on his screen. Checking them on his office computer had been risky. A computer probably under surveillance.

Reaching his desk in three strides, von Bingen held her phone in front of his face. The list of Austrian Airlines flights from Brussels to Vienna filled the screen. "I want you on the eight o'clock flight. And from now on, keep an overnight bag in the office."

"Yes, ma'am." At least she didn't tell him what to pack. Chest spread, he leaned back in his chair, lips clamped. One stroke of her pen and she could have him fired. But no way would he be her patsy. *Man, get a grip. You're a Christian. She's your boss.*

"Well—what are you waiting for? Book it now."

Heat surged up his neck. If only he could've been there for Riles. He turned to his desk and pulled up Austrian Airlines. Typed in his information and credit card number. Hovered his finger on the mouse. *Oh Riles. Forgive me.*

4

Antwerp, Day 2

Garbed in her reveal-all white leotard and tights, Pamina peeked around Riley's dressing room door. "Did you hear? The performance is SRO."

Standing Room Only. "Great." She hoped.

"*Toi, toi, toi.*" Pamina's eyes sparkled like firecrackers.

"Thanks." She hadn't a clue what *toi, toi, toi* meant. In America, they said "Break a leg" for good luck. She fiddled with her makeup brushes. Thirteen performances on that blasted hydraulic lift. Not that she was superstitious, but if Frans hadn't smoothed out her rollercoaster ride, she'd need a lot more than *toi, toi toi.* Worse still, breaking a leg would be the least of her injuries.

If she survived.

With an SRO house, maybe she should release Jacob's ticket. She tossed her makeup into her kit. Nope. Tonight she'd sing to his empty seat as if he were right there, cheering her on. Her parents would probably never make the trip overseas to watch her sing. Especially not Dad. *No daughter of mine is going to sing for a living.*

She tiptoed backstage in her combat boots and peered around the side curtain. The director wanted the house curtain open before the performance. Maybe Belgians grooved on bargain-basement staging. She scanned the front rows. Totally filled, except for Jacob's seat.

As the orchestra launched into the overture, she adjusted her spiky headpiece and crept over to Frans. "Did you fix the lift?" Somehow his thumbs up, gaze skittering left and right wasn't reassuring.

"Did you oil it?"

"*Ja*." Voice firm, Frans looked her in the eye. "It is oiled."

"Good. Thanks." She walked offstage, doing her deep breathing exercises to keep her vocal folds warmed. *Dear God, please get me through this.* If only she'd had a smooth run-through on the platform, she'd know she could make it through her arias without losing control, no cracking on the high notes.

The botched dress rehearsal was her nightmare come true. Maybe tickets sold hotter than Belgian waffles because of her flying trapeze act.

She paced the wing, sucking deep breaths and swinging her arms to relax. If only she could bribe Frans to limit the lift movements in her first aria to the opening slow section. There were almost no beats of rest in her second one, the tour-de-force aria audiences were waiting for.

Countdown to her first aria. The Queen of the Night's three trusty sidekicks were delivering their spoken lines with Prince Tamino. Soon they'd hop on their motorcycles, announce her arrival. Lucky ladies, riding onstage and off on honest-to-goodness Harleys.

Heart cowering in her boots, she stepped onto the lift. Gripped the railing with both hands. The platform shuddered upward. At least the oil job had fixed the squeal. She tried a few practice breaths. A pity she hadn't stood for the train ride from Antwerp and breathed through her arias, firmed and flexed her ribs and abs to simulate the runs and high notes.

Then she might've figured out how to stabilize her support muscles while being jerked her around like a rag doll. Instead, yesterday she'd stuffed her mouth with Burie's chocolates.

A hundred miles below, the conductor and the musician's reading lights winked like tiny shore lights from an airplane. The stage lights heated her metal headpiece, sizzling her scalp. If she didn't know better, she'd swear she'd been airlifted to the Sahara Desert. Melting makeup dripped down her cheeks. Every inch of her skin boiled and roasted beneath her black leotard and tights. Her tongue stuck to the roof of her mouth like flypaper. *Dear God, help*—no saliva.

Vocal folds needed lubrication to function well. The mere hint of nerves and a singer's throat dried out, but up here, baking under these lights ...

She scraped the bottom of her tongue over her teeth. A few measly squirts of moisture pooled in her mouth.

Why hadn't she stashed a water bottle up here? Black spots, white spots cavorted in loop-de-loops before her eyes. *God, help. I can't do this without You.* If Frans didn't lower the lift soon, she'd pass out.

The introduction to her aria wafted toward her. Yes. Yes, she could do this. Stance widened like a bad-girl biker queen, she clenched the handrail. The lift shimmied downstage then stopped, hovering fifteen feet above Tamino.

Beyond the stage, the audience was a black blur. Except for the conductor's stand light illuminating Jacob. His eyes beamed at her, and every inch of her skin tingled.

Thank You, Lord, for making a way for him to be here.

The last bar of the introduction ended. What would the lift do now? Boots glued to the platform, she launched into her aria, "*O zittre nicht.*" Sheesh. She ought to be singing "Don't Tremble" to herself.

As she sang to Tamino, commanding him to rescue her daughter, Pamina, she almost told him to rescue her instead.

Three beats later, the aria shifted into the fast section. Time for the vocal roller-coaster ride. The lift lurched to life, mimicking the direction of her vocal runs. Up. Down. Zigzags side to side.

Nausea rose in her throat. If Frans didn't stop the lift, any second now, she'd puke.

Somehow, Riley managed to support the runs, abs firm, ribs out, then nailed the high *F*. *Thank. You. Jesus.*

Applause swelled from the house, washing over her. Bravas echoed from the loges.

Staying in character, she held her stance while her hands palsied on the railing. Her arms and legs quivered like half-set gelatin. Wow. She'd survived.

The platform trembled beneath her boots. The lift bounced upward and zipped backstage at the speed of light, then swung offstage.

She staggered onto solid ground, armpits and leotard drenched with sweat. If the lift movements were any indication, things could be far worse for her next aria.

Too bad Mozart hadn't written another slow first section. But nope, he'd milked every opportunity to dramatize the queen's fury.

5

Antwerp, Day 2

The house lights rose for intermission. Imagine that—he'd survived sitting through half an opera. He'd have been more comfortable listening to country-western music back home in a Victoria, Texas, diner. Jacob scanned the three horseshoe-shaped tiers of seats rising along the green walls. The red-carpeted stairs in the ornate lobby had stolen his breath, but the matching red carpet and velvet seats were impressive.

He wouldn't have missed the experience for anything.

The plane he'd chartered to Vienna had drained half his honeymoon savings account, but seeing Riles' debut was worth it. As he scrolled through his email and text messages, the opera program and Antwerp newspapers fell from his lap to the floor.

Today's article detailing her disastrous dress rehearsal and the malfunctioning lift probably sold out the house. He snatched the pamphlet and papers from the floor. People were the same everywhere. Natural-born rubberneckers.

Ping. Why hadn't he thought to text Riles first? He reopened his text messages.

> Where are you? I'm at Schwechat Airport and you weren't on your flight.

Margot? She wasn't supposed to meet his flight. She flew home this afternoon. Fingers flying on the keyboard, he texted her.

> Sorry. Go home. I'm arriving at 2:00 a.m. Had to finish business here.

> Does von Bingen know? I heard what she told you.

> No. And I'd appreciate it if you keep my delay between us. I'll meet you at the rendezvous hotel in the morning.

> We really needed to discuss some things. In person.

His armpits moistened. Was she on the level or shooting for his job? He responded.

> What time would you like to meet?

Three dots bounced on the screen.

> 9:00 a.m.

He stifled a groan. Her info better be worth a sleepless night.

> Okay. See you at your office.

Since Riles hadn't mentioned her press coverage yesterday, he was doubly glad to be here. In case a few bad guys had read the article and sent an assassin.

He swiveled in his chair, his cop instincts kicking in, and

scoped the people milling in the aisles. Three years with the Dallas PD had greased the wheels when he applied to Interpol. That and an online/night-school master's degree and his foreign-language skills. He dug his fingers into the armrests. None of his training would save Riles if someone fired at her from the audience. He'd be sitting here, helpless. While she bled out.

He sent her a quick text.

> You were sensational.

> Thanks. I'm so glad you made it. Pray for me.
> This staging is a living nightmare.

> Sure. I'm here for you, hon.

Heavenly Father, give Riles whatever she needs to ace this performance. Surround her with Your angels.

Pocketing his phone, he scanned the house again. A sniper seated in the loges would have the best chance of hitting her.

A bell chimed, and the house lights dimmed. People traipsed back to their seats. Murmuring voices hushed, but the undercurrent of anticipation thrummed around him. He might have to learn something about opera. Especially since she'd said this role could catapult or tank her career.

As the conductor entered the pit, applause rippled through the theater. He motioned the orchestra members to their feet, then faced the audience and bowed.

Muscle fibers strung tighter than a guitar's D string, Jacob sat upright in his seat. Riles had said her next aria had been the riskiest on the lift.

ALMOST TIME for her second aria, *"Der Hölle Rache."* Dagger clutched in her hand, Riley mounted the lift. *Dear God, get me through this, please.*

The gears growled and whirred. The lift burped upward several inches, then sank to the ground.

Good. If the lift wouldn't move, she could sing this aria onstage, like a normal human being.

With a shriek and platform-rattling palpitations, the lift hiccupped upward foot by foot. Flutters rippled through her chest. Only twelve more performances. She could do this.

Pamina carried her bedroll onstage and laid down. A traditional production would've rolled a bed onstage so the soprano wouldn't have to struggle to her feet. Stage lights lit, and Monostatos crept toward her, singing his lecherous I-wish-we-could-be-together aria.

Thunder crashed from the percussion section in the orchestra pit. Monostatos fled offstage while the queen's three ladies-in-waiting *putt-putted* onstage on their Harleys. Riley's cue to enter. Pamina's cue to start their dialogue.

"Mother?" Pamina sat up on her pallet.

By now the lift should've been only five feet from Pamina. But at this height, she'd never be able to hand her daughter the dagger to kill her father.

For half a euro, she'd tell Pamina to stab the stage director.

"Mother?"

Without warning, the lift flew toward the rafters. Breath whooshed from Riley's lungs. Heart halfway out of her chest, she stifled a scream. Braced herself against the railing. What was going on? Yesterday, the lift had carried her downstage, albeit too high. Why couldn't Frans control the movement?

The metal bar wobbled beneath her one-handed grip. Instinctively, she flexed her knees for balance. Yesterday, she'd been able to lean against it. Her fingers white-knuckled on the dagger. She glanced at Jacob.

Eyes wild, he bolted forward in his chair, hands clutching the armrests.

Keeping her death grip on the metal rail, she balanced her weight between her thighs and combat boots. Maybe she should do her lines from here. Not wait for the lift to move. "Where is the young man—"

The lift jolted like a 9.0 California earthquake.

Her stomach lurched. Was Frans still trying to move the lift? Horrified gazes pinned to the machine, Pamina and the three ladies ran downstage, hands to their mouths.

The dagger wobbled in Riley's hand. Seats were costly. Management would expect the performance to continue. She finished delivering her line.

People in the front rows scrambled for their phones, aimed the cameras at her.

Great. Just great. Seconds from now her fiasco of a performance would go viral.

With everything in her she wanted to scream for help. Instead, she pointed the knife at Pamina and continued her spoken dialogue.

The aria poured from her throat, and the platform's arm plunged toward the stage. The dagger fell from her hand and clattered on floorboards.

The audience gasped.

Somehow, the words, the runs and repeated high Cs and Fs sailed from her mouth.

The orchestra segued into the four-measure interlude. Metal screeched, and the platform sloped downward, leaving the railing at an angle. Heart in her throat, she braced her legs as her hands iced on the rickety bar. Twenty feet above the stage floor, the lift shuddered to a stop.

Riley sucked a breath.

Help me, God.

The words and runs in the second section of the aria flowed from her mouth by rote memory. As she finished the last note, the lift plunged again, screeching like a banshee.

The upper end of the railing jerked free. Boots scudding on the surface, she fell to the platform. Red talons popped from her nails as she skittered toward the edge, clawing the metal floor.

She grabbed the end of the railing, wrapped her arm around the blessed pole, legs dangling off the lift, boots flailing the air over the orchestra pit.

How much longer could she hold on? If the other railing failed ...

JACOB LEAPED TO HIS FEET. Why didn't they do something—send help—stop the performance? Squinting against the bright stage lights, he glanced left, right. Steps. Steps. There must be stairs to the stage.

"Pardon me." He shoved past the people in the seats next to him and raced for the steps beyond the orchestra pit.

He scrambled onstage, darted toward Riles. Arms screaming in their sockets, he stretched upward, ribs distended until his muscles burned. No, it couldn't be. His fingers were still a foot and a half from the bottom of her boots. *God, help us.*

Fire flashed from Riles' eyes. How she stayed in character through this nightmare, he'd never understand.

Dear God, spare her. Don't let her die.

6

Antwerp, Day 2

Flicking his hand, Jacob signaled the ashen-faced stagehand to back the lift upstage.

The man's eyes bugged. He shook his head. Pointed at Riles, slashed his fingers across his neck.

"No choice. Do it." Jacob signaled him again. "Now."

With an ear-splitting screech, the lift jerked her back toward the stage.

Heart clobbering his throat, Jacob darted behind her. *C'mon, move, move*, he willed the lift. Three more spasms from the machine and the bottom of her boots floated toward him.

The orchestra launched into the fiery postlude.

Feet planted inches from the edge of the stage, he stretched upward, arms straining until his fingers brushed the tips of her boots. He was close—oh, so close. He lunged on his toes, locked his hands around her ankles, and her black-clad legs slid down his chest. Grabbing her waist, he seated her on his shoulder and stepped away from the orchestra pit. Tremors jittered her body against his.

As the orchestra played the final chord of her aria, the cable snapped. The lift crashed to the stage. The floor vibrated beneath his shoes like a barreling locomotive, threw off his balance. Abs gripped, he braced his feet wide.

Applause thundered through the house. Bravos roared over the stage. They'd done it. She'd survived. *Thank You, God.*

"Are you all right?"

"Yes, thanks to you." Her ragged breaths rasped across his scalp. "Let me down. I still have lines to speak."

"You're kidding."

"Nope."

The applause died down, and Pamina walked toward them, eyes full of questions.

And so was Jacob. Unlikely the opera house had been so grossly negligent. More likely, he was dealing with foul play. Forcing his shuddering leg muscles into a squat, he lowered Riley to the ground. If only he dared stay with her, make sure she was steady. Safe. But he backed offstage left as she staggered upstage and snatched her fallen dagger.

Flashing his Interpol ID, he walked over to the stagehand.

The man mopped a soiled cloth over his face. "I-I don't know what happened."

Jacob scanned the backstage area. Choristers. The other leads in the opera. A thin, young woman in jeans and a sweater stood near the entrance to the hall, clutching her long braid. Fear and belligerence mingled on her face like a cornered cat. Her eyes narrowed on him, then she disappeared into a group of supernumeraries.

"How much longer before the show ends?"

The man scratched his head, shoulders creeping toward his ears. "If nothing else happens, perhaps another hour."

Sheesh. Another hour to keep Riles alive.

"Miss Williams told me the lift wasn't working properly in rehearsal. Did you work on it afterward?"

Gaze ping-ponging left and right, he rubbed a grubby hand

over his mouth. "I put it through its paces. Oiled it. Checked the cables."

"Was the lift working smoothly after that?"

"Better. Just an occasional squeal. Maybe a few wobbles."

Yeah, right. Jacob bit the urge to tell him Riley could sue them for negligence.

"You know how it is, budgets are tight these days."

"And lives are precious." Jacob couldn't curb the venom in his voice. Riles might've been killed.

Shoulders slumped, the stagehand nodded, shifting his weight from foot to foot.

The musical numbers rolled past. Choruses, more dialogue, duets, and trios. All of it barely penetrating Jacob's senses.

Boots clomping on the wooden floors, Riles marched over to them, eyes piercing as daggers.

Good thing she'd given the knife to Pamina.

"What happened out there? Did you actually oil the lift?"

"Yes, miss. I did." Frans wiped his palms on his blue lab coat. "I swear I did."

"When?"

"Yesterday. As soon as the rehearsal was over."

"Thank you. I'm sorry I was rude." She wrapped her arm around Jacob's waist, the remaining red talons scraping his stomach. "If it weren't for you, this would've been my debut-farewell performance."

Avoiding her spiky headpiece, he snugged her sweaty body against his chest. "Glad I didn't take that flight to Vienna."

"Me too." The music switched and she yanked free of him. "Yikes. There's my cue. Time for the finale." Moving behind the wing curtains, she walked upstage then strutted down center stage, singing her lines.

He'd heard tales of performers finishing a show despite severe illness and injury, but how did she manage to keep going after all she'd been through tonight?

Minutes later, Frans cut the lights, and the cast lined up for a group curtain call. Pamina and Tamino stood at Riles' sides. As they whispered to her, she shook her head, wobbling that ridiculous headpiece.

One by one the singers stepped forward for a solo bow. Papageno and his bird-girl sidekick, Papagena. Sarastro, Pamina's father. Clasping hands in front of Riles, Pamina and Tamino stepped toward the orchestra pit, bowed, then moved aside. Riles walked forward and curtsied in those ridiculous combat boots. The house erupted in deafening applause.

Standing offstage, Jacob grinned. Pamina and Tamino had forced Riles into a solo bow as the lead singer.

The porter and two stagehands crossed the stage, carrying the three baskets of roses he'd ordered, eighty-five pinks, whites, and reds, and set them at Riley's feet. A basket for every month they'd been engaged. A rose for every day of those weeks. Tonight, she'd earned every one of them.

Her eyes widened, and her hand flew to her mouth. As she turned to him in the wings, a thousand-watt smile lit her face. "From you?" she mouthed. Nodding, he pressed his fingers to his lips and released them toward her. The lights glistened on the wetness in her eyes.

The conductor joined the cast onstage, kissed Riley's hand, then Pamina's. Embracing the audience with outstretched arms, the stage director jogged onstage in his black-velvet Nehru jacket and jeans.

Jacob shoved his fist in his pocket. Did the guy really think the applause was for his asinine staging?

Sweeping one foot behind him, the director bowed over Riley's hand with the panache of Sir Walter Raleigh.

Hand slipped free, she snagged one of the baskets and presented it to Pamina. Offered a red rose from the second basket to Tamino and one to the conductor.

Ouch. Jacob bit back a chuckle. Hopefully the stage director was too smitten with himself to notice her snub.

Air eked from Jacob's mouth. Only an hour ago Riles

could've died. He swallowed the lump in his throat. What he'd intended to bless her had nearly become bouquets for her coffin.

As the conductor joined the cast, Jacob spied the young woman in jeans and a sweater hurrying from the wing and headed toward the hallway, her long braid tapping her back.

He darted after her. "Stop, miss."

Glancing at him over her shoulder, she picked up her pace.

"Interpol." He flashed his ID. "Stop where you are."

She turned, crossed her arms, her face sullen. "What do you want with me?"

"A few questions. Who are you? Why were you backstage?"

"Annie Verhalen." She thrust her chin at him. "I'm the cover singer for the Queen of the Night."

The full-of-herself understudy Riles had told him about. "I suppose you think you should've been singing tonight."

"Maybe." She smirked. "You can be certain I wouldn't have turned the performance into a farce."

"So ... you're saying the lift wouldn't have failed if you'd been singing?"

Her jaw dropped. Clamped shut.

"Agent Coulter." Frans lumbered down the hall, still ashen-faced. "Come with me."

"Miss Verhalen, don't go anywhere. I may have a few more questions."

Arms crossed, Annie stomped beside him in her high-heeled boots as he followed Frans to the lift onstage. The steel arms, platform, and gear boxes lay scattered on the floor like the limbs of an extinct metal mastodon.

"Look." Joints creaking as he knelt, Frans pointed to several places along the black cables. "This has been cut." He scooted further. "Someone tampered with the screws on this end of the railing."

An invisible gut-punch stole Jacob's breath. Someone had tried to murder Riles. Pulse skyrocketing, he whipped out his cell and speed-dialed Inspector Vlincke's private number. The Antwerp police, and especially Vlincke, had been helpful when Riley and he had tracked terrorists in Antwerp last June. The inspector answered on the first ring.

"Ah, Agent Coulter. Hearing from you at this hour of the night, I presume it isn't good news."

ANTWERP, Day 2

Jacob had no choice but to leave the investigation to the police. If anyone could put fear into Annie, it would be steely-eyed Vlincke. Outside the backstage entrance, Jacob grasped Riley's elbow, the flower baskets gripped in his other hand. "Hate to rush you, but I've got a flight to catch."

Still in her slinky black costume, Riles clomped beside him in her combat boots. "After tonight's fiasco, I need to sterilize my leotard and tights before the next performance."

"What's with all the roses?" She slipped into the front passenger seat. "You aren't breaking up with me, are you?"

"No-no." He struggled to squelch the rise in his voice. Was she having second thoughts about their engagement? They'd had so little time together since the night he'd proposed on the riverboat cruise. "Actually, it was more of a guilt offering."

"Thank you, Prince Charming." She stroked his cheek with her remaining red talons. "The roses are stunning. I feel like a pampered queen."

Buckled into the driver's seat, he reached across the console and clasped her fingers. "You were phenomenal, hon."

"Right. A regular Flying Wallenda, straight from the Barnum & Bailey Circus." She worried off another layer of her red lipstick, leaving red streaks on her front teeth. "What is it with me, turning every role I sing into a Laurel and Hardy routine?"

She turned to him, her carpet-fringe lashes batting back moisture. "Last year Düsseldorf called my performance in *The Land of Smiles*, slapstick."

"Look at it this way." He pulled a tissue from his pocket and dabbed her tears. Black and silver makeup smeared the tissue. "You not only defied death, you nailed every high note *and* every one of those fast notes."

"I can hardly wait to see the newspapers tomorrow." She thumped her elbow on the windowsill. "The critics will probably trash my performance."

"More likely they'll focus on the mechanical failure of the hydraulic lift, what a trouper you are, and how brilliantly you sang." And if the press talked to anyone backstage after the performance, they'd play up the suspicion of sabotage. He jabbed the key in the starter. Somehow, he'd see the perpetrator put behind bars. For life, if possible.

He shifted into first gear, bit his cheeks to stifle a grin. If her life hadn't been in danger tonight, her antics would've been hilarious.

"Maybe now Lars will let me sing from stage level."

"If he has a compassionate bone in his body." But the guy had looked more than elated onstage. He was probably scouring Antwerp for another hydraulic lift. Easing into the traffic, Jacob updated her on his new assignment and the team meeting. His trip to Vienna. Anything to keep her mind off tonight.

"Terrorist financiers often hold prominent positions in the business sector. So do their fixers and facilitators. They're wealthy and well educated. They consider extremists expendable. But the masterminds behind the plots are often the professor or lawyer types. Their cover is deep and squeaky clean."

She rested her hand on his arm. "Wish I could help you."

"No. Stay out of it. Stay safe."

"Maybe the Priest is legit, an infiltrator in the church. You know, sent to seminary to learn the ropes, the lingo. Witches and

Satanists have been known to pass ordination, hold positions in Christian churches. It would be a great cover."

"Whoa—hold on there."

"What's so odd about a terrorist pulling it off? Anyone trying to infiltrate one of their cells lives and breathes the doctrine or he doesn't survive."

"Yeah." His palms iced on the steering wheel. Even then, discovery was only a heartbeat away. He and Noel had learned the hard way.

"Are you traveling alone?"

"I'm meeting a team member at the Sacher Hotel in a few hours."

"Hmm. Female?"

"Margot Müller. She's stationed in Vienna and the only team member with a serious lead." And the potential to blackmail him for going AWOL tonight.

"Yay, Margot. Go for it." Riles shifted toward him, a streetlight glinting on her rhinestoned eyebrows. "Is she single?"

"I didn't ask."

"Is she pretty?"

He almost blurted out yes. But so was Riles when she wasn't made up to look like a Goth queen.

"Should I be worried?" A frown bunched her glittering eyebrows. "You might decide a relationship with a fellow agent has more future than one with a traveling circus performer."

"Honey." He pulled her hand to his mouth and kissed her fingers. "She's a teammate. Not my roommate."

7

Vienna, Day 3

A few more sleepless nights, and he'd be useless on this case. Jacob stifled a yawn. The security guard behind the Interpol lobby desk returned his ID.

A manila folder under her arm, Margot paced the hallway. She thrust a Styrofoam cup of coffee in Jacob's hand. "Here. You look like—"

"Something the cat rejected from the garbage bin." Despite a fitful sleep, he'd barely managed a cleanup and a fresh suit before heading to her office. During his flight to Vienna, he'd been too worried about the sabotaged lift to doze off. "What's the new scoop?"

"So ..." She stared at him for a long moment. "Was the performance worth risking von Bingen's ire?"

"Necessary, yes." Meeting in his hotel room might've been her first choice, but no way was he compromising his relationship with Riles to hear Margot's new info. He told her about the sabotaged lift. "Given the pre-performance press coverage, the culprit may be a terrorist or someone a cast member paid to do the job."

"Yes. Our office has heard of your fiancée's prowess catching terrorists." She flicked a piece of lint from her black suit.

Margot looked every inch the up-and-coming bureau chief, a position she'd probably penciled in on her to-do list. "Yesterday you said the news was urgent."

"A priest found a body inside *Stefansdom*, the cathedral. In the tower. There was a silver cross necklace draped on the victim's chest." She pulled a glossy photo from the manila folder.

Sipping the über-hot coffee, Jacob studied the picture. The man's body had been propped next to the edge of the parapet, a jagged slit across the victim's throat. "Is he in your database?"

"Carlos Sanchez, a Spanish national. We suspect he was a courier for money laundering operations." She punched the elevator button.

"Maybe he gave himself an unauthorized pay raise."

"One of our street informants said this is the work of the Priest." The elevator doors glided open, and she stepped inside.

"How so?" He followed her, sipping his coffee.

She pushed the button for the ground floor. "Word on the street is, the silver cross is the Priest's calling card."

"Have you found other bodies with a silver cross?"

"Yes. Although we didn't make this connection at the time." The elevator opened, and she strode toward the front doors of the building. "Last night I ran data on our unsolved murders during the past five years. Three of them mentioned a silver cross necklace in the possession of the victim."

"Great work." He tossed his coffee in the trash and followed her down the steps. "So now all we do is follow a trail of silver crosses throughout Europe."

"*Ja*." Her black heels clacked on the pavement as she walked him to the parking lot. "Like Hansel and Gretel and their trail of breadcrumbs."

"Yeah. Didn't they end up at the wicked witch's hut?"

"It's also an opera."

"You don't say. If you don't mind, I'd like to visit the murder site now." He hopped in his rental car and followed her to the Sacher Hotel where they were to have lunch. Mere steps from the murder scene. Maybe he'd misjudged Margot. Giving him the photo at the hotel would have been inappropriate. These days, your waiter could be a terrorist sympathizer, or a part-time jihadist.

At the top of the Stefansdom South Tower, there was little memorable, apart from the muddy Danube River, rooftops of the historic inner city, and dark stains where the victim had bled to death. A winding staircase of 343 steps and no elevator.

But standing where the crime had been committed might reveal aspects not evident from police photos. While Margot waited, he did another slow three-sixty. What was he missing here? Why lure a man up here to kill him? Why prop up the body?

An hour later, Jacob stepped back a century in time as he set one foot across the threshold of the Sacher Hotel's Rote Restaurant Bar. Images of Viennese tortes, *Milchrahmstrüdel*, and a waltz or two danced in his head. *Focus, Coulter. You're on assignment—not a date with Riles.*

It was the type of place he'd love to bring her. Intimate, elegant. Posh in capital letters. Breathtaking chandeliers, paintings of Kaiser Josef and others he didn't recognize. White tablecloths, red damask walls, a scarlet ceiling. A perfect setting for a lover's *tête à tête* or a clandestine business transaction.

Had Riles ever eaten here? Before they'd met, she'd lived in Vienna for five years.

As he walked Margot to their table, red damask carpet muffled his footsteps. He muttered in her ear. "Why didn't you tell me to pack a tuxedo?"

"I thought James Bond never traveled without it."

"Remind me to keep mine at the office." Von Bingen ought to be grateful the Priest hadn't chosen the hotel's Grüne Bar, where a main-course tab could reach 145 euros. He seated

Margot at his side. Nothing but Gucci-heeled guests—not a silver cross in sight.

Maybe he could hold up a sign lettered, "The Priest," like drivers did at airports. *Sleep, Coulter. You need sleep.*

At a corner table for two, a Roman Catholic cardinal forked a bite of Wiener Schnitzel. His scarlet robes matched the wallpaper. Seated with his back to Jacob, the Cardinal's guest wore a suit that reeked of mega-euros, hair gelled to perfection. A pity he couldn't see the guy's face. Sunlight glinted through the window, reflected on the silver chain and cross around the prelate's neck. Surely he wasn't the notorious priest.

The Cardinal glanced his way, and Jacob opened his menu.

Menu shut beside her, Margot activated the listening device on her cell then scrolled through emails. They probably wouldn't capture anything of use among the muted conversations. Flashing him a besotted smile, she slid her hand over his, her fingertips cool on his skin. Were they posing as an old married couple? Riles would kill him. He slipped free and shut his menu.

The waiter left with their orders, and Jacob surveilled the other guests. Zeroed in on two men at the end of the dining room.

Shoulders hunched beneath his ill-fitting suit, a little man traced the base of his wine glass like a rat in a cage. A sheen glistened above his lip. Seated across the table, his dining partner towered over him. His gray suit fit his bodybuilder physique like a hand-tailored glove. And if Jacob's guess was right, the man was packing.

Gorilla Guy's razor-eyed gaze roamed the room like a seasoned pro.

Jacob's pulse quickened. A hit man, an enforcer, or had they stumbled onto the Priest? After all, the tip had claimed he'd be here today.

"Text for backup. Tail a tall guy in a gray suit, with a Neanderthal jaw and a neo-Nazi brush-cut, when he leaves." If he leaves. Gorilla Guy might be staying at the Sacher Hotel. In which case, he and Margot would stick out if they hung around this afternoon. No doubt the man had memorized every face in the room. During his Dallas cop days, Jacob had run into the type dozens of times.

The waiter delivered their meals. Stomach rumbling, Jacob tucked into his *Tafelspitz*, Austrian boiled beef, barely aware of the horseradish sauce on his tongue. His last meal had been a vending-machine sandwich on his drive to Riley's performance twenty hours ago.

Breaking off a piece of roll, Gorilla Guy dabbed it around his plate and stuffed the bread inside his cavernous mouth. He tossed his napkin beside his plate.

"Hate to leave you with the tab, but our chief suspect looks ready to bolt." Jacob laid his fork and knife on his barely touched plate.

"No problem. I'll follow the cardinal when he leaves."

"Text me your agent's number in case I lose Gorilla Guy."

While she typed in the number, Gorilla Guy flicked a finger at the waiter and pantomimed a signature in the air.

Swallowing the meat in his mouth, Jacob forked another bite. The best meal he'd eaten in weeks, and he'd have to leave most of it on his plate. He stabbed a parslied potato.

A diamond-studded signet ring sparkled under the chandelier as Gorilla Guy slid a wad of euros in the leather folder. He handed it to the waiter who bowed and backed away. Great. An untraceable transaction. Gorilla Guy muttered something to his dinner partner, who blanched, head bobbing like a Kewpie doll.

Lunch over an unpaid money-laundering debt? Hand to his lip, Jacob leaned over the table. "Think you could find an excuse to detain his lunch mate for questioning?"

"I'm sure we could think of something." Margot glanced over her shoulder toward the table in the back. "Kraus is in the lobby. I'll have him take care of it." She texted a quick message on her cell.

Seconds later, Gorilla Guy stood. One hand tweaked his

jacket button over a bull-sized rib cage while his searchlight gaze swept every patron. Landed on Jacob.

Eyes down, Jacob forked another bite. No way could he follow the guy. He'd be made in half a heartbeat. As for the man's cohort, best keep his Interpol connection secret, especially if Margot couldn't arrest the man.

Gorilla Guy strutted across the dining room, patent-leather shoes squeaking. At the doorway, his brush cut nearly scraped the top of the door frame.

As her cell pinged, Margot tilted it toward the wall. Her lips curled upward. "Our man has your man in sight."

"Good. Tell Kraus to tail him. I'm sure I'm on this guy's radar." If the suspect was the Priest or could lead them to him, maybe they could wrap up this case quickly. Once they had enough proof to make a conviction stick. Jacob dabbed his mouth with his napkin. He could almost taste the victory. With the strongman's head lopped off, the little ones might scatter, short of cash.

A BREEZE WHIPPED Jacob's suit jacket as he dashed across the parking lot at Schwechat Airport, cell pressed to his ear. "What's the scoop, Kraus?" Given the ten-car pileup on the autobahn, taking the airport train from Vienna might've been faster.

"Not good, I'm afraid."

Lead weighted Jacob's shoulders. Five years with Interpol should've taught him by now. Cases like this seldom solved themselves in a day, a week, or a month. Inside the departures lobby, he surveilled the milling crowds, families with children and luggage. A single man off to his right walked toward him. Kraus' face matched the photo Margot had forwarded. Wavy hair trimmed short, black suit hanging from his small-boned frame. Dark eyes peered from a face barely old enough to shave. Jacob scanned the room. "How bad is it?"

"I lost him on the autobahn. My car spun off the road in that pileup. By the time I arrived, he was nowhere in sight. Took me half an hour to check every airline before I found him. With a mug like his, the airline agent recognized him immediately. He's on a flight to Paris. A first-class seat, using the name Roman Lachalle."

"Probably carries a slew of forged passports in his pocket. Did you get a picture of him?"

"Not the best." Kraus tilted his cell toward him. The grainy profile captured Gorilla Guy's Neanderthal profile as he left the Sacher Hotel. "The agent said he arrived with a carry-on, barely made the boarding call."

"He may have canceled a flight elsewhere and picked the first plane out of Austria with an available seat. To throw us off scent." Had his and Margot's cover been blown as easily as the suspect's? "Maybe switching flights and IDs is his standard M.O."

"Will you be following him?"

"No. He's seen me. I'll alert our man in Lyon to meet the flight." Jacob's cell rang. "Thanks for your help."

"Any time."

Walking toward the Austrian Airlines check-in desk, Jacob took the call.

"Inspector Vlincken here. We've arrested Annie Verhalen's boyfriend on suspicion of sabotaging the hydraulic lift. Can you attend his interrogation?"

"If I can catch a flight from Vienna."

"Good. Keep me posted. He could use a night drying out in the cell."

8

Antwerp, Day 4

Straightening his tie, Jacob hurried inside the Oudaenstraat Police Station. The architect must've had a sense of humor. Why else design the exterior to resemble an enormous Belgian waffle? He crossed the lobby and shivered. Poor Riles. Vlincken grilling her here as a suspect three months ago. Her hours searching Interpol databases for mugshots of the terrorists she'd tried to tail.

The elevator doors opened. Vlincken stepped out, all six feet of him, white thatch of hair, still unruly, suit as dingy beige as the centuries-old buildings outside. Jacob's own suit looked as if he'd slept in it for a week.

"Glad you could make it." Vlincken's handshake could crack walnuts.

Trying not to wince, Jacob nodded. "Thanks for letting me attend the interrogation."

"It took some effort, but we located Annie's boyfriend, Dierck van Tromme, in a bar, drinking himself into a stupor."

"Drowning his regrets?"

"Something like that."

"Any priors?"

"Doubt he'll win Antwerp's Citizen of the Year award, but only a couple of unpaid traffic tickets." Vlincken motioned Jacob inside the interrogation room. Jacob almost gagged at the reek of sweat and urine and stale cigarette smoke.

Seated across the table, Dierck jiggled one knee like a jackhammer, hands thrust beneath his skinny-jeaned thighs. Moisture pimpled the edge of his greasy hairline. A few oil streaks across his T-shirt completed his fashion statement.

In one smooth move, Vlincken sat next to Jacob, set a recorder on the table and mirandized Dierck. "How long have you been dating Annie?"

"Hmm." Dierck flicked his head, but the lock of ash-blond hair flopped on his forehead. "Maybe ... four years?"

"Your booking record says you're twenty-eight. Annie's eighteen. Isn't she a bit young for you?"

Scarlet patches mottled his cheeks. "Well. You know. She's uh —good in—" The flush in his face faded to gray. Math wheels almost visibly whirled in his eyes. Annie had been a minor when they met.

"So, why'd you do it?" Vlincken tilted his chair back on two legs, fingers thrumming the table like snaps of a whip.

"Do what?" Dierck's voice shifted to falsetto, cracked.

"Sabotage the lift."

"I—I didn't do it. I swear."

"That's not what your girlfriend says."

Dierck's eyes bulged. "No. I don't believe you." His hands flew to the table, flexing, fisting, flexing. "She wouldn't—she didn't—" Lips clamped, he slammed his fist on the table.

"You know how women love to talk." Vlincken thumbed his well-trimmed nails. "Annie seems pretty full of herself. A real prima donna."

Mimicking a drama-queen eyeroll, Dierck snickered. "Yeah."

"The type who uses others to do her dirty work."

"I told you." Dierck scowled, squirming on the chair. "I didn't do it."

"Your booking record says you're an auto mechanic."

"So what?" Dierck's shrug morphed into a nervous tic. "It's a good job."

Jacob cocked his eyebrow at Vlincken. He should've asked beforehand if he could question the suspect. But his invitation today was a courtesy, for Riley's sake.

"Be my guest." Waving a hand toward Dierck, Vlincken thumped his chair legs on the floor.

"Thanks." Jacob slouched in the chair, scratched above his ear. "Don't know about you, Dierck, but I've never been much of an opera lover."

Another nervous-tic shrug.

"In fact, the other night was my first time to see one. How about you?"

"I go sometimes. To see my girl."

"And you hang around backstage with her, right? To keep her company."

"Sometimes."

"Like the day of the dress rehearsal."

Chin jutted, he bugged his eyes at Jacob. "So?"

"So, why weren't you there for the opening performance?"

Glances darting around the room, Dierck gnawed his lips as if he hadn't eaten in a week. His eyes flashed like the click of a mental light bulb. His mouth shifted into a gotcha smirk. "Because the tickets were sold out."

"But you were seen backstage before the performance." Jacob hadn't a clue if that were true. Or what Annie had told Vlincken.

"We found your fingerprints on a pair of cable cutters near the lift." Vlincken crossed his arms over his chest.

Sweat trickled from Dierck's temples. He swiped a hand across his stubbled jaw. Oil stains etched the skin around his fingernails. "I told you. I'm innocent. I didn't do it."

"Do what?" Jacob shot the words at him.

"Cut the cables."

"But you loosened the screws on the railing."

"No, no. I didn't do that." Dierck's shriek pulsated in Jacob's eardrums.

"For someone who claims he didn't commit the crime, you seem to know a lot about the damage."

"I—I—" Dierck's T-shirt heaved and shuddered. The soured exhales curdled Jacob's stomach.

Clearing his throat, Jacob turned to Inspector Vlincken. "What's Dierck's prison sentence likely to be?"

"I think the prosecuting attorney mentioned going for the maximum. Thirty years."

"Thirty years?" Dierck leaped from his chair. "I'm not going to prison for something I didn't do."

Fists squeezed in his lap until they throbbed, Jacob tried for a calming breath, but his gut seized. "Looks like you've caught your man, Inspector. He had motive and opportunity. Even knows the details of the sabotage."

"*Ja, ja*. And then there's the testimony of his girlfriend."

Jacob nodded. Annie hadn't looked capable of the sabotage, but she was a class A manipulator. And Dierck had been smitten.

"Annie's ready to swear you did it." Vlincken's flinty tone matched his steel-trap gaze.

"All right. All right." Dierck writhed on the chair, raked a hand through his hair. "I went backstage after the dress rehearsal. But Annie had been begging me, egging me on. You know how women are. She said we wouldn't be caught. Said it would help her career. I didn't want to lose her. She's like—really good ..." He slumped in the chair. "She's all I've got."

"So, how'd you do it?" Jacob struggled to bury the snarl in his voice.

"I told Annie I would slice the cables—" Head drooping toward the table, Dierck palmed open hands like a saintly penitent. "But not all the way through. After watching how that platform jerked around in rehearsal, I figured a partial cut would do the job ..." He cleared his throat and mumbled, "Once the lift was in motion."

"Then you went to the bar to celebrate." Vlincken sighed. "To give yourself an alibi."

"To celebrate the death of an innocent woman." The words choked off in Jacob's throat.

"No, no. It wasn't like that at all. I was scared."

"Scared?" Vlincken snorted. "Scared you'd be an old man when you get out of prison? No woman would want you."

"You've got to believe me. I'm telling the truth. When I went over to the lift that afternoon, someone had already cut the cables. Messed with the railing."

IN AN INSTANT the sabotaged lift had become Interpol's jurisdiction. His domain. Fists jammed in his trouser pockets, Jacob stared out Vlincke's office windows. After witnessing Dierck's behavior and terrified sobbing, he was inclined to believe the guy was telling the truth. And if lover boy was innocent, then they couldn't rule out terrorist sabotage.

"Almost hate to say this." Vlincke handed him a mug, the scent of coffee rising from the curling steam. "Based on our police interviews, I don't think anyone else at the opera house seemed to dislike Miss Williams."

"I agree." Jacob sipped the coffee, the heat searing a trough in his throat. He set the mug on Vlincke's ultra-tidy desk. Not a photo or file in sight. No inbox overflowing with top-priority memos.

"When we interviewed the performers, everyone said she sang brilliantly. Given all the press coverage, we're probably dealing with an outside attack."

"Yes." Jacob slammed his fist against his palm, the slap stinging his skin. "And as of three days ago, I've been assigned to track down terrorist financiers, not jihadist cells." Not assassins with a vendetta against Riles.

"I suppose congratulations are in order."

At the moment, Jacob wasn't so sure. If only he could be assigned to her case, her protection detail. Keeping her alive on the riverboat cruise had been a night-and-day job.

"There is also the matter of Annie and Dierck's intent to harm Miss Williams. Under the Belgian Criminal Code, Article 327, Dierck's confession makes them liable to a prison term from six months to five years, plus a fine of one-to-five hundred euros. Shall I call Miss Williams in to see if she wants to press charges?"

As far as he was concerned, the question was moot. "If the lift hadn't already been sabotaged, Dierck would've cut the cable."

"True. But speaking as a father, pressing charges might make for uncomfortable relationships in the opera house for Miss Williams. As an ... uh ... American singer in a foreign country. However, as a police officer, I believe they need to pay for their intended crime."

Much as he wanted to tell Vlincke to lock those two in Belgium's dankest dungeon, Riles needed to make the decision. "I'll give her your message."

"In the meantime, I'll have the security camera videos pulled for you to view. Perhaps we'll be lucky and spot the perps."

"Good." Riley's ringtone aria tinkled from his pocket. The blasted aria that had nearly killed her. He excused himself and stepped to the corner of the room. "Hey, hon, where are you?"

"At home, but the general manager of the Antwerp Opera wants to see me."

"I'll come get you." He hadn't meant for panic to grip his voice. Too late now.

"What did you find out from Vlincken?"

"Annie and her boyfriend intended to sabotage the lift."

"Wow. It's a cutthroat profession, but sabotage—"

"They didn't do it, Riles."

"Then who did? She was the only one at the dress rehearsal who seemed antagonistic."

"The case is being assigned to Interpol. The counterterrorist division."

Her gasp, the exhale *chuddered* into the phone. More than anything, he wanted to be with her. Hold her in his arms and comfort her.

"Stay in the apartment until I get there. Do not go out without an escort."

"You think those newspaper articles are responsible, don't you?"

"Yes. So does Inspector Vlincken."

"Maybe now Lars will let me enter the stage on the ground."

"I'll make certain Interpol backs that decision."

"Thanks."

"If possible, I'll hire private bodyguards. A female to stay with you in the dressing room at the opera house. A guy for backstage, if I can find someone I trust." The man Interpol had assigned her three months ago had been working undercover for the terrorists. "I—I just wish I could do the job myself."

"Me too."

Antwerp, Day 4

SEATED across the general manager's ornate desk, Riley smoothed her navy pantsuit jacket. Once they paid her, she'd buy a new outfit. Something sophisticated, for meetings with the brass. Maybe today he'd offer her hazardous duty pay to sweeten the job. After all, she could've died.

"A stunning performance, Miss Williams." Mr. de Groot laced his hands on his desk, his charcoal suit as elegant as his manner. "The likes of which ..."

"I hope never to repeat."

Breath fell from his mouth as his shoulders sagged. "Exactly."

"I'd like you to make sure the concept for my scenes is changed. No more hydraulic lifts. I enter and exit and sing from stage level."

"I assure you, there will be no more hydraulic lifts used in this production."

"Wonderful." She eased out her pent-up breath and crossed her legs.

The office door burst open and Lars, the stage director, strode across the room. "Oh. Sorry. Didn't realize you were in a meeting."

"That's the beauty of a door." Fist raised, Mr. de Groot made a knocking gesture. "Make an appointment."

"Sorry." Lars' cheeks pinked. "Just wanted to let you know the ramp is finished."

Every muscle in her body stiffened. "Ramp?"

"For the queen's motorcycle. She'll enter on her very own Harley."

Riley gripped the armrests. "Ramp—as in a slope."

"*Ja.* The audience will love it. She enters from offstage left on a levee, then motors down a seven-foot ramp."

"Not. While she's singing." Her knuckles whitened on the armrests.

Shaking his head, Mr. de Groot covered his face in his hands. "Not now, Lars."

"It's perfectly safe. Only the initial section of her first aria is sung from the motorbike while she's parked on the levee. As the orchestra transitions to the second part, she rides down the ramp and parks the bike. Struts around the stage while she sings the *fioratura* and high notes."

"Out." Mr. de Groot rose and pointed toward the door. "Now. We'll talk later."

"Well." Lars gave him a curt nod and left.

She forced a smile through her clenched jaw. "His idea is

clever for an avantgarde production, but I don't think Interpol will approve."

"Precisely. Since this is now a criminal matter, we've had to rethink things."

"Someone could tamper with the motorcycle."

"Agreed."

"Good." She sank back in the chair. "I'm sure Interpol will be comfortable with simple, traditional stage moves for the queen. If the house is worried I'll sue, forget it. The *Vlaamse Oper* is not responsible for what happened."

"That's good to know." Face ashen, he mopped his brow. "Miss Williams, I don't know how to say this ..."

Bummer. From the look on his face, he wasn't increasing her salary. Legs crossed, she bobbed her high heel from her toes. "I understand if you can't make up the canceled performance. After all, the stage was a crime scene, and until the police finished processing the area, you had no choice."

"That is most considerate of you. I called you here because the house has decided to—" Fingers skittering across his forehead, he cleared his throat. "I called you here to tell you your contract has been terminated."

Ice slewed through her veins. Spots whirled in front of her eyes. "What—terminated?" Singing the Queen was the door to an international career. Everything she and Lacy had dreamed of. "You can't do that to me."

"I assure you we can, and the decision is final."

"I—I'll sue you for breach of contract."

"I'd advise you to reconsider. Our lawyers are exceptional litigators."

"But the reviews were stellar, a sold-out house."

"Yes, very true. Our legal team advised us to terminate the contract. If there were another attack, they were concerned about multiple lawsuits from injured patrons."

She sank in the chair. How could she argue with their logic?

If someone planted a bomb, or a sniper's bullet went astray, their scenario was a distinct possibility. "Is Annie ..."

"No. Inspector Vlincken said she was involved in a plot to harm you."

What an idiot she'd been. Presuming, playing the polite prima donna. She stifled the urge to ask who her replacement was. Why look even more unprofessional? Maybe if she'd stood up to them before opening night, as Jacob had suggested, there'd have been no attempt on her life.

"Very well." She rose, body stiff. "Thank you for the opportunity to sing with the *Vlaamse Oper*. It has been —memorable."

"Thank you." De Groot stood and shook her hand. He pulled an envelope from his jacket's inner pocket and handed it to her. "You've been most gracious."

Right. Gracious. Her career was in shambles. Another door slammed in her face. Who'd want to hire a singer who attracted terrorist sabotage to their house, and endangered the musicians and the audience?

Worst of all, Dad would gloat.

9

Antwerp, Day 4

The idea of Big Brother filming citizens' every move chilled Jacob's core. But given the current world scene, maybe security cameras had become a necessity. From a law enforcement perspective, they were a boon.

Elbows planted on Vlincken's desk, Jacob blinked away his foggy vision and restudied the videos filmed outside the opera house. Three unidentified men entered shortly after three p.m., each carrying toolboxes. At four p.m., Dierck scurried from the stage entrance, mouth taut. Shortly after five p.m., Annie entered the house, followed by a steady stream of people. Probably singers, and musicians carrying instrument cases. Riles entered behind them, shoulders back, eyes sparkling.

He rubbed his forehead. Swallowed hard. He'd come so close to losing her. Clicking several buttons, he enlarged the faces in three photos, then swung his chair toward Vlincken hovering behind him, a half-drunk cup of coffee in his hand. "Think we may have found our man. Or men."

"*Ja*, if their ugly mugs match facial-recognition databases of terrorists."

"It's not much to go on, but it's a start." Jacob forwarded the jpegs to Interpol's facial- recognition database then punched print. Triplicates of three photos shot out of Vlincken's printer.

Jacob snatched the pages and spread the photos on the desk. If he were a betting man, he'd put his euros on the one in the middle. Dark-haired, pointy nose, dark eyes too close together. A runt of a man in shabby jeans, a toolbox gripped at his side. The guy was stupid enough to glance up at the camera.

"Question is, how did they know the staging would require a hydraulic lift?" Vlincken peered over Jacob's shoulder.

"Maybe someone on staff was in on this plot." Jacob slid the photo on his left forward.

The clean-cut blond with a man's purse slung over his shoulder walked toward the backstage entrance to the opera house. More likely a businessman. Jacob restudied the third picture. The man hurried toward the camera, head turtled between hunched shoulders. A lumpy sack dangled from his fist.

"The perp wouldn't have needed a toolbox to slice the cables." Jacob tapped the photo. "Or loosen the screws on the railing."

"*Ja*. A sharp knife, metal cutters, screwdrivers, an adjustable wrench could be in that sack."

"They'd have to clear the porter. He's supposed to screen everyone who enters the building."

"The porter might have been less watchful since they were dressed like workmen." Vlincken sipped his coffee. "Now, did a terrorist cell hire an outside assassin or use one of their own to do the job?"

"More needles in haystacks." But if Riles had the photos, she could watch for the men. Make sure she wasn't being tailed. Especially while he was away, following leads to the Priest.

"Tracking them down will be the challenge."

"*Ja*." Vlincken thumped his empty coffee cup on his desk. "It's never easy to find a particular rat in the sewer."

OUTSIDE THE OPERA HOUSE, Riley let Jacob help her into the car. Tears spilled into her lashes. Always the gentleman, her Jacob. Coming for her as soon as she texted him. Still clutching the general manager's envelope, she yanked a tissue from her purse. "They fired me."

"They what? After you saved their sorry tails." He tugged her to him, his lips tender on her forehead. His aftershave washed over her. "I'm sorry, Riles. You deserve better than this. What about severance pay?"

Great. Jacob the Practical. Just like Dad. All she wanted was a chance to sing the opera roles and art songs she loved and build her career. "My contract stipulated twenty-five hundred euros per performance. No pay for the rehearsal, which is normal. And I still owe my agent fifteen percent of my gross." She slipped her fingernail under the glued flap, fingered the check for €10,000. If only she could've sung all thirteen performances. Instead, she should thank God for His provision. And for sparing her life.

"Looks like hush money to me." Jacob fired the engine.

"Do you think other houses will hire me?" Face tilted up to his, she drowned herself in his blue eyes. "A singer with a risk of terrorist retribution on her head?"

The corners of his mouth slacked. An I'm-so-sorry look hooded his eyes.

"Right." Her career was over before it made it out to sea. With her conservatory degrees in vocal performance, and no general ed courses, she was limited to singing professionally or teaching voice. And a university position would require her to perform off-campus to earn tenure. More ops for terrorists to strike.

"Maybe if I go by Marie, my middle name. Dye my hair blonde. Or black. Use my sister's name and Mom's maiden name. Lacy Parker." No. Lacy should've been here launching her own career.

"Or Marie Coulter." Eyes wistful, he touched her engagement ring. Sunlight sparked fire in every facet of the diamond.

Sighing, she stared out the window. She wanted to bear Jacob's children, be his soulmate. Tag along on his Interpol assignments. But a shipboard romance and now their careers keeping them apart, she'd had little time to get to know him. After all, if they were to spend a lifetime married. What if he turned out to be like Dad?

"I want my wedding day to be special, because the timing is right for us to become man and wife, not to prop up my career."

The color drained from his face. "You aren't thinking of backing out on me, are you?"

———

AT THE STRANGE look she gave him—moisture pooling at her lashes, chin trembling—a boulder lodged in his lungs. Jacob pulled into the traffic on Frankrijklei. He couldn't bear it if she ditched him. Before she waltzed into his life, saucy-eyed, mud-splattered and vulnerable, no other woman had held his interest long enough to steal his heart.

He risked a glance at her. Wetness glistened on her cheek as she angled her head toward the window. No, this couldn't be happening.

"Stop the car!" She slapped the windowsill. "Turn around."

Inadvertently, he jammed the brakes, tires screeching on the asphalt. Horns honked, brakes squealed as cars swerved to the other lanes. "What's the matter?"

"You're going the wrong way. Burie's is at Nationalstraat Four."

He smacked his forehead. "You nearly caused a multi-car collision because of chocolate?"

"Dark chocolate is a great stress reliever, full of polyphenols. It's a mood-lifter. Besides, now I won't have an excuse to come to Antwerp. Burie's doesn't have a shop in Brussels."

"Hon ..." He reached for her hand and kissed her fingers, his lips savoring her soft skin. "How about we pray and turn to the Lord to get through this?"

"How about we do both. But stop at Burie's first."

Ten minutes later, he'd parked in the garage closest to Burie's. He stood at her side inside the shop, the scent of rich Belgian chocolate engulfing his every breath. Saliva pooled in his mouth. This beat sitting at home, biting into a truffle from a box.

He trailed her as she pointed to the pralines and truffles and molded shapes she wanted, eyes gleaming like a child. Warmth oozed through his chest. What wasn't there to love about Riles? One moment vulnerable, the next a don't-mess-with-me warrior, dangling from a hydraulic lift, determined not to lose the battle. He edged his hip against hers, inhaling the scent of her Chanel No. 5 mingled with dark cocoa.

Flashing her intoxicating smile, she nudged his ribs. "You choose some."

"All right." He pointed to the fondant-filled horses' heads, the two-tone horseshoes. "This could be addictive." If he kept this up, they'd be doing a lot of repenting.

Fifteen minutes later, Burie's sack in hand, he helped Riles into the car. He scooted into the driver's seat and pulled out the printouts of the three men who'd entered the opera house before the performance. "We don't have their names yet."

"Hmm ..." She leaned against his shoulder, tapped the photo of the shifty-eyed runt. "He was backstage the day of the dress rehearsal. Sort of gave me the creeps, the way he watched me, clutching his toolbox. Rat Eyes."

"The dress rehearsal, huh." He'd have to check the videos again, see when Rat Eyes left the opera house and have his steps traced on other cameras in the area.

Riles' phone rang, playing an Edith Piaf song.

"Frénie," she mouthed to him then told her friend about the canceled contract.

Vielle Frénau. The BFF from the riverboat cruise staff he'd

never had the opportunity to meet. His Interpol partner had interviewed Frénie in the hospital.

Placing the call on speaker, Riley held the phone near him. *"Oh là là, chérie,* this is terrible. I tell you what. You will come to London and stay with me. Armand is treating me to a fabulous suite at the Savoy. You will love it."

"Who's Armand?" Jacob whispered.

"Her super-rich French boyfriend," Riles mouthed back.

This could be the solution he'd been praying for. Send Riles to London until he and the team could nab the terrorists who'd sabotaged the lift. In the meantime, maybe they'd find the Priest too.

"Chérie, are you there, *'allo?"*

"Yes, yes. I'm here. That's really kind of you, but this isn't a good time for a visit."

"Why not? What else have you got to do?"

"Riles." He covered the phone with his palm.

"I—I want to stay here." Riles grasped his hand, her eyes pleading with him. "And be with you."

More than anything he wanted her at his side. One more trip apart, and she might decide she could live without him. He shifted in the seat. No. Her safety came first. Even if she broke up with him. "Take it. You're not safe here. You've got to get out of Belgium."

Riles scowled. "No," she mouthed at him.

For a moment, scuffling sounds muffled the call from Frénie's end. *"Chérie.* My darling Armand is sending his private jet for you. His pilot and I will arrive at Zaventem airport tomorrow morning at ten."

"Say yes." Jacob re-covered the phone with his hand. "I'll be away on assignment. I can't protect you here."

Fingers gripping the armrest, she angled her feet toward him. Classic body tells she didn't want to do this.

"That's awfully generous of Armand. Thank you. I'll be there."

"Ta-ta, *ma chérie*. I can hardly wait to see you." Frénie giggled into the phone, then disconnected.

Huffing, Riley stashed her cell in her purse. "Well, you got your wish."

"Good. With a private plane, you're less likely to be tailed to London."

10

London, Day 5 (afternoon)

The walk across the Zaventem tarmac stretched longer than the Red Sea. The last thing she wanted was to board this plane. Glancing over her shoulder, Riley searched for Jacob among the windowed walls. He could be any one of the specks visible behind the glass. Waving anyway, she climbed the short set of stairs to Armand's Lear jet.

"*Chérie,* how lovely to see you." Waiting behind the open door, Frénie darted toward her, arms outstretched. Her hug caught Riley around her ribs with a strength she didn't recall from last year. "Once again, we are together." She stood on tiptoe in her stilettos and air-kissed Riley's cheeks. "Look out, London, here come the mischief makers."

Riley stepped back. More mischief was the last thing she wanted. "London agrees with you."

"*Non, non, chérie.*" Heart-shaped face tilted upward, Frénie wisped her pixie haircut into place. The peplum jacket of her designer suit accentuated her tiny waist, the curve of her hips. "It is my darling Armand who agrees with me."

"Yes. I can see that."

The pilot stowed Riley's luggage in the entryway closet and secured the door. Sashaying beside her, Frénie escorted her across the plush carpet to a group of four leather seats. "Armand said I mustn't be seen. His flight plan named only the pilot, not that I was onboard." As she tittered behind her pink-painted nails, an enormous sapphire glinted on her finger. "I am a stowaway."

"I'm glad he let you come." Riley sat across from her. She set the Burie's sack at her feet and fastened her seatbelt. Odd, traveling into exile in such opulence. Siberian white from floor to ceiling. Credenza, the couches, and tables, the bed in the rear. Even the hue of Frénie's suit matched their oversized chairs. "You should've mentioned the dress code."

"Oh silly. Navy suits you. It's so ... so businesslike."

Businesslike. Career-minded. Yep, that was her all right.

The engines whined, and the plane taxied onto the runway. Riley stared out the window, tears blurring the tarmac. Inhaling the blast of chilled air, she summoned the feel of Jacob's arms around her, the scent of his aftershave, his lips pressed against hers as if there'd never be another kiss.

"What did you bring me?" Eyes twinkling, Frénie nudged the Burie's sack with her shoe.

"A kilo of your favorites." Riley handed her the large blue-and-gold embossed box. With her own kilo to eat, maybe Frénie wouldn't ask what else was in the bag. After all, an exiled woman needed sustenance.

"A kilo—how generous. It's a good thing I've been working out. I'll have you know I can bench press one-hundred-fifty pounds."

"Wow. Remind me never to tangle with you." Maybe she could keep up her own exercise routine at the Savoy.

The jet lifted off, wings tilting in the wind. All too soon, the airport shrank beneath her. It was only a trip to London, one hour away. At least Jacob hadn't insisted she return to the States.

"Now you must ask me all about Armand." Frénie popped a cocoa-dusted truffle in her mouth. Groaning, she rolled her eyes. Letting her savor the truffle, Riley hunted for words. "He seems to be a very generous man. A Chanel suit, the ring."

Nodding and chewing, Frénie pointed to the sizeable diamond studs in her earlobes. She licked the cocoa from her fingertips and closed the candy box. Eyes dancing, she leaned across the seat. "*Chérie,* I think he's going to ask me to marry him."

"What do you know about him?"

"Everything I need to know."

"Which is what, exactly?"

"He's unbelievably wealthy. We're both French. He thinks I'm adorable." Frénie plopped the candy box on the seat next to her. "What more do I need to know?"

"How many times has he been married?"

Tilting her tiny chin toward the ceiling, Frénie tapped her lip. "Once, I think."

"How old is he?"

"Armand told me he is forty."

"Hmm." Twelve years older. Practically a junior uncle.

"Oh *chérie*, he takes such good care of me. What's so wrong, wanting to be treasured by a man?"

"Nothing. If he's the right man for you." Jacob was the right man for her, wasn't he? Sometimes he reminded her of Dad, his need to be in control. If she hadn't won the Fulbright Scholarship to Romania, she might never have escaped his micro-managing. Luckily for her, small, high voices had a better chance of a career in Europe's centuries-old opera houses than in America.

"What business is Armand in?"

Shoulders hiked, palms out, Frénie sighed. "What does it matter if he provides well for me?"

How could her friend be so blind? "Have you forgotten the trouble I landed in, in Romania?" All because she'd fallen for a drop-dead gorgeous Arab-Romanian. Until the Security police arrested her for couriering what he'd told her were letters for his family in Europe. Not funds for terrorists.

"Armand. Is not. A criminal. You rushed into that relationship with Radu." Shaking her finger at Riley like a schoolmarm, Frénie crossed her legs. "You refused to see everything I warned you about."

"Exactly. And I don't want you to be hurt." Riley reached for Frénie's hand, but she slid it beneath her hip. "I'm sure Armand is an extraordinary man, but you need to know someone well before committing to marriage." Liar, liar. Wasn't she doing the same thing with Jacob? "When do I meet Mr. Wonderful?"

Arms crossed, Frénie pouted. "If you can't be nice, I'm canceling our lunch with him tomorrow."

"Forgive me. I just want you to be happy. To stay happy."

JEAN-PIERRE'S sleepy-eyed face loomed from the Zoom screen, navy sweater and shirt as rumpled as ever. "No Roman Lachalle cleared French customs."

"What? That can't be." Jacob *thunked* his coffee mug on his desk. "Gorilla Guy stuck out like a sore thumb. Could he have switched passports upon arrival?"

"Trust me. We combed Orly and DeGaulle airports. Roman Lachalle never arrived."

"No dead body on the plane? No officer recalled a man matching the picture Margot's agent had?"

"That is correct." Jean-Pierre's sigh reached into Jacob's cubicle. "So, now we are back to—how you say—the square?"

"Square one. Monopoly, it's a board game. Do not pass go. Do not collect two hundred dollars." Von Bingen wasn't going to like this news.

"You Americans." A grin lifted Jean-Pierre's cheeks, then slacked. "So, boss, what do we do now?"

Pray. Pray for a divine breakthrough. "Circulate his picture on the street, to informants. And businesses with known connections to money laundering, like restaurants, casinos, laundromats, car washes. Let's see if we can dig up a fresh lead on him." Somehow. "Good work. Keep me updated."

"*Merci*. I do not envy you having to tell von Bingen about this."

"Thanks." If they didn't get a solid break on this assignment, his days as Golden Boy were numbered. He disconnected the call and knocked on von Bingen's door.

Desk cleared of all but three Antwerp newspapers, she looked up at him. Her icicled gaze froze his shoes to the carpet.

Even as he read upside down, the headlines were clear. So was the picture someone had snapped of him onstage with Riles on his shoulders. "There's an update on our suspect in Vienna."

"You mean you actually were there?" The acid in her voice curdled the coffee in his stomach.

If only he'd charged the lunch instead of paying cash. "Most definitely. Interpol records will confirm I met with Margot at her office at nine. Then we visited the murder scene before staking out the Priest's lunch meeting."

"And why should I believe she wouldn't cover for you?"

"Because she wants to make bureau chief. And the security guard's sign-in records have my signature, and time of arrival and departure stamps. Same for my rental car."

Von Bingen slapped the papers shut and tossed them in her waste basket. "I gave you an order, and you disobeyed it."

"I met the terms of your instructions. I was there for the meetings." He squared his shoulders. "If I'd taken that evening flight to Vienna, my fiancée would likely be dead. We now have leads to three known terrorists involved in the sabotaged lift."

"You are skating on cracking ice, Coulter."

The knot in his tie grew tight. He didn't want to lose his job, but he'd do it all over again if it meant saving Riles.

"How much did your little private jaunt to Vienna cost us?"

"Nothing. I paid for it."

Did he detect a hint of respect in her arched brows?

"Well, then. That's settled. Don't let it happen again." Sucking a breath, she smoothed the hair behind her ear. "What was the update?"

Steeling himself, he gave her Jean-Pierre's news and the follow-up plan.

"We need a breakthrough. Fast." She sagged in her chair, fingers grooving her forehead. "While you were cavorting in Antwerp, we received confirmation of terrorist attacks slated for the EU meetings in four weeks."

The same tactic the terrorists had planned last summer. When would the EU security force beef up their manpower, their vigilance? "A man with a gorilla face like that stands out in a crowd. He's arrogant. Thinks he's invincible."

"And deadly. Do you think he killed the man in *Stefansdom*?"

"If he's the Priest, very likely."

"Or he ordered the killing." She gave him a pointed look. "Being a man of authority."

"Right." Her sub-texted threat was clear. "I'm on it."

Seated at his desk, he set up an afternoon Zoom meeting with his team. An alert dinged on his computer. A message from the facial-recognition data analyst. His pulse quickened as he opened the document and read the reports on the three men caught on the Antwerp security cameras.

Georges Babor, the man with the male purse, no priors. Guy Malpin, the little man with the bulging sack, wanted for burglary. On the streets, known as Swifty Pete. Always on the lookout for quick bucks.

Pointy nose, the man with the toolbox. Jacques Ibert, the man Riles had dubbed Rat Eyes. Resident of Brussels. Was he the saboteur? He texted Riles the man's name. Then Inspector Vlincken for more video clips of Jacques Ibert near the opera house.

Elbow planted on his armrest, Jacob cradled his forehead in his palm. Not one of them was on Interpol's lists of suspected or known terrorists.

Another dead end.

11

London, Day 5 (morning)

S unlight lasered through the overcast sky and gilded the hood of Armand's silver Rolls Royce, nearly blinding Riley. The car glided to a stop near the London Bridge train and tube station. Not the most attractive part of London. Moments later, the chauffeur opened the back door, and she swung her feet to the pavement. "Where are we?"

"The Shard." Frénie scooted out, wobbling in her stilettos. She lifted her champagne flute toward the obelisk-shaped skyscraper looming beyond them. "Let's surprise Armand."

"Is that a good idea?" Jacob wouldn't be pleased if she showed up at Interpol HQ, especially not with her BFF. Her gaze crawled up the double-sheathed glass and metal scaffolding that encased the building and riveted on the Shard's pinnacle, piercing the clouds. She gulped. The tea she'd consumed on the plane churned in her stomach. "On second thought, let's not."

"Don't be silly." Frénie handed the chauffeur her glass and grasped Riley's wrist. "Let's find out if he's in."

"I don't think that's wise."

"Nonsense. He's excited to meet you."

"Uh-huh. Let's make that on level ground." The structure looked like a work in progress. The hydraulic lift had felt like that—rickety. Unpredictable. "You sure this building is finished?"

"Yes. Thousands of people work here. The Shard has offices, a hotel, restaurants. Forty-four elevators." Heels clattering, Frénie dragged her toward the entrance, OFFICES AT THE SHARD, emblazoned over more glass walls. A series of bowed entrances with revolving doors gave the place a scalloped effect. "You can even rent a residential flat, floors fifty-three to sixty-five, almost to the top of the building."

"How many floors are there?"

"Ninety-five, but you can go only to seventy-two, the observation deck. The rest of it narrows to the pinnacle."

"That many?" Riley's voice squeaked.

"The Shard's one of the tallest skyscrapers in the UK and Western Europe. Over a thousand feet tall."

Bile shot on Riley's tongue. *Dear God, get me through this.* "Why don't you call Armand first and make sure he's in?"

"Silly. Then our visit wouldn't be a surprise."

"I-I'm not good with heights. And after Antwerp—"

"Nonsense. You'll be fine. These high-speed elevators fly you to your floor, take you to the top in less than a minute."

Great. A rocket-propelled elevator. "Did I tell you about the time someone talked me into taking a ski lift in Romania? When we reached the station, I blacked out and fell into a pile of sheep dung, my knees scraped raw."

"*Ma chérie,* I didn't know. But you must conquer this fear before it destroys you." Frénie snagged Riley's wrist and dragged her toward the bank of elevators in the lobby. "Today, I will help you do that."

"I don't think this will work." A bell pinged. The steel doors yawned open like the jaws of Jonah's great fish. Tremors ripped across Riley's shoulders. She'd never even liked fast escalators. And after the hydraulic lift—

"Come." Frénie yanked her inside and the doors glided shut. "We're only going to the fiftieth floor."

"That's. Good." Riley sank against the cold steel wall, ankles jittering in her high heels. As the elevator whisked them upward, pressure weighted her skull, pounded her eardrums. A blizzard of black-and-white dots twirled before her eyes. Darkness tugged at her mind. No, she could do this. Fingers clawing the wall, she dug her feet into the floor, struggled not to collapse. A fresh wave of nausea caught in her throat, threatening to erupt.

"*Chérie*, are you all right? Your face is green."

"Must be the lighting," Riley mumbled. No way was she humiliating herself in front of Armand.

The bell dinged, and the doors swung open. Plastering a hand on the wall, Riley staggered from the elevator, Frénie grasping her other elbow. Burning acid spurted into Riley's mouth.

Oh please God, no.

Mount Vesuvius heaved again. She leaned over the metal waste bin and vomited into the plastic-lined canister. As her leg muscles dissolved into mush, her knees thudded on the ground. No, no. Black dots swirled in her eyes. Black ... black ...

EVERY INCH of Riley's skull throbbed. A sour taste coated her tongue. Where was she? Across from her, a wall of windows, an ornate eighteenth-century desk, credenzas built to match. Beneath her, a couch upholstered in pale blue silk. Good. She was outside that horrid elevator.

A raven-haired man in a navy-blue suit bent over her, dabbing a cold, wet cloth on her forehead and cheeks. His Hollywood-handsome face and musky cologne snatched her breath. This must be a dream.

"You fainted." Even his voice was low and musical. He pressed his fingers to her wrist.

At his touch, her pulse leapt in her vein.

"Armand Découvrir, at your service."

"My darling Armand carried you to his office." Standing beside him, Frénie held a crystal pitcher of water.

"How gallant." At least he hadn't said she'd thrown up. The pools of soul-searching concern in his brown eyes nearly drowned her. Had she misjudged this man?

"Is she all right?" Sloshing water on the Persian rug, Frénie peered over his shoulder.

"*Mon petit chou* ..." Lips curled upward, he stroked Frénie's cheek. "You shouldn't have forced your friend to come up here." He pulled an armchair to the sofa and sat.

"I'm fine now, thank you." Biting back a smile, Riley dug her elbows in the cushion and hauled herself upright on the couch. She'd never understand the French endearment, calling your beloved a little cabbage.

Frénie plunked the pitcher on his desk blotter. "But she has to go down in the elevator."

"How about I take the stairs?" Only fifty times ... how many steps per floor?

"Re-laaaax." As he fixed his penetrating gaze on her, Riley squirmed on the seat cushion. "If need be, I shall carry you myself."

"Thank you, but I'm sure I can walk down."

"Have no fear, Miss Williams." His arm around Frénie's waist, Armand pulled her onto his lap. "I'll get you downstairs."

Cheeks aflame, Riley nodded.

Maybe London wouldn't be so bad after all.

ONE BY ONE his team members popped onto the Zoom call screen. From their bleary-eyed looks, eight o'clock meetings weren't their thing. Nor apparently, was a seven a.m. call to Tracy. When was he supposed to talk to his kid sister if she wouldn't take his after school or evening calls?

Earbuds in place, Jacob adjusted his laptop screen on the conference table. "Good morning. You've all seen von Bingen's alert regarding the EU."

Faces solemn, heads nodded on the screen.

"Any updates for the group?" About time he developed a lead.

Jean-Pierre cleared his throat. "Thirty minutes ago, a man was found shot at close range on the top viewing platform of the Eiffel Tower. No suspects yet, but the victim clutched a silver cross necklace in his hand."

Jacob jerked forward in his chair. This could be the break they were waiting for.

"If the cold cases Margot uncovered in Austria are related, why the sudden string of murders?" Ian fingered his brow.

"Rebellion in-house, perhaps?" Gunter removed his glasses, polished the lenses. "Taking out dissenters?"

"That's possible." Jacob tapped his pencil on the table. "So far, each murder has occurred at a high place."

"True," Margot said.

"You're saying the killer lures his victims to a high place because he's obsessed with heights?" Gunter paused his glasses midair.

"There's a pattern emerging." Jacob slowed his pencil taps. "Symbolically, the EU meetings represent a high place. Not topographically, but a governmental seat." Maybe he should've kept his theory to himself. "We may have overlooked other murders the Priest committed because he left no calling card on the victims."

"These murders need to be stopped." Margot thumped her mug on her desk. "We must become proactive, not reactive."

"And how do we become proactive with no solid leads?" Gunter asked.

"Capitalize on what we *do* have." Jacob leaned toward the screen. "The newest victim."

"Why don't we set up a sting op?" Ian planted his elbows on

his desk. "Run ads in the papers to draw out the bad guys, the Priest?"

"Yeah, the financial section." Jacob chuckled.

"Do we have time to organize it? My office is working around the clock to track suspected money launderers in Germany." Gunter pocketed his half-readers.

"Same in Vienna." Margot's lips thinned.

"Ditto for Britain." Ian sighed. "But I still think we need a plan."

"France is a big country ..." Jean-Pierre hiked his shoulders to his ears. "There's enough criminal element here in Lyon to tie us to our desks for decades."

What was happening to his team's morale? While they murmured onscreen, Jacob scrolled through the flight website on his phone then switched to the trains. He booked his ticket. Good thing he'd stashed a suitcase under his desk. He checked his watch. With hourly departures, the Thalys train would have him in Paris in less than ninety minutes.

"Jean-Pierre, meet me at Paris Nord at ten-thirty this morning."

"*Bien sûr*, of course. Always love a trip to Paris."

"Bring photocopies of Gorilla Guy's picture. Several hundred, please."

12

Paris, Day 5

I f only he could've arrived before they removed the body. As Jacob crouched on the viewing platform of the Eiffel Tower, a stiff breeze ruffled his hair, flapped the police tape cordoning off the crime scene. Jean-Pierre knelt beside him, police photos of the body in his hand. The tower had been closed to tourists today.

"According to this photo, the man was propped against the girder." Jacob pointed to the central metal structure. "Like the body in Stefansdom."

"Why the parallel?"

"I don't know." Jacob circled the platform. The panoramic view of rooftops and streets stretched for miles. Using the compass app on his cell, he moved until his position matched the direction the body had been facing. "The killer propped him up facing northwest."

"Coincidence?"

"It's odd, both bodies arranged in the same manner. Could be more than a calling card." Jacob texted Margot.

> What direction was the body in Stefansdom facing?

> Give me three minutes.

Was the killer toying with them, leaving them clues? If so, why would a terrorist financier do this? Jacob walked back to Jean-Pierre. "Have your men check every luxury hotel in Paris. With such a memorable face, a desk clerk may remember Gorilla Guy."

"*Bien sûr.*"

"And don't quit with the first place you find him. He may have booked himself in different places over multiple trips. We need dates of his stays to check for patterns. Have the hotels watched in case he returns."

"No problem."

"Thanks." He'd ask Margot to do the same for Vienna.

"Why not less expensive places too?"

"If Gorilla Guy is the Priest, I suspect he loves the lifestyle of the rich and famous. Unless he thinks we're on to him, he likely won't change his M.O."

Dusting the dirt from his trousers, Jean-Pierre grinned. "My men will appreciate the assignment."

Jacob paced the deck, drinking in the view until the three dots bounced on his screen.

> I checked the police photos, their notes. The body was facing west, slightly north.

Moving out of the breeze, he texted Margot back.

> Thanks. That matches a Vienna to Paris direction.

> The Paris body is facing northwest. I think we'll find the next victim in London.

As Riles whizzed the phone camera across her suite in the Savoy Hotel, Jacob almost lost his dinner. "Nice pad." In the background a woman with a pronounced French accent sang "I've Got You Under My Skin."

"Is that Frénie singing?"

Riles plopped on the couch, her face happier than he'd seen her in days. "Yes. In the shower. We're expecting room service soon."

"Sounds like fun." He and Jean-Pierre had eaten *coq au vent* at a bistro on the Left Bank while they hashed out possible scenarios for the Eiffel Tower murder. Then he'd checked with Inspector Vlincken for updates on the saboteur's movements on their CCTV cameras. "Did you see my text with Rat Eye's name?"

"Yes. Jacques something."

"Jacques Ibert." Good grief. Why wasn't she focusing?

"Right. Right." She gnawed a fingernail. "You don't think he's in London, do you?"

"Not that we know of."

"Good." She squinted at her screen. "Where are you?"

"In Paris." Simple digs, nothing compared to the Savoy. He told her about the murder. "As soon as von Bingen signs off on the paperwork, I'm coming to London."

"Yippee." Her squeal shattered his eardrum. "That's wonderful. Then we can be together."

"Riles, I'm coming on assignment. I think the next murder will occur in London." Somehow, he had to carve out time to visit Tracy. Find out why she was sidestepping his phone calls.

Since Riles still had her Interpol-encrypted phone from the

riverboat-cruise caper, he shared his theory with her. The strains of French-accented "Night and Day" wafted through the speaker.

"What do the silver crosses mean?"

"I wish I knew." How many more victims would die before he had answers?

Solid leads.

Suspects under arrest.

13

London, Day 6

Guidebook in hand, Riley scanned the corners for street signs. "St. Paul's Cathedral ought to be that way."

"Let me see." Frénie took the book from her and flipped through the pages.

"It can't be far now." Riley pulled out her street map and did a three-sixty on the sidewalk. "I think it's—" She did a double take at the corner across the street. The handyman she'd spotted backstage at the opera, the day of the dress rehearsal. Adrenalin shot through her veins. Rat Eyes. Jacques what's-his-name.

Had he followed her to London? But she'd taken a private plane. Heart thumping, she peered over Frénie's shoulder at the guidebook. It had to be a coincidence. Maybe he had family in the UK. And maybe she was burying her head in the sand like an I-don't-want-to-know ostrich. But if she were wrong, she couldn't stand here, waiting for him to make a move.

"Lead on McDuff." Looping her arm in Frénie's, she let her walk them down the street. Rat Eyes had turned to face a shop window. She ought to call Jacob. But not around Frénie. At the airport he'd asked her to continue to keep his job secret. "What time is lunch with Armand?"

"One o'clock. We can do the cathedral, perhaps walk the River Thames."

"Sounds like a plan." If Rat Eyes was tailing them, she'd give him a workout his feet would remember. Right now, she had an advantage. He didn't know Interpol had identified him. And alerted her. All good, unless he decided to attack.

Inside the cathedral, the marble black-and-white floor stretched for miles. The massive organ pipes lining the choir stalls, the gilded ceiling and altar snatched Riley's breath. Christopher Wren knew how to design them. A pity he hadn't lived to see the realization of his dream.

"Let's climb the stairs to the dome. It's great exercise and the view of London is fantastic." Frénie grabbed her arm. "It's only three floors. You climbed higher than that in Bucharest every day. But I must warn you, it's over a thousand steps."

"You're kidding."

"They're steps, not an elevator."

"No." Riley peeled her friend's fingers from her elbow. "Absolutely not." Not with Rat Eyes tailing them. She wasn't giving him another chance to kill her. He'd murder Frénie too. Up there, they'd be isolated. Vulnerable.

"*Ma chérie*, you need to conquer your fear."

"Uh-huh." Riley fought the urge to scan the sanctuary again for Rat Eyes. "Right."

With a sigh Frénie turned toward the altar, genuflected, and made the sign of the cross. She sat in a chair off the aisle and bowed her head.

From her seat in the row behind her, Riley texted Jacob.

> With F at St. Paul's Cathedral. Rat Eyes is sitting in the back row.

Seconds later, three dots flashed on the screen.

> Keep me posted on your whereabouts.

> Calling Ian in Manchester to notify British police.

> Thanks.

Three more dots blipped across the screen.

> Don't do anything dumb like try to follow him.

> Me, dumb?

What could be dumber than letting Rat Eyes escape? The sooner he was caught, the greater her chance of restoring her career.

As Riley slipped the phone in her purse, Frénie stepped into the aisle. She genuflected and made the sign of the cross. "If you won't climb the dome, shall we go?"

Gawking like an open-mouthed tourist, Riley glanced around the sanctuary again. Breath eased between her lips. No sign of Rat Eyes. *Thank You, God.*

"You want to see the room where Armand is holding his gala?"

Not really. "Sure."

Before she knew it, the Shard towered in front of her, all eleven-hundred feet of it. The roiling in her gut shifted. Rat Eyes. Only a few yards ahead. Pulse tattooing her veins, she scoped the area for a policeman. Why couldn't she find a constable when she needed one?

Shoulders hunched, Rat Eyes sauntered across the street and entered London Bridge Station.

"I changed my mind. Let's go for a ride."

"Now?"

"Why not? We have time." Digging her fingers into Frénie's

SARA L. JAMESON

biceps, Riley strode across the street, her feet barely touching the pavement. He was only yards ahead. She'd put an end to his stalking now.

"Why the rush—slow down." Gasping, Frénie trotted beside her like a short-legged dachshund.

Fifty feet ahead of her, Rat Eyes cleared the turnstile to the subway lines. Within seconds he'd disappeared into the crowd.

Clutching her ticket, she forced her feet to slow. Her pulse quickened. She didn't want to lose him. Which tube line would he choose—the Northern or the Jubilee?

As he loped toward the Jubilee trains, she inserted her ticket, Frénie a few steps behind her.

Leaving a subway car between them, she nudged Frénie inside the train and sat in the back. In the car ahead, Rat Eyes sat facing a window.

"You do the strangest things. Why are we riding the tube?"

"I don't know." Riley shrugged. "Sounded like fun to me."

Frénie's brows hiked. "But you ride the subway in Brussels."

"The London tube system is historic." Riley drew enough breath to fuel a two-page roulade. "Can't you smell the history down here?"

"What is the matter with you? The place reeks of dust and decades of fumes." Frénie edged away from her. "I feel like I don't know you anymore."

"I'm sorry." Riley brushed a piece of lint from her slacks. Their friendship. Another casualty of her secret life, dodging terrorists. If only she could tell Frénie the truth. But she didn't understand the meaning of don't tell a soul.

Wheels screeching, the train slowed as it rolled into the final station, Canary Wharf. Rat Eyes moved to the doors, and Riley's heart leapt.

As soon as the doors opened, he exited and loped along the platform.

Letting him walk a few yards ahead, Riley stepped from the train, Frénie at her heels.

92

"What now?"

"Let's have a look. Canary Wharf is so—"

"Historic." Frénie sighed. *"Oui,* I know."

But Rat Eyes headed for the Docklands Light Railway, an above-ground train.

Her heart skipped a beat. Had he spotted her? Was he leading her on a fruitless chase around London? When he boarded the three-car train, she nudged Frénie into the final car. Not enough passengers to risk sitting closer to him. Victory thumped in her veins. Minutes from now she'd have concrete info for Jacob. The police would arrest Rat Eyes. Maybe she could ask to sing the rest of her performances with the *Vlaamse Oper.*

But he'd been bold enough to hang around backstage. Riley angled her feet toward the doors. What if this trip was a trap to lure her to a deserted place where he'd kill her? And Frénie. The muscles in Riley's calves knotted. Sweat slicked her palms.

Feigning the gaga tourist, she peered out the windows. Surely there was an escape route among the luxury apartment buildings and wharves along the River Thames. If only she'd come alone. It'd be all too easy for Rat Eyes to dump Frénie's body into the water too.

Her friend's sighs punctuated the air. "Are you enjoying this trip?"

"Uh-huh." Riley faked a smile. "Immensely."

"Well, I'd much rather talk about Armand. And I can hardly wait to take you for a spin in my new Lamborghini."

Ride with Frénie behind the wheel? Images of how her friend probably drove sent chills across Riley's shoulder blades. "Tell me more about Armand."

"He studied international finance at the Sorbonne. He's always listening to opera at home. I—I don't know what he saw in a simple musical-theater performer like me."

Frénie doubting herself? "What's not to love about you?" Riley squeezed her friend's hand. "You ooze charm, you're a loyal friend. So, you sing musical theater—surely he appreciates you trained as an opera singer. Armand is fortunate to have you."

Twenty minutes later, the train pulled into the end station at Lewisham. The doors opened and Rat Eyes disembarked, glancing over his shoulder toward the rest of the cars.

Shrinking in her seat, Riley tucked her head. As the warning bell dinged, she leapt into the aisle, dragged Frénie with her. "Come on." Half a second later, the doors whooshed shut behind them.

"What's the hurry?"

Riley scurried down the steps to the street level. Frénie trailed behind her.

"What are we doing here—there's nothing to see."

"True." Riley's heart plummeted to her toes. No, no, no. Rat Eyes had vanished.

14

London, Day 6

Lunch with Armand at a posh restaurant in Mayfair and a tab to match. Today, she'd choose something delectable, feed the gnawing hunger pangs twisting her stomach. Flats clattering on the wooden walkway to the Greenhouse Restaurant, Riley lengthened her stride to catch up with Frénie.

"Come, we're late." Frénie scurried toward the entrance.

Steps led to the entry of the restaurant, located on the ground floor of an elegant red brick apartment building. At least the place wasn't fancy dress. The only men in suits and ties were waiters. Riley brushed a wayward curl from her temple. They'd never have made it back from the Docklands in time to change clothes.

Nothing about the place was standard fare. Not the white walls and tablecloths, nor the vases and artsy bowls. The meals on patron's tables were plated tableaux of art, too beautiful to eat. Even the cheese trolley made her mouth water.

The *maître 'd* led them to Armand's table in the corner overlooking the Zenlike garden.

Easily the best-dressed man in the restaurant, Armand had

looped a pale blue sweater over his shoulders, his silk polo shirt and slacks expensive. He rose to greet them.

"Sorry, darling." Frénie stretched upward to kiss Armand's cheek. "The train took longer than we thought."

"Train—what train?" He seated her to his left, kissed Riley's hand, then seated her to his right.

"The train to the Docklands." Frénie whipped her napkin onto her lap.

"The Docklands?" He frowned. "What were you doing there?"

"I don't know." Frénie flicked her hand toward Riley. "Riley had a crazy idea to see the area. So, we took the train and walked around some townhouses in Lewisham." She gave an exasperated look. "Why we did that instead of seeing wonderful historical sites—oh, ask her."

"There seems to be an air of mystery about you, Mademoiselle Riley." His dark eyes riveted on her. "Tell me more."

Cheeks warming beneath his gaze, Riley grasped for a logical answer. "Some guidebooks mentioned the area for its revitalization." Lame. But it was the best she could think of.

"So, you're a history buff."

"Well ..."

"Frénie told me you are a famous opera singer."

"She exaggerates."

The waiter set the first course in front of them.

"I took the liberty of ordering for us. Frénie told me you have no food allergies."

If only she had. Riley's eyes glommed on the disk of raw ground beef topped with microgreens and diced chili peppers. "Steak tartare. How lovely."

Sending up silent prayers for protection from harmful substances, she forked a bite and swallowed the mushy beef without chewing. The blob slid down her throat. Trying not to gag, she sipped her water. Armand was staring at her, his finger stroking his upper lip. "It's delicious." She forced down another forkful.

"I was wondering ... would you consider performing for my gala?"

"I'd love to." Riley dabbed her napkin to her mouth. "Thank you for asking me."

"It's in twelve days, in the Ren Room at the Shangri-La Hotel in the Shard."

"The. Shard." Her stomach knotted. Another launch into outer space. Before a performance.

"It's only floor thirty-two. Do you think you can manage that?"

"I—I think so." She'd have to. It was a chance to resurrect her career.

"*Bon*, good." He rested his fingers on her wrist. "The gala is a fundraiser for my orphanage near Brighton."

"What a wonderful cause." Slipping free, she lifted the water glass to her lips.

"Allow me to provide you a designer gown of your choice. And a fee of twenty-thousand pounds."

The water spilled into her airway. She set the glass down and sputtered into her napkin. "That's most generous. However, I would prefer to donate my services."

"As you wish. I'm sure you must have a press kit you can email me for publicity."

"Of course." Had she just turned down enough money to buy a new car? Riley pushed tidbits of beef around the plate's rim. No way could she eat this. "Tell me more about the orphanage."

"It's dear to my heart." His eyes misted. "All those poor children with no place to go."

"I tell it for you, Armand." Frénie leaned across her plate, bare of the red mass of beef. "Armand's mother and little sister were killed. By terrorists."

No wonder he loved children. "How dreadful. I'm so sorry."

Jacob would want the details, but asking when, where, and how long ago would be gauche.

Hand trembling, Armand drained his glass of red wine in one long swallow.

The waiter cleared their plates.

"You know, darling ..." Frénie tapped Armand's arm. "Riley has experienced terrorists too. When I was in hospital, she uncovered terrorists on my riverboat cruise."

His Adam's apple jolted. "Really."

"Like you, I don't care to talk about it." If she were certain she wouldn't hit Armand's leg by mistake, she'd kick Frénie under the table. Instead, she gave her a will-you-shut-up look. They needed a ladies' room talk about keeping confidences. ASAP.

What on earth had she told Frénie about Jacob and his job? Surely she'd skirted the probing questions, hadn't she?

"How's London?" Despite the miles between them, Jacob's voice warmed her through the phone.

Slippers kicked off, Riley sat on her bed. "Lonely without you. How soon are you coming?"

"Tomorrow, if I can rent a flat. Von Bingen signed off on the paperwork this morning." He sighed into the phone. "Heard from Inspector Vlincken this morning. After leaving the opera house, CCTV cameras filmed Rat Eyes en route to the train station. Another camera had caught him boarding a train for Brussels, a favorite hangout for terrorists."

"Good." Squashing a bed pillow, Riley curled on her side and hugged it to her chest. Goose down was a poor substitute for Jacob. "I miss you." She was happy for Frénie. Really, she was. But watching the two French lovebirds was more than she could bear.

"Why aren't you ladies out on the town tonight?"

"She's with Armand. He said he needed to discuss some things with her." Frénie's apology for leaving her alone had been a relief. Room service had been great. No raw beef on her plate, she'd ordered Dover Sole.

"Sounds like he can't stand to be apart from her. What do you think of him?"

"Charming. Debonair, a French Cary Grant—can't take his eyes off her." Riley brushed a flake of mascara from the pillowcase. "She's bonkers about him." She told Jacob about Armand's family, the orphanage, the gala.

"Don't suppose he said where or when the terrorist attack occurred."

"No. He was pretty choked up."

In the background, keys clicked on a computer.

"You at the office?"

"Yep. Gotta find the Priest."

"Oh." She bolted upright on the bed. "I almost forgot." Words tumbling, she told him about following Rat Eyes before lunch. "If you can wrap this up, I can come home."

"Did you get an address?"

"No. He was too far ahead of us, but I can give you the area. Maybe Interpol can track him. As you exit the final stop of the Docklands rail line, there are townhouses in Lewisham next to the station entrance. Quite nice-looking homes. Out of his price range, I'd guess."

"On it." The keyclicks double-timed. "From here on out, stay out of this. Leave it to the police. I want your promise, Riles."

"Maybe Interpol should put me on a retainer." She stifled a giggle. "After all, I've provided valuable intel."

The sound of a mug *thunked* on his desk. "No. You're not trained, you're not armed. As far as that saboteur is concerned, you're number one on his hit list."

A shiver flickered down her spine. "You sure know how to give a girl sweet dreams."

"I don't want you going out by yourself."

"How about swimming laps in the hotel pool, Daddy may I?"

"This is no joking matter."

"I know." She sank on her wannabe-Jacob pillow. "Sending you kisses." Caressing the pillowcase, she smooched into the phone. "Love you." If she couldn't be with him, after her opera audition for Regents Opera Company tomorrow, she'd hire a pianist to accompany her performance at the gala. Another perfect excuse to leave the hotel.

15

London, Day 7

The cathedral-like arches of St. John's Church rose above Riley's head. A sigh escaped her lips. How great to be auditioning, doing what she did best, what she loved most.

Readying her body for her aria, she expanded her chest, positioned her feet on the diamond-pattered marble floor. Her audience of two, the general manager and the conductor, had chosen seats halfway back in the sanctuary.

She stood beside the piano, where Felix, the company's pianist, dove into the intro to "Der Hölle Rache." With the first chord, the impassioned music catapulted her into the zone. The words and melody soared from her mouth and soul. Three minutes later, she moved to the bend of the piano, catching her breath, shedding the evil queen's persona.

She shifted her posture and launched into the nineteen-page tour de force, Zerbinetta's aria from *Ariadne auf Naxos*. Fifteen minutes later, she drew a calming breath. She'd nailed it today. Every high note, every run. Stepped into the character of the evil Queen of the Night, the captivating, flirtatious Zerbinetta.

"Brava, Miss Williams," the conductor said. "A stunning

performance." Face impassioned, he turned to the general manager, their murmurs too soft to hear. The general manager shrugged, one palm out.

Maybe they were discussing the terms of a contract, which role to offer her.

The conductor leaned forward in his seat. "Do you sing Adele, from *Die Fledermaus?*"

"Yes, of course." She turned to Felix. "Mein Herr Marquis," please."

Chin tucked, the stage manager shook his head, fingers tweaking his eyebrow.

While Felix riffled through her aria book and creased the page open, she stepped into the persona of the saucy maid, pretending to be a noblewoman at the masked New Year's Eve ball. Auburn curls she could cover with a wig, but her height— nothing she could do about that. Oh, well, she'd beguile the bow ties off these guys, and they'd forget she was five foot nine. Maybe.

Playing to the conductor as if he were the Marquis, she oozed every ounce of Viennese charm she could muster.

If she couldn't finish her gig in Belgium, maybe doors would open for her in the UK.

When she finished singing, the conductor applauded. "Truly one of the finest auditions I've heard in a long time. Beautiful voice, flawless technique, and riveting stage presence. I'll make sure your agent knows."

"Thank you. You're most kind."

"I'd like to offer you a contract. However, Mr. Van Cleef, our general manager ..." He gestured to the man beside him. "Is concerned your sabotaged performance in Antwerp could pose a serious risk to the safety of our company and the audience."

Blood boiled in her veins. She hadn't included those reviews in her press kit. "But Interpol has identified the man responsible. They expect to make an arrest." *Soon.* This couldn't be happening to her. Not again.

Why did the opera world have to be so small? She'd never live this down.

"Unfortunately, despite your brilliant audition, Mr. Van Cleef has urged me not to ignore the potential danger. I wish you well in your career, Miss Williams."

Blast that stupid hydraulic lift.

ANOTHER OPPORTUNITY, destroyed.

At least Felix had agreed to accompany her performance at the gala. From the sidewalk, Riley cast a final glance toward the church's stone façade, the cozy brick buildings around it. Not a major opera company, but it would've been a chance to prove terrorists wouldn't dog her every step. If this kept up, her agent might drop her. "I'll never live down that performance."

"Oh *chérie*." Frénie patted her arm. "Perhaps over time, people will forget about Antwerp."

"In the meantime, my career is dust. A coloratura's timeclock isn't as limiting as a ballerina's, but the days of the high notes are numbered. Every coloratura knows that."

"There is a solution. Marry Jacob and make babies."

"I want the satisfaction of achieving something in my professional life before I stop and raise a family."

"Being a good mother and raising children is a serious calling."

"I know. But I'm not ready to do the 24/7 housewife bit. Changing diapers, doing dishes, vacuuming floors."

"Let's do something fun. See the sights. Buckingham Palace, Parliament, Big Ben. But no more trains and subways." Frénie snagged her phone from her purse. "I'm calling Armand's chauffeur to drive us."

"Armand might need him." Riley glanced at Frénie's shoes. Good. Flats for once. "Besides, I like traveling like the British do. Double-decker buses, the tube, trains."

"Thousands of people travel by chauffeur-driven cars."

"Not in my circle." The less beholden she became to Armand, the better she'd feel. "Let's visit the Churchill War Rooms." Maybe focusing on Churchill's desperate battle to save Britain in WW II would numb the sting of today's audition. Right now, she could use a double dose of his courage, his stamina.

"You are so not fun."

"Come on." Looping arms with Frénie, Riley headed for the Fulham Broadway tube station. Once Jacob arrived, maybe he'd let her tag along on his assignment. They'd made a good team on the riverboat cruise, once they'd ironed out their suspicions of each other. Then she could give Frénie a break from her constant company.

"This museum better be exciting."

"Trust me. You'll be glad you came." A few more days sitting on the sofa, snarfing Burie's chocolate and reading novels while Frénie muttered sweet nothings to Armand on the phone would be disastrous for her hips. Riley brushed dust from her pantsuit. Today she'd walk off all those calories. She had a performance coming up, and a trim figure was part of her professional package.

Twenty minutes later, entry fee paid, Riley handed Frénie a headset. As she joined the throng, the reconstructed rooms whisked her back into Churchill's battle to save Britain. Bakelite rotary-dial phones, telephone switchboards, Imperial typewriters. Tiny fans on the girders to dispel the clouds of cigarette and cigar smoke. If it were up to her, she'd spend days here.

"Wow." She sidled in front of the Cabinet Room viewing window. The room where Churchill had held court with generals and ministers of state, plotting Britain's next moves in the war against Hitler. Her fingers itched to touch the wall maps with color-coded thumbtacks and Churchill's chair where he'd smoked his cigars. She almost asked Frénie if Armand could arrange a private tour inside the war rooms.

"*Ma chérie*." Frénie pincered Riley's elbow. "How did the staff stand this? The ceiling is closing in on me." Short breaths huffed her blouse. "Bombs going off overhead, shaking the place."

"You're sensing the oppression they must've had to squelch. Try taking a deep breath."

"I can't imagine having to live down here." Color leeched from Frénie's cheeks. "The smells. The bodies. Hundreds of people cloistered around you." She peered over her shoulder toward the entrance. Sighing, she turned and followed the crowd shuffling toward the next exhibit.

Since when had Frénie become claustrophobic? Maybe they should skip the museum portion and just view the glassed-in rooms. The queue inched toward the lockers and massive wooden storage desks lining the narrow halls. No wonder the place was getting to Frénie. Riley glanced at the new herd of visitors rounding the corner behind her.

Near the end of the group, a gangly Ichabod-Crane-type man and a plump woman gawked at the exhibit rooms along the hall. The lady whipped her head toward the wall sign indicating the outdoor weather, and miniature tropical fruit on her green hat bobbled.

A small man with greasy hair moved behind the woman. Rat Eyes? Height was right. Hair was right. But she needed to see his face clearly.

Pulse hammering her throat, she turned and faced the front of her line. Frénie must've gone on ahead. If only she could be sure the man really was Rat Eyes. This morning she'd been so determined to forget the opera audition she'd ignored the people around her.

Forcing the stiffness from her leg muscles, she walked toward the next room. Her fingers iced as she slipped her cell from her purse. If he was Rat Eyes, was he here to harm her?

"There you are." Frénie zipped back through the line and grasped Riley's arm. "Remind me to buy you a leash."

"Sorry." She started a text to Jacob.

"Not now." Frénie slapped her hand. "Wait until we get out of this rabbit hole."

If only she dared tell Frénie about Rat Eyes. After the riverboat-cruise events, she'd probably believe her. But she'd promised Jacob to say nothing. Breath shuddered into her mouth. Right now, she needed a good dose of the British carry-on-and-keep-calm spirit. No problem with the carry-on bit, but the keep-calm part ...

The line trickled forward.

So did the group behind them. The woman with the green hat, the man beside her. Hard to tell who stood behind them. Maybe the guy had ducked down. Or peeled off to a side exhibit.

If he intended to attack her, she had to protect Frénie. Alert Jacob. Separating might be safest. Up ahead, a signpost pointed to the rest rooms and the Switchroom Cafeteria. "Need to make a pit stop."

"Now?"

"Yep. Excuse me." Riley threaded past the line, headed for the ladies' room. She fought the urge to look over her shoulder. Run for the rest room.

Once inside, she bolted the stall door and sank against the wall. Fingers shaking on the keyboard, she texted Jacob.

> I think Rat Eyes is following me.

Heart thumping her chest, she gave Jacob her location.

Waited for the bouncing dots.

Nothing.

Three minutes later, still no response.

Cold sweat prickled her hairline. Maybe he was in a no-phones meeting with von Bingen. But she couldn't hide in here forever. She dialed his number. Four rings later, the system kicked her into his voicemail. Whispering, she left him a voice message. What if he couldn't check his messages soon?

The rest room door squeaked open. "Riley, are you okay?"

"Be right out." Phone stashed in her purse, Riley flushed the toilet.

"I cannot stand this anymore." Breathlessness riddled Frénie's voice. "I must get out of here." Her tone shrilled toward a high *C*. "Text me when you're done. I'll meet you outside the museum." The rest room door slammed.

Now what? Riley unlocked the stall. Dribbling icy water over her soapy hands, she glanced in the mirror above the sink. A haunted look etched her eyes, lips thinned to a gash, skin paler than a ghost. If only she could've asked Frénie if Rat Eyes was waiting outside the door.

Heart in her throat, she stepped out into the hall. Retreating from the museum wasn't an option. If she tried to backtrack to the entrance, he'd catch her, attack her.

And if she beelined for the exit, Rat Eyes would follow her. Stalk her until he'd fulfilled his mission. She forced her feet toward the line in front of her. Mercifully, the fruit-hatted lady's group was stalled about thirty feet behind her.

The woman stepped out of line and squinted at a placard on the wall. As the tall man joined her, Rat Eyes slipped behind the next couple.

Her stomach flipflopped. No doubt now. Definitely Rat Eyes. His group trudged forward.

Up ahead, the crowd cleared from the front of the glassed viewing wall. She'd have only seconds to make this work. *Dear God, let the exhibit room door be unlocked.* Feet wobbling in her shoes, she closed the distance to the couple ahead of her. Ripped off her headset. Thirty seconds from now, she'd be completely exposed.

The group behind her walked closer. Soon they'd turn the corner and see her. She darted down the narrow side hall to the door for the GHQ, Home Forces exhibit room. Neck muscles almost rigid, she turned the doorknob. The door squeaked open. Pulse throbbing her temples, she strolled between the desks and mannequin soldiers as if she worked for the museum. If Rat Eyes spotted her in here, she'd be trapped.

Breath caught in her chest. No witnesses at the viewing window. Ducking behind a row of black filing cabinets and a wooden desk in the back of the room, she sank to the floor, tucked her knees to her chest. Air eked up her throat, shuddering her ribs like a washboard.

Dear God, don't let him see me.

What if he decided she'd left the museum and waited outside, stalked Frénie until she met her? She whipped out her cell and dialed 999, the British equivalent of 911.

Words burbling from her mouth, she told the dispatcher about Rat Eyes, the sabotaged lift, Jacob's connection to Interpol. "I think there's an Interpol Red Alert out on this guy."

"Do you know his name?"

She rubbed her forehead. What had Jacob called him? "Jacques something. I—I don't remember. I call him Rat Eyes." She scrabbled inside her purse for the folded picture of Rat Eyes Jacob had given her. Gone. No way had she taken it out of her handbag.

"Where are you now, miss?"

"Inside the Churchill War Rooms, the GHQ, Home Forces room, behind a desk in the back of the room." A squeak crept into her voice.

"Try to stay calm. Help is on the way."

Calm? She was a loose-cannon American, not a well-brought-up Brit. Next thing she knew, the woman would suggest she pour a cuppa. The desk leg dug into her spine. The chill from the floor seeped through her skin. Teeth chattering, she prayed verses of protection from Psalm 91.

The doorknob rattled.

16

London, Day 7

Riley shrank against the desk in the exhibit room. Why had she hidden here? A chill from the floor seeped inside her slacks. The wooden beams, girders, and buttresses closed in on her.

Footsteps crept toward her.

Her lungs seized. Eyes squeezed, she scrunched lower. Idiot. She should've scoped the room for some sort of weapon.

"Miss Williams? PC Delaney here." As the constable stepped behind the desk, his black cargo trousers seemed to stretch up a mile. His police number was stitched on the shoulder of his black shirt, a radio and camera clipped to his black stab-proof vest. A metal baton dangled from his fingers. His colleague waited near the door.

Her muscles jellied. Safe. For the moment. *Thank You, God.* Grasping the side of the desk, she wobbled to her feet. "Thank you for coming."

"Step into the hall, please."

At least his handcuffs and pepper spray were still attached to his equipment belt.

A crowd gaped at her through the glass, some snapping photos.

Great. Her one chance to stand in this historic room, drink in the atmosphere, and step back in time. Instead, she was caught on camera with the police as if she were being arrested.

As she left the room with the two constables, she glanced toward the hall, the next exhibit rooms. Her body steadied. No sign of Rat Eyes.

PC Delaney motioned her to the Annex preceding the room.

With their notebooks out and recorders activated, she told them everything. "My friend was feeling claustrophobic and left by the main entrance. She's waiting for me outside. I think. Since Rat Eyes saw her with me, I'm concerned for her safety as well."

"You think this man was following you because of the press coverage, your part in uncovering terrorists?"

"Special Agent Jacob Coulter with the Brussels Interpol office can confirm this. He has a picture of Rat Eyes, and his name."

"We'll escort you from the building." PC Delaney pocketed his notebook.

She swallowed a groan. The one museum she wanted to visit, and she'd barely seen half of it. "Thank you."

The other exhibit rooms passed in a blur as the policemen escorted her toward the exit. People stared and edged away from her as if she was a mortal danger to society.

Heat flamed her cheeks. Innocent, and she was branded a criminal.

She emerged from the museum, constables in tow.

"There you are." Frénie marched toward her, hand on her hip.

"Please, Constable. My friend mustn't find out about this. Jacob wouldn't like it." Riley slipped him her business card. "She and I are staying in room 614 at the Savoy."

"Why are the police with you?" Frénie stopped a few feet from them.

"Just following up on a situation, miss. Would you mind stepping over there?" The other constable motioned her to the side of the building.

A situation. She'd never hear the end of it. Turning her back to Frénie, she spoke sotto voce to PC Delaney. "Do you need anything else from me?"

"When we've located this man and know his identity—"

"Jacques Ibert, that's his name."

PC Delaney scribbled the name on his pad. "We'll need a formal statement from you, preferably at the police station."

"Of course. You know where to reach me. Thank you for rescuing me today."

"We're stationed outside the building so we can't take you to your hotel. Sadly, with budgetary restraints, we can't offer you protection in the UK."

"No problem." She hoped. Jacob ought to be here soon.

As they walked away, Frénie sidled next to her. "A police escort—what have you done?"

"Nothing."

"This I do not believe." She shook her head. "For fifteen minutes, I leave you alone, and you get into trouble." She narrowed her mascaraed eyes at her. "Did you try to steal something?"

"Of course not." Riley scoped the lawns, the trees of St. James' Park across the street. The bus stop farther down from the building. Lots of people, but no sign of Rat Eyes.

"Come. We will take a taxi and be done with sightseeing." Frénie steered her toward the intersection. "Some Burie's chocolate and a good book is what we need."

"Uh-huh." And a cuppa. No. Make that a potta. Riley paced the sidewalk, eyes peeled for a taxi, and Rat Eyes among the pedestrians. She couldn't live her life on the lam, holed up in hotel rooms in foreign cities. The trip to London had proven that. But a life looking over her shoulder every five seconds wouldn't cut it either.

"All this pacing—you are like a lion in a cage." Frénie's steps double-timed to stay with her. "Ever since you subbed for me on the cruise, I think I do not know you anymore."

"I'm sorry." Riley raked her fingers through her hair. The cruise job *had* changed her. Not only because of Jacob in her life, it was the simmering threat of danger, the need for constant alertness for stalkers planning her death. She slipped her phone from her purse. Maybe that's how Burie's chocolate had wrapped its seductive finger around her heart. If she could switch her cravings to tea, her waistline and hips would thank her.

Head down, she pulled up panicked texts from Jacob.

> Where are you? Call me.

Ten minutes later. Another.

> Call me now. Please.

Her fingers flew over the keyboard.

> I'm fine. He got away before the police arrived.

> Headed back to the hotel now.

Passengers queued in front of them to board the oncoming double-decker bus.

No sign of Frénie. Riley clutched her shoulder bag to her side, scanned the area to her right. She'd been so lost in thought. Had Rat Eyes snatched her friend? "Frénie, Frénie."

Massive hands tackled Riley's waist. Before she could turn, a knee crashed into the small of her back.

Heart thumping, she stumbled toward the street. "Hey!

Watch it!" Her feet splayed left and right. Rat Eyes? No, too big, too tall.

With the force of a locomotive, her assailant rammed her kidneys.

Groans gripped her throat. Flames radiated from the blow. He thrust her forward, her shoes skidding toward the edge as if they'd been greased. "Stop, stop!"

One more thrust and she flew into the street, arms flailing the air. Her palms and knees slammed the pavement like a sledgehammer, pounding her teeth. Breath whooshed from her lungs.

The bus barreled toward her.

A scream clawed up her throat. She was going to die. Fire lanced every bone in her body, seared her muscles. Why couldn't she make her limbs move? *Dear God, help.*

A thousand miles away, pedestrians' shrieks wafted through her addled brain.

Tires squealed, horns honked as cars veered out from behind the bus.

Brakes screeching, the massive bus loomed in front of her like a crimson fireball. The stench of burning rubber and street dust filled her nostrils.

Her diaphragm seized. If she didn't get out of the way, she'd be run over.

Waves of heat poured from the monstrous engine and shrouded her body.

Tears spurted into her lashes. *God, spare me.* Fingers clawing the pavement, she forced her leaden torso to roll toward the curb. Her racing pulse throbbed inside her temples. She'd never clear the edge of the bus. Instinctively, her muscles stiffened, tight as rigor mortis.

RILEY BRACED FOR IMPACT.

The vehicle skewed left, right, shrieked to a stop. The underbelly of the front end inches from her head.

Breathless gasps heaved her ribs. Black dots swam before her eyes as her limbs melted into the asphalt. *Thank. You. God.*

The doors whipped open. The driver darted toward her, orange reflective vest billowing away from her navy-blue uniform. Face ashen, she squatted beside Riley. "Are you all right, miss?"

"Just peachy." Riley managed to uncurl from her fetal ball and wobbled onto all fours, trembling like a traumatized animal. "Thanks to your great brake job."

"For a minute, I thought you were a goner."

"Are your passengers okay?"

"I'll find out in a minute. I was yelling, telling them to hold on. That we were going to have an accident. Hopefully they gripped the railings." The woman grasped Riley beneath her arms. "Up you go now." She hefted Riley to her feet, but her leg muscles had dissolved to mush.

"Oh *mon Dieu*, you are so lucky." Frénie darted beside them, eyes wide. She wrapped her arm around Riley's waist, and together with the bus driver, half dragged Riley onto the sidewalk.

"Thank you." Ankles tottering, Riley shuffled between them to the broad steps near the Churchill War Rooms, purse clutched to her chest.

A pair of constables darted into the area.

If these attacks kept up, she'd be on a first-name basis with half the London police force.

Moving aside, the bus driver spoke with the constables, pointing where the attack had come from. The compassion in the female officer's gaze almost undid Riley. Somehow, she had to hold herself together until she reached the hotel.

"What happened?" Frénie sat beside her. "Are you all right?"

"Yes. As soon as we can leave, we're taking a taxi."

"*Bien sûr*, of course."

"PC O'Malley." The female constable knelt in front of her. With her dewy skin, she looked all of eighteen. "Do you need medical attention?"

Riley shook her head, setting off sparklers in her eyes. "Nothing seems to be broken." She examined the stinging abrasions on her palms, the torn fabric and bloodied skin around her knees. A good washing and bandages should suffice.

"Can you describe the person who pushed you?"

Standing beside her, PC O'Malley's partner recorded the interview and scribbled notes in a tiny journal.

"It happened so fast—" Riley huddled on the steps, hands jittering on her knees. "I'd never seen him before."

"So, you did see someone?" PC O'Malley asked.

"N—no, I didn't see him." The chatter in her teeth battered her molars. "B—but the size of his hands, the force of his shoves. Y—yes, I'm pretty sure it was a man."

One thing she was sure of, Rat Eyes hadn't been the attacker. His hands were much smaller. And he was too short to have kneed her in the back. Which meant she'd been targeted by a second assassin.

17

London, Day 7

Still wrapped in her bath towel, Riley inched one leg toward the toilet seat, every muscle and ligament screaming as they flexed. She dabbed antiseptic on the abrasions on her knee. Flinched as the liquid stung her skin. Frénie whimpered from her seat on the edge of the bathtub.

The pain was better than risking infection. When the flames in her nerve endings subsided, Riley switched legs. A couple of ibuprofen around the clock and she'd be good.

"I don't understand why someone would push you in front of a bus."

"Neither do I." Teeth clenched, Riley scrubbed the embedded dirt from her palms. In less than an hour, shades of magenta and purple had mottled her skin.

"And your police escort from the museum—what are you involved in?"

Trying to stay alive. "Nothing."

"This I do not believe. That man tried to kill you."

Sighing, Riley tossed the used pads in the waste basket. "Maybe he caught my performance and didn't like my singing."

Frénie's eyes saucered. "You think he followed you here from Antwerp?"

"No, I was joking. I haven't a clue who pushed me." If only she had the answers. She downed the pills with a glass of water.

"Wait until I tell Armand." Frénie's hand flitted to her hair. "He'll be so upset."

"Let's leave him out of this, okay?"

"Why? He cares about you."

"It isn't anyone's business."

Frénie bolted to her feet. "How can you say that—if I'd stood next to you, I could've been pushed in front of the bus too."

"I'm sorry." Watching Frénie's ashen face in the mirror, Riley cleaned up the mess on the counter. "By the way, where were you?"

"Hailing a taxi. I'm going to order room service." Frénie flounced from the bathroom.

"Thanks. Sounds great." Muscles and abrasions protesting, Riley slipped into her pajamas and a robe, then texted Jacob.

> Survived being pushed in front of a bus this afternoon. Am fine.

Three dots bounced on the screen.

> Can you talk now?

> No. Soon.

> Okay. Call me ASAP.

Thirty minutes later the room service waiter arrived, pushing the linen-clad table. As he removed the domes from their plates, Armand rushed through the door. "Riley, how are you?"

"Fine, thank you." Eyes beaded on Frénie, Riley shot her a

mutinous look. Frénie hiked her shoulder to her ear, palms out. Right. Miss Innocent. Traitor was more like it.

"Let me see." Armand reached for her hands.

Steaming inside, Riley held out her palms.

"Not too deep." He cradled her hand in his, tilted her palm toward the lamplight. "You were fortunate. And your legs?" Heat flooded her cheeks. "They're fine thank you." She flipped the edges of her robe over her knees.

"Excuse me." He rose from the couch and signed the room service ticket, slipped a hundred-pound note inside the leather folder. Giving him a curt bow, the waiter left. Armand sat next to Riley on the couch, Frénie hemmed in her other side.

This was almost as bad as the police escort out of the Churchill War Rooms.

"Our poor Riley." Armand touched her wrist. "You've been through so much."

"It's nothing." Flickering a smile, she slipped her hand free. "I'll survive."

"I certainly hope so." At the indignation in his voice, Riley bit back a smile.

"And you haven't heard the worst of it." Frénie launched into her version of the fiasco at the museum.

The muscle pulsing Armand's jaw was so like Jacob when he was upset, worried about her. At least Armand had the grace not to ask her for details.

Lurching to her feet, Riley shuffled to the dinner table. "I'm starved. Let's eat."

"Come join us, Armand." Frénie pulled him to his feet.

Great. Just when they needed to have a private girls' chat. Riley forked some smoked salmon and shrimp cocktail on her plate, a few mini quiches, chunks of Brie and Camembert and sliced baguette. "If you'll forgive me, I'd like to eat in bed. Today's adventures were exhausting."

"Of course." Armand smiled. "Call us if you need anything."

"Thank you. You've been most gracious. And thank you for the lovely meal." Riley shut the bedroom door behind her and settled in the easy chair beside the window. Nestling the plate on her lap, she forked a bite of smoked salmon. Protein. That's what she needed.

Between bites of shrimp, she called Jacob. He picked up on the first ring. "Hi, can you talk now?" She kept her voice to a whisper.

"Yeah. What's up. Thought I'd go berserk this morning when you didn't answer me. And then, your text about a bus—"

"Sorry, it's been a zoo here." Munching on a bite of Brie, she brought him up to date. "I need protection." She wiped her fingers on the napkin. "I wish you were here."

"I'm still trying to negotiate a short-term lease for a flat there."

"I think I'd be safer in Brussels."

"Yeah, I'm beginning to agree with you."

"Great. Then I'm booking a flight home." She hovered the knife over the Camembert. But if she left, she might not find out what Rat Eyes was up to. And if Jacob came to London ... "On second thought, I think I'll stay a while longer."

"Riles ... what are you cooking up?"

She popped the last shrimp in her mouth and mumbled around it. "Nothing."

"I don't believe you."

"How is it two men are hunting me now?" Had the bus attacker followed her inside the museum? "He must be a lot taller than I am. After all, he rammed his knee in my spine hard enough to send me flying. Maybe he's working with Rat Eyes. If not, who's behind Tall Guy's attack today, and why?"

Clicks at the keyboard sounded in the phone. Jacob's breaths huffed at her ear. "I wish we had more information."

"Since my focus was on the bummer audition, I suppose Rat Eyes could've tailed me to the museum."

"Riles, I don't like this. I wish I could be there to protect you."

"Me too."

18

London, Day 8

What else could go wrong today? Payment for his flat lost in transit. The flight to London delayed two hours. Text messages from Riles, saying they had a double date with Armand and Frénie for dinner tonight. But he'd prayed and felt God urging him not to cancel that.

Stifling a yawn, Jacob rubbed the grit from his eyes. After a day of meetings and travel, his suit needed a good pressing. A fresh tie and shirt. The vase of red roses from the Savoy Hotel flower shop tucked to his chest, he knocked on Riley and Frénie's door.

A petite woman in a magenta silk suit flung the door open. "Finally. I meet the magnificent Jacob Coulter who has won my best friend's heart." Frénie air-kissed Jacob's cheeks, French style. Stepping back with the panache of a Hollywood starlet, she motioned him inside.

"And I have the pleasure of meeting the irrepressible Frénie." The bouquet felt like an albatross. Idiot. He should've brought flowers for Frénie too. Armand had been generous to Riles.

"Riley has told me so much about you. Well, *non*, she hasn't."
Frénie's eyes twinkled at him. "You are a man of mystery."

"Just a humble civil servant."

"Bravo. That's an improvement over waiting tables on a cruise ship." The rocks glistening in her earlobes were a couple carats' worth of diamonds. "And now working in London."

"Temporarily." The knot in his tie squeezed his throat. All this woman needed was a bare-bulb interrogation lamp.

"Confidentially, I missed Riles." Whose idea was this double date? Riles would never expose him on an assignment. "It seemed a good way for us to spend time together."

"Hmm, a man of independent means. *Bon.*" The way Frénie assessed his suit made him want to squirm.

"Where are you staying?"

"I rented a flat." He needed to turn the tables, fast. "How's life away from the riverboat cruises?"

Arms spread, she pirouetted on the carpet. "I love it. You saw my cabin, *non?*"

"Cramped, aren't they. Where's Riles?" She should've warned him they'd be playing twenty questions.

"Still dressing."

The bedroom door opened, and Riles limped into the room.

Either she'd taken a prescription painkiller or was downing ibuprofen. Being tossed on the street must've been excruciating.

Eyes aglow, she hobbled toward him, her turquoise dress rustling at her knees. Her thousand-watt smile washed over him, and his chest nearly burst. Once again, he'd come close to losing her.

Frénie took the vase of flowers. Nodding his thanks, he swept Riles in his arms and buried his face in her hair. He drank in the scent of her perfume. "Thank God, you're okay."

She tilted her face toward his ear. "I've missed you so much."

"Thought I'd go nuts today, counting the hours until tonight." Von Bingen's last-minute meetings hadn't helped either.

Sniffing the roses, Frénie set the bouquet on the coffee table. "They're lovely."

"Yes, they are." Riles brushed her lips across his, and he hungered for more.

"You ladies may need a wrap tonight. It's a bit chilly." If only he and Riles could've dined alone, ordered room service.

Easing away from him, she smoothed a wrinkle from her dress.

Wearing a cream-lined magenta coat, Frénie returned from the bedroom. She handed Riles the Belgian lace shawl he'd given her the night of their first month's engagement.

How fancy was this restaurant? He straightened his tie. Maybe he should've listened to Margot's warning to keep a tux in his office travel bag.

In the corridor, he punched the elevator button. Good thing von Bingen had authorized a rental car. "Where are we eating tonight?"

As he held the elevator door open, Frénie stepped inside. "Armand reserved a table at La Gavroche, in Mayfair."

Jacob nearly choked. A Michelin two-star French restaurant with a tariff of $600 per person. At least he was appropriately dressed. La Gavroche meant "street urchin."

En route to the restaurant, he kept tabs on vehicles behind them. There'd been too many attempts on Riles' life. And he'd sent her to London to protect her.

The red brick exterior was understated elegance, the interior, conservative reds and black. Most guests were casually dressed. The knots in his shoulders relaxed. The wealthy felt no need to flaunt their money.

Armand rose as the *maître 'd* walked them to his table. Jacob stifled a grin. After waiting tables on the riverboat cruise, being the waited upon should be pleasant, especially in a place known for stellar service.

"Jacob Coulter." He shook hands with Armand then stood aside as Armand kissed Frénie's cheeks and Riley's hand. While

Armand seated Frénie, Jacob helped Riles and took the chair beside her. As his lips brushed her ear, he whispered, "Haven't been on a double date since high school. They've come up in the world."

Chuckling, Riley placed her napkin in her lap. Despite her artfully applied makeup, the lighting deepened the shadows beneath her eyes.

This invitation seemed more like a polite summons, not friends on a date. He flicked his napkin open on his lap. A pity he and Riles hadn't discussed this before they came. "Thank you for the invitation, Monsieur Découvrir."

"Please. Call me Armand. We are friends."

That was fast. "Armand." Riles could've added suave to her list of the guy's attributes.

"I took the liberty of ordering us a memorable meal." Armand flicked a hand at the waiter. "No food allergies, right?"

"Correct." Jacob flexed his fingers in his lap. He'd add control freak to Armand's character list.

Settling his elbows on the armrests, Armand studied him, a bemused smile at his lips. "What field are you in, Jacob? Frénie tells me you are a spy."

Jacob choked on his water. Von Bingen's orders were to stay undercover. "Where did you get that idea?" Surely not from Riles. She'd warned him about Frénie's tendency to blab. Was her probing intentional or curiosity?

"But ..." Frénie said with an impish grin, "You were on the riverboat cruise with Riley."

"Yes." He dabbed his napkin to his mouth. Had he overlooked press coverage on the terrorists mentioning him by name, connecting him with Interpol?

"When I rejoined the cruise, the crew were full of stories about the terrorists on board." Eyes laughing at him, Frénie toyed with the stem of her wine glass. "And how you disarmed them at the captain's table the last night of the cruise."

"Coincidence. One of the passengers drew a weapon. Now I work for an import-export firm. Office work, mostly."

"In Brussels, *non?*" Frénie sipped her wine.

Staring toward the table, Riles fidgeted with her engagement ring in her lap.

What had he gotten himself into? "And you, Armand, what business are you in?"

The waiter served their first course with the flair of the well-trained.

"I run a charitable organization, an orphanage in the UK."

"How admirable." Inherited wealth must be footing the bill for their four-course meal tonight. His background checks on Armand had been innocuous. An upstanding citizen, no convictions, no known vices. No known shady business deals or associates.

Jacob picked at his smoked salmon salad. *Admit it—you don't want to like the guy.* Maybe it was jealousy. The wealth, the gifts he tried to shower on Riles, the extravagant lifestyle. Tucking people in his back pocket through sumptuous meals. The fish in Jacob's mouth soured. Maybe that's how the little man in Vienna felt, eating with Gorilla Guy.

Sizing up the patrons, Jacob studied the beefy man with a walrus mustache, chatting with three men. His expensive-suited tablemates bore the hallmarks of armed enforcers. Bodybuilder physiques, don't mess-with-me faces.

Armand caught his stare and glanced toward Beef Boy's table.

Fat hands splayed on the table, Beef Boy nodded, lifted his index finger in Armand's direction.

Cutting Beef Boy a curt smile and nod, Armand turned back to Jacob, mouth tight.

"You know him?" Beside him, Riles' posture went on alert.

"Not well. He owns a townhouse on my street." Armand twisted the gold signet ring on his pinky. "Although he's seldom there."

A snapshot of the guy could be useful. But impossible, sitting with Armand. "What's his profession?"

"Not one that would interest a man in import-export work."

"Try me."

Wine glass lifted to his mouth, Armand's sip turned into a long draught. He dabbed his napkin to his lips. "Rumor has it he gambles."

"Is that all?" Jacob snorted. Probably the best excuse Armand could come up with over a sip of wine. If La Gavroche was a typical hangout for terrorist financiers, he should've asked von Bingen for a hefty expense account. "What's his name?"

"Why all the questions?" Elbows on the table, Armand steepled his fingers. "Given your profession, of course."

Jacob pushed back his plate. Armand was playing cat-and-mouse with him over *foie gras* and chocolate soufflés. But why—because the man desired Riles?

"*Mon chèr*, after capturing those terrorists on the riverboat, Jacob is probably curious." Frénie patted Armand's sleeve. "The little gray cells and all, like Hercule Poirot."

"Yes." Jacob flashed her a smile. Maybe he'd been too harsh on Frénie. "Just wondering if I'm seeing my first Russian oligarch."

An amused smile playing at his lips, Armand motioned the waiter to refill his wine glass. "I believe he goes by Yousef Mandouri."

"Wrong again—not Russian." Jacob faked a chuckle. Somehow, he needed to wangle a photo of the men. If he'd known the dinner would be profitable for Interpol, he'd have worn glasses with a hidden camera. No matter. As soon as possible, he and his London guy Ian would pay Yousef Mandouri a visit.

DINNER OVER, Jacob helped Riles into his car. Thankfully, Armand drove Frénie back to the Savoy himself. Jacob climbed in the driver's seat and fired the engine. From now on he'd do his own cooking. At home. Unless Yousef Mandouri was eating out.

"I swear I didn't tell Frénie you work for Interpol." Riles tugged the hem of her dress toward her knees.

Reminding himself to check to the right, he eased the car into the traffic. "She's not as naïve as you painted her."

"So, it seems." Riles glanced out the window. "It's a little late to give her the loose-lips-sink-ships lecture. And after the bus incident, things were chaotic."

A Porsche cut in front of him, and he slammed on the brakes. Somehow, he needed to activate damage control, or the French couple could become a problem. "You don't discuss my cases with your family, do you?"

"No. Never. They have no idea what you do for a living."

Good. He could still use Riles as his sounding board. He downshifted for a turn.

"Do you think Yousef Mandouri is connected to the Priest?"

"It's possible. Von Bingen assigned me to the UK because of the Paris murder. The body faced London. Paired with Ian's arguments that London is a money laundering capital." Jacob hoped there wasn't a connection between the murders and the latest attempt on Riles' life.

"You're good at your job. Von Bingen chose well." Riles placed her hand on his knee and squeezed his thigh. Shock waves zinged his nerve endings. "You'll catch the Priest."

Right now, he wanted to pull off the road and catch her in his arms, smother her with kisses and caresses. Instead, he headed for the Savoy. Ian was waiting for him at the flat to discuss developments in the case. Jacob's first roommate since college.

To justify him taking the day off tomorrow, they'd have to pull an all-nighter. Maybe they could line up enough info on Yousef Mandouri to round up his dinner partners at La Gavroche.

"If you're free, I'd like you to come with me tomorrow to see Tracy. The school ends early Wednesday afternoons." Thankfully, Ian had encouraged Jacob to connect with his sister.

"I'd love to meet her."

"Thanks. Tracy's been putting off my Zoom calls, so I haven't seen her all year." He raked a hand through his hair, drummed his knuckles on the steering wheel. These days, a thirteen-year-old could get into all sorts of trouble. Drugs. Boys—no. *Don't go there*. If only their parents were here to raise her.

Riley covered his drumming hand in hers. "I'm sure she's fine."

"I don't have the heart to force her to spend her school vacations with me while I'm at work all day. And she'd rather stay with her best friend's family." From now on, if he could manage it with his job, that would change.

19

London, Day 9

I f they didn't get a break in this case soon ... Jacob drained the last drops of his coffee and set his loaner mug on CT specialist Marcus Rayborn's desk. Early this morning he and Ian had requested to liaise with CT, the Counter Terrorism branch of the Met. If the need arose, they could also work with MI5. Despite the coffee, the last half hour bringing Marcus up to date had left Jacob's mouth drier than a wad of cotton.

Brown eyes razored Jacob and Ian as Marcus nodded, scribbled notes. Slender as a beanpole, he'd seldom smiled as they spoke. The assigning Met officer said Marcus had been instrumental in uncovering terrorist cells in the Paddington station area two years ago. Cells about to launch attacks on Parliament.

"Was Yousef Mandouri on CT's radar?" Jacob asked.

"For money laundering." Marcus leaned back in his chair, palmed his short Afro. "But nothing specific linked him to terrorist financing."

Tie askew, Ian hunched over his laptop. Dark circles rimmed his eyes.

They'd stayed up until the wee hours, digging into Yousef's business ventures. Searching for anomalies, shell corporations, gambling preferences. The document Ian had forwarded to Marcus when they arrived spit out of the printer.

"Let's pay a call on Mandouri." Marcus whipped Ian's pages from his printer and slapped their copies on the desk.

Forty minutes later, Marcus parked in the garage closest to One Canada Square, a skyscraper in Canary Wharf.

Jacob inhaled the salty air and tang of fish, his all-too-brief moments outdoors. Sunlight silvered the River Thames as it lapped the piers. For a moment, the gulls squawking and circling overhead transported him to South Padre Island, Texas. A million miles away. A place he hadn't visited in years. Thanks to years in a French boarding school, university, and parents living overseas. Why couldn't they have accepted mission assignments stateside?

The elevator whisked them to the fortieth floor. Inside the office, an attractive receptionist stood behind the black-veined marble counter. The gleaming gold and silver logo of Mandouri Enterprises emblazoned the white marble wall behind her. Business must be even better than their research had indicated.

As classily dressed as her surroundings, the smiling young woman adjusted her hijab. "Morning. Do you have an appointment?"

"No." Ian flashed his Interpol badge. "We're here to speak with Mr. Mandouri."

"I'll see if he's in." Her face an unreadable mask, she rose and smoothed her pencil skirt. She disappeared down the hall, heels clacking on the marble floor.

"Right." Turning his back to the hall, Ian leaned an arm on the counter. "As if she didn't know."

"Maybe we should've stationed a team around the exits," Marcus said.

Heels tip-tapped on the floor. The receptionist stuck her head around the corner. "Mr. Mandouri will see you now."

Inside the office, a wall of windows overlooked the sunlight dancing on the River Thames below. A barge laden with rail cars glided past the wharves.

Mandouri waited behind a massive desk, his throne-like chair fit for a Middle Eastern potentate. He seemed tall and beefy enough to have pushed Riles in front of the bus. But then, so were his three dinner guests.

Today he wore a raw silk suit in ombre shades of gray, a black turtleneck sweater, and a gold bracelet thicker than a bicycle chain. Jacob's gut knotted. He forced his gaze from the silver cross necklace around Mandouri's neck. Identical to the ones on the Priest's victims.

"Great view you have here." Jacob extended his hand. Mandouri mangled it like minced meat.

"Don't I know you from somewhere?" Mandouri's eyes narrowed on him.

"We've never been introduced."

"Hmm." Swiping his tongue over the front of his teeth, Mandouri settled his shoulders against the back of his chair, his belly rounding against the sweater.

As they sat in front of the desk, Marcus pulled out a field notebook and pen. Ian flashed his Interpol badge.

"If you don't mind, Interpol has some questions for you," Ian said.

Shrugging, Mandouri said, "Why should I mind? I have nothing to hide." His lips spread, quivering the tips of his walrus mustache. "I'm an honest businessman."

Yeah, right. "Do you do business in Vienna?" Jacob crossed his ankle over his knee. "And Paris?"

"Sometimes." Mandouri's tone was guarded. "Why?"

"Nice necklace you're wearing." Ian settled in his chair. "Where'd you buy it?"

Mandouri's tongue made another circuit around his teeth. "Why does Interpol care about my necklace? You aren't religious, are you?"

"Are you?" Ian asked.

"Yes." A smirk crossed Mandouri's face. "About some things."

"Such as?"

"Invasive questions for no apparent reason."

"Were you in Vienna six days ago?" Jacob asked.

"I might've been." Mandouri cracked his knuckles. "What's it to you?"

"Where did you stay?" Jacob asked.

"At the Sacher Hotel."

"And your meals—did you eat them there?" Mandouri hadn't been at the Rote Bar Restaurant when he and Margot had staked out the place.

"I don't recall."

"Do you travel alone?" Ian asked.

Marcus's pen scratched across the page.

Cheeks flushing, Mandouri splayed his hands on his desk. "What business is it of yours?"

"I'll take that as a no. We're investigating a series of murders," Ian said.

"Do I look like a murderer?" Mandouri's bushy brows shot north.

As far as looks went, Mandouri could pass for a Mafia Don. A man capable of having others do his dirty work. Like the three goons at his dinner table last night.

"WHAT DID YOU THINK OF MANDOURI?" Jacob said as they headed to the underground car park.

"Guilty as sin." Marcus pushed the key fob, and the car doors clicked.

"Thanks to your dinner engagement last night, we have two strong contenders for the Priest. Mandouri and your Gorilla Guy," Ian said.

"And maybe the guy who pushed Riles in front of the bus."

Jacob fastened his seatbelt. "But Mandouri didn't wear the cross necklace to dinner last night."

"Manchester is making detailed searches into his banking records and business deals," Ian said.

"I'll request a Met plainclothes team to tail Mandouri and his henchmen," Marcus said.

"Good. Jean-Pierre can check Mandouri's stays in Paris."

"We'll need every piece of evidence for the court." Marcus turned into the Met car park.

"Thanks, guys." Jacob hopped from the car. He ought to stay and help Ian, but this might be his only chance to see Tracy. "Couldn't do this job without you."

"Hey, what are partners for?" Ian flashed a grin. "Your kid sister needs you."

20

Near Brighton, Day 9

As Jacob drove into the grounds of Chumley Girls' School, hordes of preteen and teenaged girls spilled from the Georgian red brick building, chattering and laughing. The saliva fled his mouth. Would he recognize Tracy? It had been so long since she'd taken his Zoom calls.

He fingered the gift box on the stick-shift console Riles had wrapped for him. "You think she'll like it? I mean—I know you did a great job, but ..."

Squeezing his biceps, Riley smiled, melting an inch of his angst. "Choosing gifts for a thirteen-year-old girl, someone we don't really know ... it's the thought that counts."

"Yeah." He yanked the knot in his tie. "Hope you're right." He helped her out of the car.

The gaggle of girls darted past them and headed out the main gates. Once again, the school door swung open. Decked out in her school uniform, Tracy trudged down the steps, blonde ponytail swishing her shoulders.

Air caught in his chest. Clutching the gift in one hand, Riles' hand in the other, he quickened his pace. Fifteen strides and they reached Tracy. He snugged her to his chest, and her hands stiffened at her side. "Hey sis, it's great to see you." He introduced Riles.

"It's great to meet you." Riles flashed the dazzling smile that always left him weak in the knees. Tracy's pretty face pinched.

"Hi." Her eyes glommed on Riley's ring finger, shot to his.

"We're engaged." He brushed a stray hair from Tracy's cheek.

"Oh. That's nice."

"We haven't set a date." He could hardly blame her reticence. She barely knew him. Blinking, his eyes swept her voluptuous figure. Man, he needed to do the birds-and-bees chat, ASAP. "I brought you a little something."

"Thanks." She pulled off the ribbon and paper, opened the lid. As she held the delicate gold chain in her fingers, the tiny diamond glinted in the afternoon sunlight. "How sweet." She dropped the necklace in the box, closed the lid. "Thank you."

Air seeped from his lungs. He'd passed the first test. "Do you want me to put it on you?"

"Sure." Her gaze locked on his. "You picked it out?"

Heat scalded his face. "Well, actually ..."

"Oh." Shoulders drooping, she eyed Riles with the intensity of a trained interrogator. "I guess you bought it."

"Your brother bought it, I picked it out." Riles' cheeks pinked. "His job leaves little time for fun, not even with me."

Man, he'd blown it. He hadn't even taken the time to buy a gift for his sister.

"But I'll bet he picked out your engagement ring."

"Yes, I did." Jacob spread his palms. "I'm sorry, Tracy. I should've found time to shop for your gift myself. Next time, I will."

Her gaze dull, she stared toward the main gates so long he wanted to sink through the pavement. She hiked a shoulder. "It's okay."

"Where'd your classmates go?"

"To town. Wednesdays, we're allowed to shop, buy treats and stuff."

"Sounds like fun."

"Yeah." She kicked a pebble with her shoe. "Kid stuff."

"How about we see the sights instead?"

"Sure. Let's go to the Royal Pavilion. It's a really cool palace. My treat," Tracy said.

"Hey, that's my job."

"Nope. I've got money."

Was he sending her too much allowance? British entry fees were stiff. Riles on one side, he draped his arm around Tracy's shoulders and walked her to his car.

"Why are you here? I mean, you've never come to see me before."

"That's not true. I came. Once." The week before he started with Interpol. Five years ago. She'd been a sweet kid, then. Vulnerable, underneath the stiff veneer. He'd been a senior in high school when she was born. By the time she was toddling around the coffee table, he was hundreds of miles away, living in a college dorm. Spending summers on overseas jobs.

Twenty minutes later he pulled into the car park. The minarets and domes, the lacy stone filigree of the Royal Pavilion's exotic exterior looked as if the building had been transplanted from India or the Middle East. Not the kind of place he'd have expected his kid sister to enjoy. "Wow. Some seaside resort."

"For the royals, of course." Inside the palace, Tracy pranced up the faux bamboo staircase as if she lived here. "You must see the banqueting room. It's way beyond fabulous."

"Do you come here often?" Riles drew beside Tracy on the stairs.

"Yes. It's my favorite place in Brighton."

Whoa. He wasn't sending her enough money to visit the palace *that* often. He caught up with her. "That must eat up a lot of your allowance."

Flipping her ponytail over her shoulder, she darted ahead of him on the staircase.

The grandeur of the banqueting room snatched his breath. The wallpaper on the staircase was exquisite, but the Chinese wallpaper painted to look like individual pictures was special. Gaudy crystal chandeliers designed like enormous lotus blossoms, hung overhead. The floorboards creaked beneath his feet as he crossed the room.

Arms extended like a ballerina, Tracy glided toward the dining table the size of a soccer field. Gold candelabras and cutlery, bone china, and crystal glassware had been laid for an unforgettable meal.

Sighing, she clasped her fingers to her lips. "Can't you imagine dining here, using this beautiful china, slipping food in your mouth on solid gold silverware?"

Where had she developed such values? Certainly not from Mother and Dad. If they knew about this, they'd be appalled. "It's probably the everyday ware."

"Oh, you." She elbowed his ribs hard enough to crack them.

He winced at the searing pain.

"You have to ruin everything, don't you?"

Blast. He'd done it again. His teen years weren't that far behind him but relating to his sister was like connecting with an alien from outer space. If only they'd shared a common childhood, living with their parents. Maybe she'd have recognized his joshing.

"I agree. It takes your breath away." Riley stepped beside her. "Eating like this must be an incredible experience. Which piece is your favorite?"

As Riles and Tracy strolled along the table chatting, Jacob glanced toward the entrance to the room. His gut lurched.

Gorilla Guy.

Standing in the doorway, watching Riles and Tracy.

140

Was Gorilla Guy following Riles? Had he pushed her under the bus? He was tall enough, had massive hands.

Heart racing, he glanced around the room like Joe Schmoe tourist, then turned back to the table. How long had Gorilla Guy been standing there? If he was the Priest, he was packing. He curled his fists in his pockets. Why did Interpol keep their agents unarmed?

He glanced up from the epergne centerpiece, and his stomach plummeted. Gone. He'd lost him again. If Gorilla Guy had crossed the room to the kitchen or salon, squeaky floorboards would've alerted him.

Sidled next to Riles, Jacob whispered, "I'll be right back. Keep an eye on Tracy. The man from Vienna's here."

Riles gripped his sleeve. "You saw him?"

"At the doorway. Text me if you leave this room." Calf muscles urging him to sprint, he forced himself to stroll to the door. Surveilled the hall, the closed doors. No sign of the man. Taking the steps two at a time, he headed down the main staircase.

Cell out, he texted Ian and brought him up to date.

Is Brighton a known money-laundering center?

Willing the three bouncing dots to morph into text, he didn't know whether to be excited or worried. Now he had a firm connection with Gorilla Guy to the UK. The Priest could be using the palace as a drop for payments, clandestine meetings. And if Gorilla Guy had recognized him, and connected him to Riles and Tracy, he'd led the guy to his kid sister too. Jacob jogged around the side of the castle and peered into hidden alcoves, scanned the trees and gardens.

As he returned to the main entrance, Ian's text came through.

Checking into this. Thanks for the tip.

Great. A euphemism for no idea.

Bring Marcus up to date.

INSIDE THE ROYAL PAVILION TEAROOM, Riley slathered her
scone with clotted cream and strawberry jam. For safety's sake,
she'd suggested eating inside, rather than on the terrace. But the
shrubs, flower beds, and massive trees ringing the velvety lawn
had been tempting. Possibly also to the man Jacob was seeking.
And if he were a sniper …

At their small bistro table, Tracy stirred her tea. The sugar
should've dissolved minutes ago. "Where's Jacob?"

Probably texting Ian. "The men's room?"

"He's taking forever." Tracy slapped the spoon on her saucer,
thumped her back against the magenta upholstered chair. "What
do you see in my brother anyway?"

Dabbing her napkin at her lips, Riley composed her answer.
"I realize you don't know him well, but he's a kind man.
Considerate, witty, honorable, trustworthy. On several occasions
he's saved my life."

"As in—literally?" Squinting at her, Tracy snatched a bite of
her apple tart.

"Yes." Riley told her about the hydraulic lift, the ridiculous
staging.

"You're an opera singer?" Tracy snarfed another bite of the
tart. "How cool is that."

"It's a tough way to make a living. But I enjoy learning new
roles and performing them onstage. How about you? What do
you want to do with your life?"

Tracy shrugged. "Have lots of money."

"You know …" Riley kept her tone gentle. "There's nothing
wrong with being wealthy, but there's so much more to life. Have
you made good friends at school?"

"Yes, one." Tracy pulled a frayed snapshot from her purse and handed the picture to Riley. "My BFF. We're roommates."

Both girls were dressed in school uniforms. Their heads touching, Tracy beamed at the camera, her arm draped around the dark-haired girl's shoulder. Judging from her current physical development, the picture was several years old. Riley returned the picture to Tracy. "She's as pretty as you are."

"You think I'm pretty?" Tracy pulled at her lip, the vulnerability in her eyes so raw, Riley wanted to take her in her arms and hug her.

Instead, Riley met her gaze, settled her smile on Tracy. "Most definitely." Best not tell her she had Jacob's deep blue eyes, his generous mouth, and high cheekbones.

SHOULDERS SAGGING, Jacob made his way to their table. How had Gorilla Guy managed to vanish?

"Your tea's cold." Tracy's voice was flat.

"Story of my life, sis." He gulped a few sips. "Couldn't be helped."

His sister snickered.

Brows knit, he mouthed at Riles, "What?"

"Girl talk."

Tea and muffin gulped, he walked them to the car, Tracy strolling beside Riles. Jacob jammed his fist in his pocket. He couldn't even make it off the batters' bench with his own sister.

As soon as he pulled into the school's car park, Tracy hopped from the back seat. "Thanks. It was fun."

"We should be thanking you." Jacob managed a fleeting smile. "Hostess with the mostest."

"Any time, bro."

Did she mean that?

"We'll hold you to that." Winking, Riles flashed Tracy a smile.

With a nervous chuckle, Tracy backed away from the car.

Go for it, Riles. Maybe there was hope yet.

Without a backward glance or wave, Tracy loped toward the main building, ponytail swishing the air.

Elbows on the steering wheel, he cupped his forehead in his hands.

"Cut yourself some slack, Jacob. She's a teenager who feels abandoned by her family. It'll take time to build her trust."

"Yeah." Cell in hand, he scrolled to the grainy picture of Gorilla Guy taken in Vienna and handed Riles his phone. "This is the guy I was tailing. Have you seen him before?"

"No. I'd remember that face, his jaw."

"Keep a lookout for him. Today he saw us together. He may remember me from Vienna. If he's our man known as the Priest, last week he murdered two people. He leaves a silver cross necklace on his victims."

Shivering, she huddled in her seat. "You think he had business in Brighton?"

"It's possible." Every muscle on edge, Jacob headed toward London. His gaze darted from mirror to mirror, tracking every vehicle around them. For the first time since his assignment had begun, he wasn't following the Priest's trail of dead bodies, he was on hot on his tail.

And he'd led Riles smack into the heart of it.

21

London, Day 10

I f the resident entering the building hadn't let Riley inside without buzzing Jacob's flat, her surprise would've been spoiled. Grocery sacks weighting both hands, she knuckle-rapped Jacob's door. He'd better be here.

Knocking again, she studied the hallway. Nice updates to a century-old building. Forest-green paint, contemporary sconces, Art Deco prints on the walls. She pressed her ear to the door. Maybe she should've called first. The lamb steaks wouldn't keep long.

The bolts shot back. Jacob stood in the doorway, clutching a bath towel around his waist, water trickling between the hairs on his legs. "Hey, what's up?"

Insides turning to mush, she held up the grocery bags. "Surprise. Chef à go-go."

"Wow, thanks. I'm sure it beats what Ian and I have in the fridge."

Rats. She'd forgotten Ian would be here too. All she'd wanted was a nice quiet evening with Jacob. Alone.

One hand on his towel, he reached for three of the bags. She scooted past him, her arms brushing his damp chest. The end of the hall opened into a living room cum kitchenette. In decorator terms, cozy but modern. A couch, coffee table, and a TV perched on a console. Perfect for one person.

Shoulders aching from slogging groceries for five blocks and up a hesitant elevator, she set her sacks on the minuscule counter. She smoothed the wrinkles from her silk dress. Wiggled her burning feet in her high heels. Why did her best-laid plans always go south?

The last time she'd cooked for Jacob, they'd nearly broken up. She shoved aside the memory of that riverside picnic. Her attempts to convince him she wasn't working with the terrorists.

He unpacked his bags on the bistro table and held up the two lamb steaks. Grimaced. "Will this be enough?"

"Sure. Chefs specialize in the unexpected." She'd dice the lamb, carrots, and potatoes for a stew. Ian deserved a homecooked meal too. "Why don't you dress while I start?"

"Back in a jiffy."

"Great." Meat prepped, she turned on the gas burner and melted a chunk of butter in olive oil.

"Sous-chef reporting for duty, ma'am." Heels snapping together, he saluted her.

Knife paused over the onion, she chuckled. Hard to resist his goofy grin, damp hair spiking from his head like a kid. His suit trousers and blue shirt brought out the cobalt in his eyes. No tie, but his polished loafers gleamed beneath the kitchen lights. The evening might be redeemable yet. "Grab a knife and chop the carrots, please." She turned back to the counter, diced the onion and garlic.

"At your service, madame." Slipping behind her, he tied an apron around her waist. His lips nuzzled the back of her neck, sending shivers down her spine. "I've heard from the Antwerp police. Inspector Vlincken thinks you should press charges against your understudy and her boyfriend."

Shoulder blades jammed toward her spine, she grabbed a

carrot, whacked it to pieces. Why did he have to be all business? Didn't he realize why she'd brought dinner? "That'll grow warm fuzzies between European and American artists."

"Riles, you can't be serious. Whether or not Annie considered the consequences of her plan, she let her boyfriend take the fall. Under Belgian criminal law, they're guilty of plotting bodily harm."

"Do we have to talk about this tonight?" She slammed her knife on the counter, threw the chopped onion and carrots in the sizzling butter. Drops of hot oil stung her cheek.

"No, but it'd be wise to bring closure to part of this mess."

"I don't want to hear about it tonight."

"Why not? Next thing we know, terrorists will be recruiting that pair."

Garlic added to the onions, she attacked the potatoes under the running faucet. Bits of peel and tap water splatted on her dress. Rats. She dabbed the apron on the water-spotted silk. Knowing her luck, she'd ruined her best date dress. "But they didn't go through with the plan."

"Only because someone else had already cut the cable." He took the potatoes from her. "And when the police were searching for answers, neither she nor lover boy stepped forward. They were content to let the perpetrator escape."

Lips taut, she tossed the diced lamb into the skillet, salted and peppered the meat.

"Don't be such a softie." Working beside her, he chunked the potatoes, then dropped them into the sizzling fat. "Does Annie remind you of Lacy? I know they don't look alike but—"

Her twin sister, who'd never share the operatic career they'd dreamed of. Thanks to Leukemia. Riley shrugged, added the stock to the stew. "Maybe. But Lacy was a mezzo-soprano, not a coloratura."

"Yeah, right, a low voice? But hon, you could've been killed. And the other singers onstage, the guys in the orchestra pit."

"You don't get it. The opera world is small."

"You're wimping out because you're afraid what other houses would think." He slapped his knife on the counter. "What's gotten into you? Where's your sense of justice, bring down the bad guys?"

Acid churned her stomach. At this rate, dinner would be a disaster. "If I listen to you, I'd be doing this out of a vindictive heart. I'd be no better than a lynch mob."

"Maybe if we catch a few more terrorists, you'll get your thinking straight."

"Maybe." Then again, maybe not. She slapped the glass lid on the skillet.

As Jacob set the table for three, the bolts shot back on the door. Footsteps thumped down the hall. "Do I smell a homecooked dinner?" Ian peered around the corner, his gaze shifting between them. "Uh ... did I arrive at a bad time?"

"No, no." Riley turned to the sink, swiped the wetness from her cheek.

"Right on time, pal." His body pressed close to hers, Jacob tucked a stray curl behind her ear. "I'm sorry. Please forgive me for being so—so—"

"Obtuse."

"Yeah. Obtuse. It's your decision."

Not trusting her voice, she nodded. Was tonight a sample of her life once she and Jacob married? With them both pursuing high-stress jobs, would they ever have time to enjoy each other? And yet, she loved helping him solve his cases. Tracking down the bad guys.

"Want to come with me to check out Armand's orphanage tomorrow? I was hoping a surprise visit might be productive."

"Sure. I'd like to know what singing the gala I'll be singing at is funding."

22

Near Brighton, Day 11

The engine cut, Jacob squeezed Riles' hand as he scoped the
parking lot of the Saint Aminta Orphanage. Two white-
paneled vans, three modest-priced cars, a Range Rover. "What
do you think?"

"Hard to tell from here." She straightened her navy jacket,
smoothed the knees of her matching slacks.

A three-story Georgian-era building faced the main gate. The
red-brick façade and white- window frames seemed well
maintained. According to his GPS, the property was twelve miles
from the nearest village. "At ten in the morning, I expected more
signs of life."

"Me too."

"Unusual name for an orphanage."

Phone in hand, Riles did a quick web search. "Aminta in
Greek and Latin means protector. From what I've observed of
Armand, the name fits."

Jacob grunted. As long as the guy kept his hands off Riles.
"It's too quiet. No children laughing. Keep your eyes peeled for
the unusual, will you?"

"Always happy to assist Interpol."

"Glad to hear it." He leaned over the gearshift box and kissed her. Moved in to deepen the kiss. Carpe Diem. No. Make that Carpe Kissem.

"Um, great perks with the job."

"Yeah." He waggled his eyebrows à la Groucho Marx. "There's more where that came from, doll."

"Do tell." She slid her arm behind his neck, her nails feathering his hairline.

Jolts of electricity shot through him. "We'd better head up to the building." He helped her from the car and walked her toward the front steps, letting his hip graze hers.

"How do we play this?"

"Off the cuff." But when Riles met his parents during the riverboat cruise and pretended to be his fiancée, she'd shocked them all. Especially him. "Wait. Within reason, okay?"

"Sure." She looked at him as if he were nuts.

Inside, the entry hall was Armand-style elegance. A brass carriage light hanging from the ceiling, pale blue walls, a royal-blue carpeted staircase leading to the next floor. Jacob knocked on the office door to his right. Footsteps pattered and the door opened.

"Yes?" The gaunt woman reminded him of a sparrow. Maybe it was her plain brown cardigan and skirt, mousy brown hair stringing over her shoulders. "Well—what are you selling? We're not interested in religious pamphlets, if that's what you're peddling."

Should he play the friendship-with-Armand card?

"We'd like to talk to you about adopting a child." Riles slipped her hand through his arm.

A nervous tic jerked his diaphragm. Adoption. Was there no end to Riles' creative leaps? He laid his hand on top of hers. Might as well play the game.

"This is a bit unusual." Rapid blinks fluttered Ms. Sparrow's eyelids. "We normally schedule appointments."

"We were in the area and hoped you might make an exception." Jacob slipped his hand around Riley's waist.

"Of course. I'm Isabel Martin." A smile flickered across her mouth. "I'll be taking your application." She darted inside the open office door.

Jacob walked inside the doorway. Utilitarian, with a contemporary desk and filing cabinets. Electric tea kettle on the credenza.

"What sort of child did you have in mind?" She pulled forms from her desk drawer, snatched a pen and a camera.

"Well-behaved, thoughtful, kind, loving, obedient." A chuckle aborted in his throat. Every quality he wished he'd seen in Tracy. But then, she was now a teenager.

"Honey ..." Riley clasped his hand. "He was kidding, of course. We'll know the one for us once we've met the children."

"All of them?" Ms. Martin's eyes widened.

"Yes." Riley flashed her irresistible smile.

"How many children are there?" Jacob cleared his throat. "Girls, or boys as well?"

"Well, um ..." The woman slicked her lips. "Why don't we do our interview first?" She opened the double doors into a salon across the hall, done in Armand-royal blue.

As he and Riles settled on the sofa, Ms. Martin pulled an encyclopedia from the bookshelf. She sat in the armchair across from them, slid her forms on the book. Pen poised. "Your names, please."

"Jacob Coulter, my fiancée, Riley Williams." As long as Armand didn't find out they'd been here, he might not regret Riles' crazy scheme. Strike now, explain later.

"Passports, please."

Flashing a smile, he handed her the documents. She flipped through them and photographed the information pages.

"How often do you receive requests to adopt a child?" Jacob crossed his legs.

"Such information is confidential."

Riles scooted against his hip. "How long does it take to process the adoption?"

"Well ... there are the appearances in court, various meetings ..." The woman hurried through the rest of the questions on her form, pen scratching on the page. Addresses. Family history. Doctors' names for health verification. Character references. Employment history.

"I'm so eager to meet the children." Riles clasped her hands to her chest. "May we see them now and tour the facility?"

"Excuse me for a moment." Ms. Martin laid the application on her chair.

As soon as she shut the door, Jacob moved to her chair and read the forms. They'd have to sign an agreement for background checks. The final line required the approval and signature of the orphanage's administrator. Armand.

No way could he afford a background investigation on his employment. Not on an undercover assignment. "Riles, this isn't going to work. We can't sign these forms."

"Okay. Leave it to me."

"Fine." Why had he been surprised she'd say they were adopting when she'd blithely announced their non-existent engagement to his parents?

The door opened. Armand stepped into the room, wearing jeans, a shopworn shirt, and a sardonic smile. "Jacob. Riley. What a nice surprise."

———

"ARMAND." Plotting strategy against Gorilla Guy was one thing, but improv theater was out of Jacob's league. "Great to see you."

"I understand you wish to adopt."

"Actually, it was Riley's idea." *Great, Coulter. Pass the buckaroo.*

"Yes." Riles gushed. "I love children. I thought your orphanage would be a perfect place to see if adoption would be possible. Since we aren't British citizens."

Seated in the armchair, Armand crossed his ankle over his knee, bouncing his sockless athletic shoe. "I'd love to help of course." He folded his hands in his lap. "After the required background checks."

"Great." Jacob slouched on the couch and extended his arm along the back cushions. *Good play, Armand. Ball lobbed back in my court.*

"We'd love to see the children and tour the orphanage." Riles leaned toward Armand. "After all, I'm donating professional services to support your work."

Chin ducked, Jacob bit his lip, squeezed off his grin. *Brava, Riles.*

"Of course. Follow me." Armand rose. "Most of the children are at school at the moment." He jogged up the blue-carpeted stairs. "Only the little ones are here right now."

"Meet Lucy and David." He opened the double doors to the first room off the hallway. As he entered, the little towheaded boy and girl squealed and darted over to him, arms outstretched. A nanny seated in a corner rocking chair rose as they entered. Nodding at Armand, she stroked the wrinkles from her uniform.

To Jacob, the children looked about two years old. Possibly twins. Both born with Down syndrome. His heart melted. With everything in him he wanted to scoop them into his arms and hug them, play with them.

Standing beside him, Riles looped her arm in his, laid her head on his shoulder. "Aren't they precious?"

Dolls and wooden blocks lay scattered on the rug. Low-rise bookshelves lined the walls, filled with children's books, wooden puzzles and stuffed animals, coloring books and tubs of crayons. Everything a child could want.

"Papa Armand."

Kneeling, Armand whisked them into his arms and kissed their cheeks. "*Mes petits choux.*"

The girl wrapped her chubby arms around his neck. "Wuv you, Papa." She planted a noisy kiss on his cheek.

"Are these your children?" Shock riddled Riley's voice.

"*Non, non.* I am not their biological father. All the children call me Papa Armand." He stood, wetness glistening in his eyes. "They are like family to me."

"Do you have any infants here?" Riley linked arms with Jacob.

"At the moment, three." He kissed Lucy and David and motioned them back to their toys.

In the nursery, heavy drapes were drawn, the room dark. Jacob stepped inside, Riles at his side. Six cribs lined three of the walls. A changing table and shelves of baby supplies were near the door. A red light flashed on a baby monitor, its microphone crackling. Odd, no nanny around. Maybe the woman next door was in charge here too.

"Come meet Peter while Nanny's stepped out." Armand walked to the crib beneath the window. "His mother overdosed on drugs. Today he's three months old."

Arm around Riles' shoulder, Jacob peered in the crib. His nostrils twitched at the stench of dirty diapers. The baby was tiny for his age, his flailing fists jittery. Signs of his mother's drug problem.

Scooping the infant as if he were made of loose feathers, Armand kissed the baby's forehead.

Peter's kitten-like mewing almost undid Jacob. The baby was so helpless. So needy. He clenched his fist. Jammed it inside his pocket. All because someone lured his mother into the world of drugs and addiction.

Cooing to the infant, Armand laid him on the changing table and unfastened his onesie, wiped the diarrhea from his bottom and changed his diaper. When he finished, he laid Peter in Jacob's arms.

A dull ache weighted his chest. He hadn't held such a tiny baby since Noel's son had been born. Tears clogged his throat. He hadn't expected this. If holding someone else's son affected him so deeply, what would it be like when he held his own child?

Nestled at his side, Riles stroked the baby's black hair. She looked up at Jacob, tears glistening in her eyes. "He's beautiful."

Peter's eyelids fluttered open. Muttering nonsense, Jacob stroked the baby's knuckles and his fist unclenched. Tiny fingers clutched Jacob's pinky and sucked every inch of his heart into its grasp.

"So." Armand lolled against the crib, arms spread along the railing. A half smile quirked his lips, not reaching his eyes. "We do have something in common."

Much as he hated to admit it, the man was right. Jacob gave him a curt nod. With Peter snuggled to his chest, Jacob planted soft kisses along the infant's forehead, the skin pure velvet beneath his lips. As he tucked the baby into his bed, Riles hovered beside him, her cheek on his shoulder. She trailed her fingers over Peter's silken hair, his tummy.

Riles at his side, he followed Armand into the hall.

At the top of the stairwell, Armand paused. "Are you ready to sign the forms?"

"Peter needs a home, a loving family." Jacob grasped Riles' hand, met Armand's gaze. "We have some things to chat about first. Decisions to make."

"Yes," Riles murmured.

The sardonic smile returned to Armand's face. "As you wish." He saw them to the front door.

"Thank you for letting us crash in without an appointment." Riles flashed Armand a smile.

"Anytime." Rigid lines threaded Armand's mouth.

This morning he'd come here to ferret out Armand's secrets and expose him as a fraud. Instead, Armand had parried him like a master swordsman. Ever since the Frenchman had walked into the room downstairs, he'd been reading him, testing him.

Definitely not an opponent he'd want to face on a battlefield.

AUTUMNAL LEAVES CRUNCHED under Jacob's feet as he walked Riles back to his car. "What did you think?"

"Armand would be brutal at ping-pong."

"The sparring was that obvious, huh?"

"Darling, your face is as readable as *Green Eggs and Ham*."

"Gotta work on that." If he intended to survive field assignments. Bad guys reading his intentions could be deadly.

"Don't." She leaned against the car door and stroked his cheek. "It's one of things I love about you."

Longing to ask her what else she liked about him, he started the car. At the village city limits, he downshifted to a crawl as they passed a red telephone box, quaint lanes with picture-perfect buildings straight out of an Agatha Christie novel.

"You don't like Armand, do you?" Riles shifted in her seat toward him.

"He makes my skin itch. Maybe because he fits the financier profile. Wealthy, gives extravagant gifts, lives lavishly."

"If those are the red-flag traits, Interpol must have a gazillion candidates."

"Yeah. That's the problem. Sifting through the innocent, the dupes. The wolves in sheep's clothing. Guess I was counting on the orphanage panning out to be a phony. But the place seems aboveboard. Competently managed."

"Even though there were so few children."

"Yeah ... They were probably at school." Gauging the oncoming traffic, he eased into the roundabout behind a rusty tractor and its threshing blades. "And frankly, I don't like the guy."

"You're jealous because he's been so solicitous of me."

"Yep. Can't deny it."

"Oh, Jacob." She leaned over, kissed his cheek. "That's sweet."

"So why does a man of Armand's vast wealth host a gold-plated gala to raise funds for a well-maintained orphanage that lacks nothing?"

"People like to be needed, to feel they're doing something good in this world. The gala provides an opportunity to be a part of his good work." Tears pooled in her lashes. Sniffling, she pulled a tissue from her purse.

"Peter got to you, didn't he?"

Her smile tremulous, she squeezed his fingers. "To both of us."

"Yes."

23

Brighton/London, Day 11

Jacob dropped Riles off at the Savoy, wanting far more cuddles and kisses than possible with the gearbox between them. Inside the flat, Ian squinted at his laptop screen at the bistro table. Jacob hung his raincoat on the coatrack.

"Ah, the intrepid explorer returns." Hands behind his neck, Ian arched his spine. "Did you manage to plant our flag on the hill?"

"I wish." More like a mutt retreating with his tail between his legs. "Think I opened a can of worms. Sandwich?" Jacob set a loaf of bread, packages of ham and cheese on the kitchen counter.

"Thanks." Ian's face split into a grin. "As long as you leave the live bait off mine."

"Right." Over sandwiches, he brought Ian up to date.

"Maybe there aren't a lot of orphans in the area." Ian pushed away his empty plate. "Or he's placed most of them with families. Besides, you were there during school hours."

"Maybe the paneled vans in the car park shuttle the kids to school." Jacob brushed the breadcrumbs from his lip. "With most of his business in London, why set up an orphanage miles from the nearest village?"

"Fresh air for the children?" Laptop open on the table, Ian pulled up the orphanage website. "Looks too deserted to hide a surveillance team. And we have no legal grounds to suspect him."

A pity. The guy was too suave. Too handsome. Too— "Let's focus on Gorilla Guy and Mandouri. Where we'll find the next victim."

"Ask Marcus for plainclothes surveillance teams on potential sites. Maybe we can prevent a murder."

"I'll check with von Bingen for a budget to fund the surveillance." Jacob texted her.

"High places in London ..." Ian pulled a pen and a sheet of paper from his laptop case and scribbled notes. "Possibly historic, or politically significant. Big Ben, the London Eye, the Shard in Southwark, two other office buildings. One Canada Square in Canary Wharf, and One-ten Bishopsgate in the City of London, our primary financial district. St. Paul's Cathedral, Parliament, Buckingham Palace ..." He threw down his pen. Scrubbed his jaw. "The list is endless."

"We don't have the manpower to cover them all."

"So, we choose a couple of them. Where is the Priest most likely to hit next?"

DIGGING her toes into the plush carpet beneath the linen-covered tea table in their suite, Riley tilted the teapot, letting the steaming liquid trickle into her cup. She nestled a smoked-salmon finger sandwich on her saucer and stretched out on the living room sofa, the couch pillows propped behind her. Something about the orphanage didn't add up.

If only she could worm her way into Armand's townhouse. His office in the Shard had revealed nothing, other than a successful businessman. Today he'd been baiting them. Knowing once they saw Peter's emaciated little body, Armand would have them wrapped around his emotional pinky.

The suite door opened and Frénie waltzed in, couturier shopping bags dangling from her fingers. *"Oh là là,* you should've come with me."

Arms laden with dress and hat boxes up to his chin, Armand's chauffeur followed her inside the living room. Riley sat up on the couch and slipped on her heels. He laid the boxes on the coffee table, nodded at her, and closed the door behind him.

"You must see what I bought." Frénie whipped open a dress box and lifted an emerald-green silk suit from the tissue paper. She held the fabric against her body. *"Chic, non?"*

"Very." But Frénie would look smashing in anything. "Did Armand take you shopping?"

"Non, he was busy at the orphanage today."

"If you don't mind my asking, has he entrusted you with his credit cards?" Cheeky, but she needed to know.

"Sometimes he shops with me and chooses what I buy. I think he enjoys shocking the salesclerks trying to fit all those thousand-pound notes in the cash register." Frénie flipped the lid off the first hat box and perched an emerald-green fascinator on her pixie haircut. She tilted her chin left, right. "Cute, *non?"*

"Yes. Armand will love it." Sipping her tea, Riley glanced at the price tag and choked.

"Today, he gave me cash."

"So, you saw him to pick up the money?" Riley poured herself another cup of tea. With a £1,500 slip of a hat, she could only imagine the cost of the garments.

"Non, he'd left it in an envelope with his chauffeur."

"That's trusting."

Fingers pressed to her lips, Frénie giggled. "And I spent every pound of it." She flopped into the easy chairs and slipped her feet from her stilettos. "Seventy thousand."

A piece of salmon caught in Riley's throat. Coughing it up,

she set her plate on the coffee table. That was more than she'd spend on clothes in ten lifetimes.

"If you'd been here, I'd have shared. You could use some new suits."

"That's very generous of you." But she'd prefer to earn her own way. "Does he often give you exorbitant sums of cash to spend?" Hadn't Frénie heard of Sugar Daddies?

"If he's leaving for a business trip, or like today when he couldn't shop with me."

"Wow." Riley reached for her teacup. "Sounds like you ought to insure your wardrobe."

"And the jewels too."

When Frénie had helped herself to the plate of tea treats, Riley snagged a cucumber-and-watercress finger sandwich. More than ever, she wanted to snoop inside Armand's house. "When is Armand's next trip?"

"He leaves tomorrow night."

"Off to some Caribbean Island?" Laughing, Riley wiggled her shoulders. "Wouldn't you like to tag along?"

"He never tells me where he's going." Her smile slipped. Frénie whisked her napkin from the tea table, slapped the linen on her lap.

"Maybe he's a secret agent, a spy."

"Armand?" Frénie paused her salmon sandwich at her lips. "Could be."

But were spies so well paid?

"WE'RE TOO LATE. The Priest has struck again." Sighing, Ian disconnected the phone call.

"Where, when?" Pushing back from the bistro table in his flat, Jacob rubbed his brow. These murders made him feel like a puppet. But who was pulling the strings?

"The bodies were found an hour ago at One Canada Square, in Canary Wharf."

"Bodies—a double murder?"

"Looks that way. A silver cross on each victim."

"Why the change in MO?" Jacob took his coffee mug to the sink.

"Guess we'll have to ask the Priest." Ian shut down his computer and unplugged it from the wall socket. "Shall we visit the crime scene?"

"Yes. Call Marcus. Ask him to meet us there." Jacob grabbed his raincoat, Ian lagging a few steps behind as he phoned their partner.

Canary Wharf. The area where Riles had followed Rat Eyes. One Canada Square. The same building where they'd interviewed Yousef Mandouri.

Forty minutes later, he parked in the underground garage off Montgomery Street. Ian put an Interpol placard on the dashboard.

"Canada Square isn't the tallest building, so why commit the murders here?" Jacob stepped inside the elevator.

"This area is a financial center." Ian pushed the button for the fiftieth floor. "Except for the ground floor, the building is primarily let as office space. Many of them banks."

"So, the murders could be another message. Or an attempt to pin the blame on Mandouri."

"Yes. But I wouldn't rule out Mandouri's involvement." Ian blocked the elevator door open. "He was rather arrogant the other day. He may think we'd never make an arrest charge stick."

"Who found the bodies?"

"The window washers." Ian pushed the button and the doors glided shut. "Their BMUs—building maintenance units—are stored on the roof. Guess they saw more than they expected this morning."

The doors opened and Jacob stepped out of the elevator, Ian at his side.

"In 1992, the Irish Republican Army attempted to detonate an improvised explosive device beneath the building, at the tube and Dockland Light Railway stations. From then on, the observation deck was closed to the public."

"The murderer could've been buying time before the bodies would be discovered."

Overhead, the sound of rushing water poured through the pipes in the pyramid roof structure. Marcus stood outside the blue-and-white police tape while crime techs worked the scene.

Jacob nodded at him, flashed his Interpol ID lanyard at the constable on guard duty, then clicked the compass app on his phone. Which way had the killer positioned the victims' bodies?

PC Jenkins walked over to the police tape. A lean man, graying temples, probing eyes. "You the men from Interpol and CT?"

"Yes." Jacob introduced himself, Ian, and Marcus. "We think this case is related to bodies found in Vienna and Paris. The MO fits."

"Come along."

Following the PC's lead, Jacob stepped over the police tape and stopped ten feet from the bodies, Ian and Marcus beside him. "How were they killed?"

"Gunshot wounds."

The woman lay sprawled on the floor, legs akimbo. The man was propped against the wall. Jacob's gut twisted. Rat Eyes. "The male victim is Jacques Ibert, a resident of Brussels. Interpol has a Red Alert on him. We suspect he sabotaged a hydraulic lift during an opera performance in Antwerp."

"Glad to have you aboard. It isn't often we resolve a case on the spot." PC Jenkins chuckled. "How about the female?"

Black hair poked from a shoulder-length auburn wig, the curls and style reminiscent of Riles' hair. Jacob's pulse ratcheted. Although her raincoat resembled Riles' coat, the woman seemed several inches shorter. An oversized safety pin fastened a piece of paper to her chest. "What's the note say?" He pointed to her body.

Snapping his fingers, PC Jenkins signaled the techs. "Could you bring over a photo of the woman and that paper on her?"

A constable snapped a picture and handed Jacob his phone. His head reeled. A page of music. "Der Hölle Rache," one of Riles' Queen of the Night arias. He forced himself to study the woman's face, the coffee in his stomach threatening to erupt. On a dark night she might pass for Riles. "The victim resembles my fiancée, who was on the sabotaged lift."

PC Jenkins blanched. "Looks like these murders are a personal warning. For you."

LAST TOENAIL PAINTED, Riley capped her bottle of pink polish. Frénie would've insisted on a professional pedicure, but since she was out with Armand, the evening had been deliciously quiet. A linen-clad room-service table with miso-glazed salmon under a silver dome, and Patricia Bradley's newest suspense novel.

If she weren't careful, this high living would spoil her. Riley returned her pedicure case to her luggage. Jacob's ringtone pealed on her phone. "The William Tell Overture," the theme song for *The Lone Ranger*. She let the music play for a few bars then took the call. "Tonto speaking."

"Riles, I don't want you going out alone while we're here. Ever. Not without me or an escort." His words spilled so fast she barely understood his torrent.

"Why?"

He told her about the double murder.

"Canary Wharf." Legs wobbling, she sank onto her bed. "Rat Eyes is dead?"

"Yes, but the female victim was dressed to look like you, wig and all. The killer left the first page of your Queen of the Night aria pinned to her chest."

"Wow. The killer must've seen me, followed me to the train." Heartrate galloping, she clutched the bed pillow to her chest. "Do you think Gorilla Guy killed them?"

"It's possible. But the other victims were criminals engaged in money laundering. We have no such evidence against Rat Eyes. The victim dressed like you is a warning."

"Okay." She swallowed a gulp. For a second, she almost wished they were back on the riverboat cruise, Jacob's room only a loud scream away. Forcing her thoughts off the murders, she told him about Frénie's shopping trip.

"I wish I'd never insisted you come to London."

"Then you wouldn't have found the Priest."

"I *haven't* found him." His voice snarled in her ear.

"You will. I'm certain of it."

The door to the suite opened and shut. "I think Frénie's back."

"Wonder where she and Armand go."

"I don't know. His place, maybe?" Riley smooched into the phone. "Love you."

"Try to get some rest, hon."

After the news he'd delivered? "Sure."

The kiss he blew into the phone caressed her ear. She disconnected the call as Frénie floated into the bedroom, lipstick and hair mussed, red splotches on her neck. Standing on tiptoe, she twirled in a circle, arms outstretched like Julie Andrews on the mountaintop. "I am *so* in love."

"I'm happy for you. Really." Riley crawled beneath the duvet on her bed. "Is Armand still leaving on his trip tonight?"

"*Oui.* With a bed on the plane he arrives rested the next morning."

"How convenient. I'd love to see his townhouse. Do you think we could visit it tomorrow?"

"Why now?" Frénie slipped into her nightgown, a lacy affair that must've cost thousands. "I know he plans to have you and Jacob over."

"Unfortunately, Jacob is awfully busy. I'll bet Armand's home is stunning inside. Do you have a house key?"

"*Non.*" With circular strokes, Frénie massaged oil on her face and eyelids. "Either Armand or his chauffeur takes me there."

Most likely Armand's home had a security system. Picking his lock wasn't an option. Riley shoved three pillows behind her and sank against them. If she managed to pull this off, she wouldn't be making the trip to Armand's house unescorted. Even with Rat Eyes' death, her bus attacker, and whoever killed the woman at Canary Wharf, were still alive. "Does Armand have live-in staff?"

"*Oui*, a maid. I think she lives on the top floor." Cleansing pad in hand, Frénie turned to her. "Why all these questions?"

"We don't have any sightseeing plans. Why not do Armand's house. His neighborhood?"

Frénie's eyes narrowed. "Why?"

"Because, my dear friend, sometimes a person's home reveals a lot about who they are, what they think and believe."

Face pale, Frénie slapped the cotton pad on her forehead. She threw the pad in the waste basket. "Why are you trying to drive a wedge between Armand and me?"

"That's the last thing I want to do." But if a peek inside his house would protect Frénie from marrying the wrong man, she'd run the risk.

"You know ..." Frénie stomped to her bed and slid between the covers. She rolled her back to Riley, yanked the duvet over her shoulders. "As soon as the gala is over, I think you should return to Belgium."

The words slashed Riley's heart. Her best friend. Ever since they roomed together in Bucharest. "I care about you." She flicked off the bedside lamp. "Think about it. Good marriages are built on honesty."

24

London, Day 12

If Jacob knew where she was, he'd have her hung from a British yardarm. But he couldn't snoop inside Armand's townhouse and she could. If their luck held.

From the front stoop, Riley glanced at the renovated townhouses on the deserted cul-de-sac. Each several centuries of restrained elegance, deceptively expensive. If Armand lived here, it must be a posh address. Riley jogged Frénie's elbow. "Knock again."

"Maybe we shouldn't do this."

"Nonsense. You're practically engaged. What could go wrong?"

"Knowing you, plenty."

But she had to find something, some lead to help Jacob. "Knock, please."

As Frénie reached for the brass knocker, the front door opened. The woman's black dress, white ruffled apron and cap starched to match, looked as if Armand had snatched her from Downton Abby.

Dark eyes stared at them from her thirtyish-something face.

"Mademoiselle Frénie?" Slavic consonants tinged the maid's accent. "Monsieur Armand is not at home."

"I know, but may we come in? Armand's planning to invite Riley over and she couldn't wait to see his place."

"I—I don't know ... this is highly irregular. I don't have his permission."

"Trust me." Frénie flicked her wrist. "He won't mind." Hands clasped over her purse, Riley beamed the woman a beatific smile. "Armand asked me to perform on his gala."

"*Oui*. Riley is a famous opera star."

Wincing inside, she knuckled Frénie's back. *Don't overdo it.*

"You won't stay long—I mean, I don't want to lose my job."

"He'll never know we were here." Frénie breezed past the maid, Riley at her heels.

Marble black-and-white tiles formed a checkerboard on the foyer floor. Twenty feet above them, a crystal chandelier gleamed on the Louis XV chairs and baroque commodes. Riley restrained a low whistle. Priceless antiques. Lamps, figurines, a massive Flemish tapestry consuming one wall. Business must be booming. No wonder Frénie was gaga for the man.

Resisting the urge to tiptoe, Riley followed Frénie into a Zenlike room with a bubbling fountain, Swedish chrome and leather armchairs, a glass-topped coffee table. Riley sat beside her on the white leather couch.

"I'm famished. Do you suppose we could take tea?" Frénie laid her purse on the couch.

The maid blanched. Her fingers skittered over her apron.

"Whatever you have on hand will be fine. Some cucumber sandwiches, perhaps?"

Biting back a grin, Riley strolled over to a credenza.

Five votive candles flickered in front of a triptych of photos. The outer two were headshots of older, bearded men. Armand's father, grandparents? In the center picture, a teenaged Armand draped his arms over a woman and a young girl's shoulders. Given their resemblance, probably his mother and little sister.

Behind Armand, crumbled building fronts formed mounds of rubble on the street, the furniture in the apartments exposed to a world of voyeurs. She'd assumed Armand was born in France. But the photo had been shot in a war zone. From the looks of it, somewhere in the Middle East. Or maybe Northern Africa. Algeria, perhaps.

The dark-haired girl looked about four years younger than Armand. Like her mother, the girl wore a cross necklace. Christians. A chill chased across Riley's shoulders. With the girl's pixie haircut and heart-shaped face, she was a dead ringer for Frénie. Turning, Riley caught the maid drilling her with dagger eyes. If she didn't watch out, the woman might call Armand. "What a lovely family."

Huffing, the maid left the room. Cutlery clanked on the counter. Water dribbled.

"The family photos seem to have been taken in the Middle East. I thought you said Armand was born in France."

"Yes." Smoothing her skirt, Frénie shrugged. "I guess."

Another puzzling piece of Armand's past and Frénie was ignoring it. "Have you noticed how much you resemble his sister?"

"*Oui.* That is one of the first things he told me after we met."

"Hmm." Riley picked up her purse from the couch. Sounded a bit creepy to her. Wooing a woman who looked like your dead sibling. Maybe Frénie ought to encourage Armand to seek emotional healing before they went any further with their relationship. "Where's the loo?"

"First door to your left off the entry hall."

Tiptoeing to the foyer, Riley bypassed the door to the loo and eased open one of the adjacent double doors. Hundreds of books lined the floor-to-ceiling shelves along the walls. She crossed the thick Persian rug to the desk. A silver-framed photograph on the massive desk was angled toward the leather chair. Her breath hitched. An enlargement of the same picture

Tracy had shown her at the Royal Pavilion. Cell out, Riley snapped a duplicate.

Sliding back his desk chair, she opened Armand's center drawer and rifled through the papers. She pulled out the stapled top sheets. GUEST LIST FOR THE GALA. Squelching her excitement, she photographed the pages and forwarded them to Jacob.

Three dots bounced on her screen.

> Where did you get this?

> I'm in his study.

> Get out of there now. Before he catches you.

> Right. On it.

"What are you doing in here?" Frénie appeared at the door and Riley gasped. "Tea's almost ready."

"Coming." Heart still clobbering her chest, Riley picked up the frame. "Who's the girl in the picture?"

"Armand's daughter." Frénie crept from the doorway.

Fingers shaking, Riley forwarded her cell photo to Jacob.

> Did you know Tracy's BFF is Armand's daughter?

Three dots flashed on the screen.

> How do you know that?

> This is the same picture Tracy showed me at the Royal Pavilion.

> You said you were leaving. Get out NOW.

I'm on zzzzzzz—Thumb jabbing a key on her screen, Riley glanced up.

The maid stood in the doorway, her withering glare shriveling Riley in her shoes. Eyes saucers, Frénie pressed her fingers to her mouth.

"HEY IAN." Jacob thumped his tea mug on Marcus's desk at CT HQ. "Riley's trapped in Découvrir's house."

"How do you know?" Ian rolled back from his guest cubicle desk.

"She's texting me from his study. My gut tells me she's in trouble."

Looking up from his computer, Marcus frowned. "What's she doing in his house?"

"His girlfriend took her there." The last thing Jacob wanted to do was implicate Riles with a PC in the room.

"Is he there?" Marcus asked.

"She didn't say." He held out his phone and scrolled through her messages as Ian peered over his shoulder.

"Wow. The guest list for the gala. Now we can vet his patrons, run down possible suspects." Ian's lips pursed in a low whistle. "You should put Riley on our payroll."

"If she lives long enough." Not bothering to restrain the snap in his voice, he pulled up Armand's address on his phone. Another advantage of working for Interpol. Then texted Riles.

> On the way.

"I'll drive," Marcus said.

"Always wanted to see how the elite live." Ian grabbed his jacket from the back of his chair.

"Thanks." Then he'd try to contact Riles en route. Jacob's cell rang. Brussels. Von Bingen's number. No way. Not now. "Coulter here."

"I'd like a progress report. Now. The bureau chief wants to know what you've been up to."

"Two minutes ago, we received a fresh lead." Raincoat over his arm, he sprinted toward the elevator as he told her about the guest list.

"That's all?"

"Ma'am, this is the biggest break we've had. Some of these guests could be the financiers we're looking for."

"I need results, not excuses."

"We're working on it, ma'am." And he owed the only break they'd had to Riles. Riles, who needed him right now. Counted on him to be there for her. By the time Marcus reached Armand's house, who knew what might have happened to her. He darted inside the elevator Ian had held open. "How long before we reach her?"

"Given the traffic, maybe twenty minutes. Maybe less, with the siren on."

His nearly-too-late dash to save Riles in Strasbourg gripped his mind. Finding her on the fourth-floor window ledge, the killer about to shoot her. No.

This time she'd be okay. She had to be.

25

London, Day 12

"What are you doing in Mr. Découvrir's private study?" Fists on her hips, the maid strode to the desk.

Heat singed Riley's neck. She'd made a royal mess of it. "I'm really sorry." If Armand found out, he might break up with Frénie. At the very least, he'd never trust her again. "I shouldn't be in here." No point fibbing about looking for the loo.

"You could cost me my job." Crimson splotched the maid's cheeks.

"I'm so sorry." Riley edged away from the desk. "I never meant to hurt you."

"Don't you understand?" She stepped toward Riley, thrust her face inches from Riley's. "I need this job."

Riley glanced toward the hall. A large man slipped behind the Belgian tapestry, his back to her. Her heart plummeted, her feet riveted to the floor. Armand? No, too tall. Too massive a build. Supposedly the maid was the only live-in staff.

The fabric undulated, then flattened. If only she could've seen his face.

Fingers pincering Riley's arm, the maid shoved her to the door. Jerked a thumb at Frénie. "You leave too."

The door slammed behind them. Bolts shot into the lock.

She'd nabbed the guest list, but at what cost? Now she'd have to face Armand at the gala, feign innocence while she squirmed inside. Worst of all, she'd lost Frénie's respect.

Sobbing, Frénie covered her face in her hands. "How could you do this to me? You've ruined everything. Armand will never trust me again."

"I'm so, so sorry." A millstone dragging on her heart, Riley walked her down the steps.

"Do you think she'll tell Armand?" Frénie blotted her eyes with a tissue.

"Maybe. If she thinks that would protect her job." *God forgive me. I used Frénie.* But she'd never meant to hurt her.

"THERE THEY ARE." Air shuddered from Jacob's mouth. At least they were unharmed. *Thank You, God.* Frénie stomped past the red and white brick townhouses on the cul-de-sac. Riles' stride stretched to catch up with her. Marcus braked, and Jacob leaned out the passenger window. "Hey, Riles, over here."

Snagging Frénie's elbow in her hand, Riles pointed toward the car. Frénie shook her head, folded her arms across her chest.

Ian whistled through his teeth, gawked at the homes. "Genteel. Conservative elegance. I'm impressed."

"Wait here." Jacob left the car and walked over to Riles and Frénie.

"Leave me alone. You've done enough." Weeping, Frénie broke free from Riles' grasp.

In two steps, he was at Frénie's side. "In the car. Now. You can discuss this at the hotel. Neither of you is safe here."

"And it's all her fault." Frénie glared at him.

"I'm sure it is." He took her arm, then Riles' and marched

them to the car. Riles' face was etched with remorse and—did he dare hope—pink with shame.

As she slid across the back seat next to Frénie, Ian winked at her. "Good show, Riley. Excellent intel."

Blushing, Riles ducked her head.

Jacob slammed his car door. Why egg her on? She wasn't a trained field agent. In this business, people were murdered for less than searching someone's desk.

ALMOST SICK TO HER STOMACH, Riley flicked on the lights in their living room. After enduring Frénie's silent fury in the car, walking to the Savoy might've been less stressful. In less than fifteen minutes she'd destroyed seven years of bosom-buddy friendship.

Cell tossed on the coffee table, Frénie snatched a tissue from the box and blotted her eyes. She plopped on the couch.

Riley joined her at the far end. She wouldn't be surprised if her BFF threw her out. Told her to find her own hotel space.

"You and your insane schemes. You've ruined everything. Now Armand will break up with me." Frénie threw the navy pillow between them.

"Has Armand proposed to you, given you an engagement ring?"

Whipping her shawl over her shoulder, Frénie swung her legs away from her. "I think this is none of your business."

"That's what friends do. They protect, come alongside in tough times."

"You've heard the saying, two makes company, three is a crowd, *oui?*"

The words knifed Riley's heart. Here she sat, destroying the last shreds of her friend's *naïveté*. "We've been BFFs a long time." Reaching over the pillow, Riley touched Frénie's sleeve. "And I treasure our friendship."

"Then why are you poisoning my relationship with Armand?" As flames flashed from Frénie's gaze, Riley cringed. "Until you arrived, everything was wonderful."

"I know. But you need to move forward with open eyes. Eyes that don't sweep questions under his Persian rugs. Not knowing how your husband makes his money, who his friends are, could boomerang on you." If Jacob had lied to her about his job, she'd have been devastated by his lack of trust. "By the way, are you sure Armand was raised in France?"

"Yes. I—I don't know. His family is Catholic." Frénie sprang from the couch and crossed her arms, paced the carpet. "Enough of these questions. I will prove your suspicions are wrong." She shook her finger inches from Riley's nose. "And you will apologize to Armand."

Riley gulped. "Deal."

Seconds later, Frénie's cell rang. She looked at the caller ID. Her face paled. "It's Armand." Fingers trembling at her lips, she backed away from the coffee table.

"Take the call. If he mentions our trip to his house, you can apologize profusely, say you had no idea I'd do anything like that. Blame it all on me."

"Trust me. I will."

Hand shaking, Frénie held the cell a few inches from her ear. "*Allo*, my darling." A tremor crept into her voice, a child expecting a spanking.

Pillow tossed aside, Riley scooted next to her. Breath trapped in her throat. With her free hand, Frénie gripped Riley's palm, icing her skin. Riley's head grazed Frénie's as she listened to the conversation.

"*Mon petit chou*, I have a surprise for you."

The held breath escaped Riley's mouth. Good. He hadn't threatened to ditch Frénie. Reading his tone was tougher. Cool? Flashing her a smile, Riley motioned Frénie to respond.

"You do? How nice. What is it?"

His chuckle reached through the phone. "If I told you, it wouldn't be a surprise, would it?"

"No. But I am ... so excited." Her voice flatlined.

"You don't sound pleased."

Nodding encouragement, Riley circled two fingers in the air.

"I am, I am."

"*Bon*. My plane lands tomorrow at ten. Meet me at the Connaught Hotel, the restaurant Hélène Darroze, for lunch at noon."

A tic pulsed the muscles around Frénie's eyes. "I—I want to bring Riley with me. She—she needs company."

The silence on Armand's end stretched several seconds, Riley's stomach triple knotted. Did he know about their escapade in his house? Was this meeting a setup?

"But of course, my darling."

26

London, Day 13

Ignoring mums and nannies corralling toddlers beside baby carriages, Riley focused on the men in Hyde Park. Men on benches feeding the birds, reading newspapers, ambling along the lanes, cells in hand. Of all these people, she'd be hard-pressed to pinpoint a stalker.

She looped around the statue of Diana, the Huntress, in the rose garden. If she were being watched, staying in the open might expose whoever had been tailing her in London.

Three dots flashed on her text message screen.

On my way. Be there in ten.

Maybe she should've told Jacob to bring Ian.

As she rounded the statue again, Jacob strode toward her, raincoat flapping in the breeze, gaze roving the area. He planted a quick kiss on her cheek. "Everything okay here?"

"I guess so." Riley dragged her shoe across a clot of dirt. "Does Mandouri own the house next to Armand?"

"Not that we know of. He owns the one across the street. At

first glance, the owner's a Michael York. Digging further, we discovered Michael doesn't exist. Nor does the shell corporation he supposedly works for."

"It's a lead then, right?"

"At the moment, it's a dead end."

"Oh." She stomped another dirt clod into powder. "What's going on here?"

Hands thrust into his pockets, Jacob looked over his shoulder to the left, then the right. "I wish I knew."

She strolled beside him to a vacant bench near the statue and sat. "Don't you have any leads on Gorilla Guy?"

"He seems to have vanished from the planet." Jacob plopped on the bench beside her, stretched an arm behind her shoulders.

"Maybe you were closer to uncovering his identity than you think." She inched closer to him. "You were making things too hot for him."

"Right. Following his trail of blood-soaked breadcrumbs, finding dead bodies in every high place in Europe. We're always too late, unable to block his next move." He fisted, unfisted his hand in his lap, shifted his feet on the pavement. "Ian and Marcus's stakeouts at the Royal Pavilion haven't turned up anything, or anyone suspicious." Jacob raked his fingers through his hair. "Riles, until we sort this mess out, I want you to stay away from Armand and his house. His maid may have told him you searched his desk."

She stifled a shiver. "What about his gala? And I'm meeting Frénie and him for lunch today."

"When did that come about?" A growl twisted Jacob's tone.

"After yesterday's fiasco, Frénie's barely speaking to me. But when Armand called and ordered her to meet him for lunch today, she was afraid. She asked if I could join them. At the Hélène Darroze Restaurant in the Connaught Hotel."

"Hang on a second." Phone in hand, he texted Ian.

> Riles is meeting Armand for lunch with Frénie. Can you cover it?

> You're on a first-name basis with Découvrir?

> Yeah. Makes me want to shower every time I think about it.

> Well done. Remind me to get to know you better.

> And courtesy of Frénie and Armand, I'm invited to his charity gala.

"When Frénie wanted you to come to lunch, was Armand quick to respond?" Jacob texted Ian the name of the restaurant.

"Well ..."

A muscle in his jaw twitched. "What time?"

"Noon."

Three dots bounced on his screen. "Ian's on it. He'll be at the restaurant. Don't acknowledge him. Since Armand knows me, it'd look odd if I crash your party."

"I assume the hair clip you gave me on the cruise still has the GPS and mini-mic you planted in it."

"Yes. Wear it. I'll set up the connections so Ian can hear you."

HOPEFULLY RILEY'S pep talks with Frénie would prop her up enough to fool Armand. Entering behind her, Riley stepped over the threshold of the Hélène Darroze Restaurant in the Connaught Hotel. Funky modern style with peach walls and curved leather and velvet seating. Dark wood tables, no tablecloths.

With three Michelin stars and an astronomical bill to match, no doubt it would be a meal to remember. She tugged at the collar on her blouse, smoothed a nonexistent wrinkle on her black jacket. If only she could relax and enjoy the food. But she'd have to look Armand in the eye, and pretend she hadn't invaded his privacy, while her stomach did flipflops.

As the *maître d'* escorted them to their table, Armand rose, natty as ever in a navy-blue suit, and tweaked his silver tie. Bending toward Frénie, he kissed her cheeks, pale beneath her makeup. Subconsciously or not, she'd chosen her Chanel suit. White, the color of innocence.

"*Mon cher*, my dear." Her smile flitted off her face, glances darting left and right.

"*Mon petit chou ...*"

If he didn't quit calling her a little cabbage, Riley would barf. What was wrong with her? She'd convicted a man in her heart on circumstantial evidence. And he'd been so tender with the children at the orphanage. Scooting beside Frénie on the semi-circular booth, Riley laid her napkin on her lap.

At a nearby table, Ian had propped his menu upright. Today he wore thick-framed glasses. Probably loaded with a camera and microphone.

As an Interpol agent, he'd be unarmed. But at the table next to him, dressed in a business suit, was the male constable who'd taken her statement after being thrown in front of the bus. She bit back a smile. Good. Someone Armand wouldn't recognize.

"How lovely to see you again, Riley."

She startled. How long had Armand been watching her? "You, too, Armand. How was your trip?"

"*Bon.*" He shrugged. "As usual."

"Shall we order?" Frénie's gaze glued to her menu.

Orders placed, Armand cupped Frénie's hand, his large palm swallowing her delicate fingers. Her chin trembled. A few more seconds of this and his little cabbage would burst into tears and admit what they'd done. He was no fool. Surely he read her hunched shoulders, downcast eyes. What would he have done or said if the two of them had met alone?

The silence stretched over the table. Heels piercing the carpet, Riley dug her fingernails into her palms in her lap. If he kept up this cat-caught-the-mouse game, she'd leap up and confess her guilt. Anything to save Frénie from this humiliation.

"Today, on such a special occasion, I have suffered a great loss." Armand sighed.

"Oh?" Riley met his gaze. She hardly knew which end of his loaded stick to pursue. "What a terrible dilemma."

"*Oui.* Today was to be a special surprise for my beloved." With a smile so tender Riley almost melted, he tilted Frénie's chin until her lashes fluttered upward. The whites of her eyes rimmed her pupils, her fear palpable across the table.

No woman should be afraid of her boyfriend—or did she expect him to break off their relationship?

"But when I arrived home, my trusted maid had vanished." His knuckle traced the curve of Frénie's cheekbone. "Now I must hire someone new." Flecks of irritation punctuated his melancholy tone. "These days good help is so difficult to find."

"That's awful." Had the man who snuck behind the tapestry reported the incident in the study to Armand? "What happened to her?"

"I have no idea." He released Frénie's chin, and she huddled in her seat. "Maria had been with me more than ten years." The man truly looked brokenhearted. "But then, one suffers many sorrows in life." With another sigh, he opened a manila envelope, set the pages in front of Frénie. "I wanted this to be our special day." His gaze slid over Riley.

Probably his hint three was a crowd. Ignoring the jibe, Riley sipped her water.

Jaw slacking, Frénie fanned out pictures of castles and massive country estates on the table.

On the first sheet, someone had inked in a price tag with

more zeros than Riley could count. Given the enormity of the house, Frénie could disappear in there and never be found.

"Botwillian Estate. What a stunning property." Surely Ian caught that.

"Oh." Frénie let out a gasp. "Is this for me?"

"I've been searching for the perfect home for us." The moisture spilling from his half-hooded eyes seemed genuine. "For my little bride."

"Bride, house?" Lips quivering, Frénie looped her arm in his, and laid her cheek on his sleeve. "Oh, my darling sweet Armand." Her pent-up tears flowed with little hiccups. "And I thought—"

"Thought what, my sweet?" Taking the silk hanky from his breast pocket, he stroked the wetness from her cheeks, and lined her forehead with tiny kisses. "Nothing, no one shall ever come between us." His gaze bored through Riley.

She sagged against the velvet cushion. If only she could sink through the floor.

He knew.

27

London, Day 14

Cell to his ear, Jacob drummed his pencil on the couch while keyboard clicks on Margot's computer filtered through his phone. Shafts of morning sun lit the beveled edge of his glass-topped coffee table, splintering the rays like a prism. The recent Zoom meetings with the team had been fruitless. While Ian was out, Jacob filled her in on Riles' discoveries, the situation.

"Maybe you should add her to our list of paid informants."

A muscle tic pulsed his cheek. Why did everyone want him to put Riles in more danger? All they cared about was the outcome. Not whom they used. "Not happening." He spat the words like a nail gun.

"You want my advice—let Riley continue to spend time with them. If they're guilty, I suspect she'll draw them out for us."

"And send Riles into the jaws of death?"

"Agents risk their lives every day."

"Riles. Is not. An agent." He leapt from the couch, paced the tiny room. No way could he do this to her.

"Let's focus on your Gorilla Guy and Yousef Mandouri."

187

Margot's soothing tone did nothing to lessen the knots in his gut. "We've found records of Mandouri's stays in Vienna over the past three years and those of several men traveling with him. His last stay was the same dates as your Gorilla Guy. So, Mandouri could be the Priest. His meals were harder to trace, apart from those in the Sacher Hotel and room service. We're circulating his picture among our street informants."

"Great work, Margot. Send me what you've found, please."

Finally. The first glimmers of a breakthrough on this assignment. Two viable suspects. While only one of them might be the Priest, both had verifiable connections to money-laundering ops possibly tied to terrorist cells. "Thanks, Margot. Talk to you later."

He punched off, and Riley's ringtone sounded on his phone.

"Morning, lover boy."

At her teasing tone, heat surged through his body. "Hey, hon. Good to hear your voice."

"Wouldn't you love to see me too?"

Picturing her twirling an auburn curl around her finger, her saucy smile, dissolved the last of his resistance. He fought the urge to tell her he'd fetch her. "I'm waiting for my trusty forager to return." He almost said, "with his kill."

"Oh. Ian. I thought once you were in London, I could be with you. Not locked up in an ivory tower. Besides, Frénie wants me to go see the estate with her."

"Riles, we've been over this a thousand times." Out of habit, he walked to the window and checked the street below. "Every time you leave the hotel, trouble follows. So far, you've been lucky—no, God's protected you."

"If I go with Frénie to see the estate, I should be safe. No one seems to have her in their sights. Besides, she and I need to repair our friendship." Riles' sigh reached into his phone. "If that's possible."

"Do that in your suite." He hated himself for sounding harsh, but her life was at stake.

"Don't you want a firsthand report on this snazzy house?"

"I can find pictures online." He opened the first of Margot's documents on Mandouri's stays in Vienna.

"But I'm her bridesmaid. I'm supposed to do things with her, hold her hand."

"Riles, you're safest in the hotel suite."

"So far."

The seriousness in her tone tore through him. Whoever was masterminding the attacks could figure a way to access their suite. And if her assailants knew Frénie was away ...

Raking his hand through his hair, Jacob paced a loop around the couch. *God, help me. What should I do?* Maybe Riles was right. She'd be safer with Frénie. "Okay. But stay in touch with me every hour."

"Yes, Master." She smooched into the phone. "Agent Riles reporting for duty."

"Riles—" But he was speaking to a dead phone.

MAYBE SHE SHOULD'VE SPENT MORE time in prayer this morning.

Feet dragging, Riley followed Frénie across the dimly lit private garage, past rows of Bentleys, Rolls Royces, Jaguars, and Daimlers berthed in stalls like prize stallions. Not once had she ridden with Frénie in Romania during their conservatory days. How experienced a driver was she?

The blue-coated mechanic had left the scarlet Lamborghini outside the stalls with the hood facing the open garage doors.

"*Voilà*, my new baby." Key fob in hand, Frénie punched the button. The sleek doors slid up in the air like a pair of wings.

A nervous chuckle caught in Riley's throat. "This thing doesn't fly, does it?"

"You are so *drôle*, so funny." Frénie climbed in behind the steering wheel, red stilettos perched on the pedals, chin clearing the top of the steering wheel by only a few inches.

Muttering a fervent prayer, Riley lowered herself into the cream leather seat. She stowed her purse and umbrella at her feet, raincoat over her lap. Palms damp, she fastened her seatbelt, doublechecked the clasp.

At least she'd worn sensible flats. No telling how big the estate was. As the doors glided closed, the dashboard dials glowed to life like the cockpit of a Boeing 737. "Sure you know how to drive this thing?"

"Of course, silly. Armand made me take English driving lessons before he let me keep the keys."

"Good." Riley riveted her spine to the seat. Maybe they'd survive this outing.

Stick shoved into Drive, Frénie floored the gas pedal. Tires screeching, the Lambo shot into the traffic like a red blur.

Eyes glued to the vehicles careening out of their way, Riley drove her nails into the armrest, almost puncturing the leather. Horns blared, fists raised at them through windshields. *Dear God, spare us. And the other drivers.* "Remember, drive on the left, the left."

"Quiet. You're making me nervous."

"*You* nervous?" Riley was tempted to make the sign of the cross over them.

At the first stoplight, Frénie pumped the brakes. "Hmm, they feel *un petit* soft."

An agonizing ninety minutes later, Frénie signaled to exit the A23/M23.

The tires screeched on the asphalt. Fumes from burning rubber grayed the air as she decelerated. Somewhat. The swirling storm clouds that had followed them from London grew ominous.

"Now we'll see what my baby can do on this country lane."

"Lane. As in, room for only one vehicle, either direction?" Riley's gulp blocked her throat. As they headed down the skinny ribbon of asphalt, a breeze flattened the grain in the fields. Or maybe it was the Lambo's speed flailing the stalks. Foot pressed to a phantom brake pedal, Riley's shoe rammed through the carpet. "And as for what your baby can do, I've already seen enough."

"Don't be such a scaredy-cat."

"I value my life. Yours, others on the road."

"Remind me never to bring you with me again."

Beads of sweat prickled Riley's hairline. "Consider it done."

Frénie's sandal floored the accelerator, and the Lambo whizzed past gorse hedges hemming the curving asphalt. Sheep skittered across the pastures, fleeing for the hills.

The first drops of rain splattered the windshield, splotched the asphalt. If only she hadn't offered to accompany her. "Roads are most dangerous when it first starts to rain. Before oil has washed off the surface. It would be awful if anything happened to your beautiful car."

"Oh, all right." Frénie eased her foot from the accelerator and the car slowed.

"Thank you." The cramps in Riley's calves loosened. Now that the vehicle wasn't passing at a dizzying speed, she glanced out the window. Not a single manor house or estate on the road. "Are you sure we're headed the right way?"

"*Mais oui*, of course." Frénie tapped the GPS map screen on the dashboard. "Computers never lie."

"Uh-huh." Definitely not her experience with them.

"Only twenty more miles."

The sky blackened and the droplets gave way to a deluge, pelting the windshield. Gusts of wind buffeted the car, shimmying it left and right. The wheels scudded through water sluicing across the road.

"Slow down." A shriek ripped through Riley's words. "You'll hydroplane."

Her foot lifted from the accelerator, Frénie squinted through the windshield. The wiper blades slapped curtains of water side to side. The headlight beams splayed across the blanket of fog.

For a moment, the mist parted. Massive trees lined the right side of the road. Faded orbs of light loomed in front of the Lamborghini, approaching them far too fast.

Look out!" Bracing herself for the impact, Riley plastered her hand to the armrest, shoes driven through the floor.

"I see it, I see it."

Frénie slammed the horn, swerved to the right, braked hard. The Lamborghini spun like a whirling Dervish. Rammed the side of the oncoming white panel truck. With a sickening howl, metal crunched, glass tinkled on the pavement, jarring every bone in Riley's body. Her head shot forward. Thudded against the head rest.

Fire seared her nerve endings. Her heart hammered her throat. They were going to die. *Dear God, spare us.* Whooshing like rocket launchers, the airbags whacked Riley's chest and face, snatched her breath. *God. Help.* Black velvet descended like a curtain.

28

London, Day 14

Six hours since Frénie and Riles had left town and not a single message from her. Seated in his loaner cubicle at CT HQ, Jacob texted her again. Why had he listened to her? Once again, he tried tracing her whereabouts on her phone GPS.

Dead.

As if the car had dropped off the face of the earth.

On his computer, he entered the database for vehicles registered in the UK and pulled up the records for Frénie's car. He switched to police reports for accidents on the A23/M23, the most likely route for their trip. Acid pitted his stomach. Two semis jackknifed by the wind. Several cars headed toward London stalled in heavy rain. Three rear-end collisions. Breath eked from his mouth. None of the accident details matched the Lambo.

Why else wouldn't Riles have checked in with him?

She hadn't mentioned an appointment time nor the estate agent's name. The ditz in this equation was Frénie.

Discreet estate agents and all-cash deals were common in the

UK to protect the anonymity of über-wealthy purchasers. A major hurdle he and Ian faced uncovering terrorist financiers who invested millions in untraceable funds.

He texted Ian again.

> Any info on the estate agent?

The three dots bounced on the screen so long Jacob's pulse ratcheted into overdrive.

> You aren't going to like this.

FRÉNIE. Lamborghini.

Fire seared every bone and muscle in her body. Groaning, Riley inched her hand toward her abdomen and pushed away the deflated airbags. How long had she been unconscious? A storm. Spinning, spinning. Crashing into—headlights?

Crumpled beside her, Frénie slumped forward, chin on her collarbone. Eyelashes brushing her cheeks, arms limp at her side. Riley felt for a pulse below her friend's jaw. Slow, but there. *Thank You, God.*

Gritting her teeth, she angled toward the driver's seat and shook Frénie's shoulder. "Frénie, you okay?"

Seconds later, her eyelids batted. "Huh?" Her voice sounded a trillion miles away. "What happened?"

"An accident."

Purple splotches had blossomed across Frénie's forehead. "Where are we?"

"Somewhere in England on a deserted country road with no house in sight. And blessed to be alive." Rain drizzled through the shattered windshield and trickled between Riley's knees. Poking her thighs, she lifted her legs, wiggled her arms. Nothing broken. Her watch read four o'clock. Judging from the faint light in the overcast sky, it was afternoon.

The Lambo's front end had smashed into the side of a white paneled van, the car's hood pleated like an accordion. The truck driver's door was shut, but a back door stood open.

Had anyone been hurt in the crash? She was no expert on British law, but Frénie might be arrested. Years of instinct had kicked in, swerving to the right, like a French or an American. The other driver wouldn't have expected her to hit him. What if he hadn't survived the crash?

Riley pulled her phone from her purse, punched 999. No rings, the battery eighty-percent full. "No phone service."

"Oh dear." Frénie unclicked her seatbelt and moved her legs, feet still strapped into her stiletto sandals. "And Armand is out of the country."

"Where is he this time?"

"Germany, I think. He told me not to expect to hear from him today. Meetings, you know." She jabbed the button to lift her door. The motor whirred but nothing moved. "Try opening your door."

"Wonder how often people drive this road." One push on the button and the door jerked upward with the unpredictability of the hydraulic lift. Cool, moist air rushed inside the car. "Bingo." Breath wisped from Riley's mouth. "If you can manage it, crawl over the console." Grabbing her raincoat and umbrella, she eased out of the car. "I need to check on the people in the van."

Hugging her ribs, Frénie shivered in the rain, her four-inch stilettos sinking in the mud. Riley opened the umbrella and handed it to her.

"We should've brought a picnic basket."

No, they never should've made the trip in the first place. Riley flicked the rain from her eyes. If only Frénie weren't so impatient. She'd ruined Armand's surprise. Now she'd have to fake it when he showed her their new home. That is, if they made it back to London without him finding out where she'd wrecked the Lamborghini.

Riley flung the raincoat over her head and peered in the driver's window. Empty. Deflated airbags. No bodies. "Whoever they are, they're gone."

"They left us here?" Frénie's voice shrilled dangerously close to a high *F*. "Stranded?"

"Looks like it." Riley snapped cell photos of the vehicles, the impact, the van's empty driver and passenger seats.

"Why would anyone do such a thing?"

"Good question." Especially since Frénie was probably at fault for the accident. Four empty water bottles, wadded napkins, a grease-stained fish-and-chips bag that still smelled of freshly fried food were scattered in the rear of the van. Riley's stomach growled as she photographed the interior, the license plate. "With no phone service, who rescued them?"

"Maybe the cell tower was still working right after the accident." Frénie tiptoed closer to the van.

"It's odd they didn't help us. Unless ... they were up to something illegal. Something they dared not let the police find?"

"You mean like drugs or something?"

"Possibly." Riley dragged her shoe on the pavement, scraping off the mud.

The umbrella jittered in Frénie's grip. "It will be dark soon." Her voice rose to a wail. "What should we do?"

"You can't walk in those shoes."

"Oh, I wish I'd listened to you." Teeth chattering, Frénie wiggled one stiletto in the mud. The ooze *thwacked* as her foot came free. "We could be cozy at the Savoy."

"We'll sit in the car and pray. Survive overnight on a bottle of water and my two Burie's truffles."

Frénie's jaw slacked. "You brought only two chocolates?"

"I'm trying to cut back."

"*Oh là-là*. What a time to start." Frénie rolled her eyes.

"Jacob will wonder what's happened to us." Riley headed for the car. "He'll send for the cavalry." She hoped.

———

ONE BY ONE Jacob's team members entered the Zoom call screen. Forcing his jaws to unclench, he sucked a breath. He needed to focus on finding Riles, not updates on the Priest. The background captured the standard cubicles of the CT HQ, Ian seated at the adjoining desk. He introduced Marcus as a special guest to the group, then updated the team on Riles' discoveries, the visit to the orphanage.

"Immigration notified us Découvrir flew into Berlin yesterday," Gunter said. "I've tagged so many billionaires, I was surprised the system pinged him."

"Berlin? Is he setting up a new business venture?" Margot asked.

"We don't know yet. But Yousef Mandouri entered Germany last week. He spent two days in Munich, then flew to Berlin," Gunter said.

"Maybe Mandouri's finding London too hot right now," Marcus said as he scribbled notes on his pad.

"Gunter, if you could put a team on their activities and report back to us, that might shed some light on their trips," Jacob said. The last thing they needed was Mandouri expanding his criminal activities. He had no proof Armand was engaged in anything illegal. But Mandouri was proving interesting.

"Jean-Pierre, what's the news from France?"

Rumpled-looking as ever, Jean-Pierre leaned toward the screen. "Mandouri and his close associates have flown to Lyon for the day twice now. He visits casinos, gambles, and they harass local small businesses. We suspect he's trying to take over new territory, move in against established crime bosses here."

"So is Mandouri the Priest?" Gunter asked.

"I think it's very possible." Jean-Pierre rubbed a hand across his mouth.

"I wouldn't rule out Gorilla Guy, as you call him. The man he dined with at the Sacher Hotel agreed to talk, for a reduced sentence. He confirmed Gorilla Guy was his contact for money laundering through his garage. He's a mechanic," Margot said.

Who was the Priest—Mandouri or Gorilla Guy? Jacob rubbed his forehead. If only they could be certain. The EU meetings were drawing close. And von Bingen was expecting answers.

29

Near Brighton, Day 15

The first rays of sun struggled through the clouds, and Riley opened her eyes, her body stiff from her fetal-ball curl on the van's cold metal floor. Soon she'd have to find a makeshift restroom. Frénie still huddled back-to-back, her ribs rising and falling against Riley's spine.

Ten minutes in Frénie's car, rain drizzling on their legs as night fell, had been too much. Chilled and almost hypothermic, Frénie'd insisted they move to the van. Riley prayed the owners wouldn't return, if they were criminals.

If no one drove by soon, she'd leave Frénie here in her ridiculous stilettos and walk for help. Teeth chattering, Riley eased from beneath the raincoat and draped her half of it over Frénie's body. Near the van doors she speed-dialed Jacob again. Her heart sank. Still no service. *Dear God, please send help.*

Monster storms had pummeled the UK in recent months, wreaking havoc. Could Interpol phones track a person if cell towers were down?

She slid from the van, shoes squishing in the mud. On one side, grassy knolls, a copse of trees. Shoulders slumped, she massaged the throb in her temples. Yesterday she'd been so terrified by Frénie's driving, noting places they could shelter hadn't topped her to-do list.

A faint *putt-putting* sounded in the distance. But from which direction? She crossed to the middle of the road.

Minutes later, a tractor crawled over the hill, driving down the center of the asphalt. "Frénie, wake up." Waving madly, Riley dashed toward the vehicle. "Stop, please stop."

Belching black smoke, the tractor slowed, circular threshing blades clanking behind. The grizzled driver squinted at her. Then toward the Lambo. Pulling off the side of the road, he killed the engine and climbed down. "What happened, miss?"

Trying to control her clattering teeth, Riley told him about the accident, the flight of the van's occupants. "We need to call London and notify the police."

"Them blokes leaving you like that, sounds suspicious to me." He whipped off his dirt-stained jacket and wrapped it around her shoulders. "Looks to me like you need to see a doctor."

"Thank you. M—my f—friend is in the back of the van."

The raincoat belted around her waist, Frénie tottered toward them, heels wobbling in the mud, arms wind-milling in the air. The farmer lumbered over to her, gripped her elbow, and led her onto the asphalt.

"Where's the nearest phone booth?" Riley joined them beside the tractor.

"In the village, eighteen miles from here. And the force constabulary." Scratching his head, he eyed his tractor. "Not sure how to get you ladies there."

"How about we stand behind you, Roman-chariot style on that rear ledge?" Inside, Riley cringed. Not her most brilliant idea. The rusted joints looked as unstable as the hydraulic lift.

"Sounds a mite dangerous. Sure you're up to it?" He gave Frénie a onceover. "Tell you what. You're a wee one. If you sit on my lap, I can see over your head. Then you—" He gestured to Riley. "Hang on behind me."

A gulp caught in Riley's throat. What had she gotten herself into? "Okay."

"We were on our way to see the Bodwillian Estate. My fiancé is buying it for my wedding present."

Mouth working like a guppy, the farmer rubbed dirt-smudged fingers across his forehead. "Miss, I work there. Bodwillian isn't for sale. The estate has been in the family over four hundred years. The Duke will leave the property to his son."

WHERE WAS RILES? Last night she hadn't answered his calls or his text messages. Jingling the change in his pocket, Jacob paced the hall outside Marcus Rayborn's cubicle in the CT Unit HQ. The trip to the estate shouldn't have kept them away overnight.

Especially since Ian had said the estate wasn't for sale. Armand was arrogant. Convinced he could talk the owner into selling for some you-can't refuse-me price. "Marcus, can you check for new accident reports?"

"Sure." Marcus tapped his computer keyboard.

Snatching a pencil, Jacob tapped a panic-stricken SOS on the desk.

"A report came in a few minutes ago. Yesterday afternoon a car matching that registration was involved in a wreck on an unclassified country lane."

Lead settled in Jacob's stomach. "Any injuries?"

"Other than a few bruises and severe chills, both women are fine. The accident occurred on a lane with no route number, intended for local traffic. Which describes sixty percent of all roads in the UK. The driver reported the brakes felt mushy. Cell towers in the area are down from the storm. They hitched a ride to the local police station. But the driver of the other vehicle fled."

"Fled?" Jacob's antennae went on alert. "Can you locate the wreck?"

"Yes." Marcus peered at the computer screen, clicked an entry. "I'll drive you there."

"Thank you." Thank God they were all right. Jacob's cell rang inside his pocket. He snatched the phone. An unidentified number and caller. "Hello?"

"Jacob?" Riles' voice shrilled in his ear.

"Where are you, hon?"

"At the police station in the village we drove through after you and I left the orphanage. I'm calling on a landline. Cell towers are still out from the storm."

"Stay put. Marcus and I are on our way to the accident scene. Then we'll pick up you and Frénie."

The trip was the longest sixty minutes of his life as Marcus zigzagged between the lanes of traffic, veering so close to lorries and automobiles the car shuddered. Jacob gripped the armrest. With Marcus at the wheel, the Indy 500 would feel tame.

Minutes later, Marcus slowed and killed the siren. He pulled off the country road and parked near the blue-and-white POLICE DO NOT CROSS tape cordoning off the wreck. Two white police cars with reflective blue-and-yellow checkerboard designs on the side, the word POLICE on the hood and emblazoned on the sides of the cars, were parked off the road.

"We'll be speaking with the Accident Investigation Team." Marcus unfolded his lanky body from the driver's seat.

The Lambo's crumpled front end had folded into the white panel van. Oddly, other than the creased side, the van seemed to have suffered little damage.

Ice coursed through Jacob's veins. He struggled for a breath. Once again, he'd come close to losing Riles. *Thank You, God, for sparing their lives*.

Given Riles' shove under the bus, who was the intended victim of the crash—Riles or Frénie? According to the police report, it was Frénie's first solo drive and only 150 kilometers on a car maintained by a respected mechanic. He headed for the vehicles.

But how could a saboteur have known Riles would be in the car? Chills walked across his shoulders. Unless she was being tailed.

With Marcus at his side, Jacob stepped over the blue-and-white police tape and flashed his Interpol ID at the PC in charge. Three PCs were onsite. One poked under the hood, photographed the area, the damage from various angles. The moves were clear. A classic check for sabotaged brakes.

Moving to the white van, Jacob snapped photos of the interior and the license plate. As soon as he found cell service, he'd forward the info to Ian. He stood back from the wreck. The cars had crashed on the right shoulder of the road. Frénie should've pulled to the left side to avoid a collision. Under British law, the police could arrest her. If she left the country, they couldn't force her to return to face the court.

Neck corded tight, he stared at the van. Hadn't there been white panel vans parked at the orphanage? Which was near the village. And near the scene of the accident. He motioned Marcus over.

"What's up?" Marcus hitched his equipment-laden belt toward his waist.

"There's a chance the van belongs to the Saint Aminta Orphanage, run and founded by Armand Découvrir. I'd like to have plaster casts of the tires and mud samples taken from their vans and this one. See if we have a match."

"On it." Marcus strode back to the PC in charge.

The PC in charge walked over to him. "Last night the passengers from the Lamborghini slept in the back of the van. Any DNA from previous occupants back there has been disturbed, possibly destroyed. The front seat is another matter."

"But a night sleeping in that car could've killed them."

"Quite possibly, yes." The PC scratched his temple. "How do you see the accident tying in with your case?"

"I'm not sure yet. Perhaps the license plate or the vehicle registration papers will tell us."

"Missing from the glove box."

"Figures." Nothing about his assignment had been easy. "If you find proof the brakes were tampered with, the accident is connected to my job here."

"The examining officer said the brake lines were cut in several places."

Acid roiled the coffee in Jacob's stomach. Dear God, not another attempted murder. They had to get to the bottom of this. Fast. "Mind if I leave and check on my fiancée?"

"She's one gutsy lady." The PC chuckled. "You should've seen her riding into the village, standing on the back of a tractor like Joan of Arc."

An invisible fist punched Jacob's gut. "Sounds like Riles."

As soon as Marcus braked the car outside the village constabulary, Jacob unlatched his seatbelt. "Excuse me." Feet itching to run, he strode toward the building.

Inside the waiting room, Riles and Frénie sat on plastic chairs, swathed in blankets. Riles dropped hers on the seat and walked over to him. He folded her into his arms, laced his fingers in her auburn curls, and buried his nose in her hair. "Oh Riles. I thought I'd—"

"Shh." She put her finger to his lips. "Don't say it. I'm fine."

Crimson rimmed the tip of her nose and eyes. Hard to tell if it was from crying or a night shivering half to death. He swallowed the lump in his throat. "Can you tell me what happened?"

"The fog was thicker than a duvet. We may have hydroplaned in the downpour, but the van wasn't visible until it was meters from us, headed straight into our headlights."

"It must've been terrifying." Blinking at the moisture in his eyes, he stroked a curl from her temple. "Any sense of who was at fault?"

"Well ..." She shifted her eyes toward Frénie. "But whoever was in the van left us for dead." Her voice shook.

Fire surged across his chest. How many more attacks on Riles or Frénie before they solved this case? He pulled her to his chest. "We'll do our best to catch them. Let's see what Frénie has to say." Arm latched around Riles' shoulder, he walked her over to Frénie's chair.

Brushing a lock of hair from her forehead, Frénie tilted her chin up at him. "*Merci*, thank you for coming for us." As she stared into the distance, her cheeks sagged. "What will Armand say when he finds out I destroyed my Lamborghini?"

Jacob bit the words on his tongue. *If Armand loves you, he won't care.* Dreading what he had to tell her, Jacob cleared his throat. "The police are certain the brakes were sabotaged."

"*Un saboteur—*" Her fingers trembled to her mouth. "*Non*, that can't be. They come after Riley, not me."

"This time, we're not sure Riles was the intended victim."

"Victim? Why would anyone want to harm me?"

"Can you think of anyone with a grudge against you, someone jealous of your relationship with Armand?"

Her cheeks slacked. "*Non*."

"Either the saboteur didn't know enough to sever the brake line cleanly, or it was intended to occur over time, to make the crime less obvious. Which suggests you were the intended victim."

"*Non, non*." Frénie's shoulders shrank inside the blanket.

"How about someone who works for Armand, someone connected to his business ventures?"

She clutched the blanket to her throat, her gaze darting left and right.

"Frénie, this was no accident." Jacob squeezed her shoulder, her muscles rigid under his fingers. Was it shock from the wreck or fear? "If you know something, or suspect someone, tell me. Please. For your sake. And Riles'."

30

London, Day 16

The early morning sun dappled the apartment wall behind the bistro table. If this kept up, he'd need sunglasses. Jacob carried his cereal bowl and spoon to the dishwasher. A few more short nights, and he and Ian would be toss-ups for president of the sleep-deprived club.

While he worked on tracing leads to Mandouri's ops in Vienna, Ian had tracked down the ownership of the van, registered to the Saint Aminta Orphanage under Armand's name. The rest of the night Jacob had tossed on his bed, Riles' near-death experiences tormenting his nightmares.

"Any news on the mud and plaster casts?" Jacob poured himself another cup of coffee. Today he'd brewed it double strength.

"The plaster cast taken at the accident matches one of the vans at the orphanage." Ian fiddled with his laptop at the table, nursing a mug of tea. "The dried mud on that van also matches the mud at the scene of the wreck."

"Which means we have some questions for Armand. How about a search warrant for the orphanage?"

"I'll have to file an application in person with the duty Superintendent. Cite the reasons for the request, what we expect to find there, define exactly what we wish to search. He decides whether to fill out the paperwork. Or not. Then I repeat the process with the magistrate who issues the warrant. Thankfully, the place is manned 24/7."

"The longer we have to wait for the warrant, the higher the chance the van's cargo might disappear from the orphanage."

"What do you think they were transporting?" Ian plugged in the electric kettle on the kitchen counter.

"Drugs? Or, given the food wrappers, possibly illegal immigrants. The driver of the van must've called for help. Another van from the orphanage arrived and transported everyone and the contraband to safety. Lucky for us they didn't remove the license plate." Jacob chuckled.

"I'll request a warrant to search for drugs and illegals."

"Whoever sabotaged the Lambo's brakes didn't expect the crash to happen near the orphanage. If Riles and I hadn't made a surprise visit there, we wouldn't have seen the village or the vans."

"Maybe whoever is behind these attacks is nervous, making mistakes." Ian attached a travel lid to his mug of tea and grabbed his raincoat.

"And busy covering their tracks while we're waiting for that search warrant."

MORE THAN ANYTHING, she needed a five-hour nap. Riley turned her back to the shower head, letting hot needles of water pummel her scalp, her shoulders. After the trauma of the accident, the ride with Marcus and Jacob to London, comforting Frénie—hysterical one moment, furious the next—her throat muscles were a mass of knots.

Twenty-four hours from now she'd be singing at the gala. And a night in the raw damp hadn't done her vocal folds any good. Bath sheet wrapped around her torso, Riley stepped from the steamy shower stall. All she had to nail were a few Schubert *Lieder* and the Queen of the Night's arias. On a stable platform. For once.

Fog swiped from the bathroom mirror, she touched the slight bruising the airbag had left on her cheek. If it were an inch higher, she could skip the rouge.

From the living room, Armand and Frénie's voices wafted into the bathroom. Whisking on underwear and a robe, Riley crept from the bathroom. Light from the living room spilled into the bedroom. Frénie must've left the door ajar.

Should she close it, or would that attract attention to her? Instead, she tiptoed to the wardrobe, slipped into a pair of black slacks and a turtleneck sweater.

"*Mon petit chou*, listen to me. Please. I've already told you, wrecking the Lambo doesn't matter to me. It's just a piece of metal."

"You let us drive off in that car." Frénie's voice rose to a wail. "We could've been killed."

"I swear I had no idea the brakes were bad. I came as soon as you texted me. Tommy is a first-class mechanic. He services only the best cars. Please believe me."

"How can I trust you? You lied to me."

"*Mon petit chou* ..."

A slap sounded. "Stop it. Take your hands off me."

Should she intervene? Riley gripped the door handle.

"When were you going to tell me the Bodwillian Estate isn't for sale?" Frénie's sniffles morphed into gulping sobs. "And never will be."

The silence dragged into seconds. "Where did you hear that?" Armand's tone was smooth as a stick of butter.

"From a man who works there."

"Oh, my sweet, I wanted to surprise you. But keeping a

secret, your little indiscretions of the mouth ... I thought it best to leave you a rabbit trail."

"Oh." Frénie's voice perked up. "You knew I'd try to find the house."

"Exactly."

"Then we *are* getting married, *oui?*"

Poor Frénie, having to propose. Next, she'd be asking him for the ring.

"My dear sweet, there will never be a woman as precious to me as you are."

Leaning against the bedroom wall, Riley pictured Frénie's up-tilted chin, eyes glistening with adoration, fingers playing along his arm. Oh Frénie, wake up.

Armand had sidestepped her question.

"Oh, another present?" The sound of ripping paper and a gasp trickled between the gap in the doorway. "It's exquisite." Breathlessness fluttered through her voice. "I shall treasure it always."

More gifts. No ring. And no commitment to marriage. Sick at her stomach, Riley squeezed her brow. Why couldn't Frénie see past the tinsel and hear what he wasn't saying?

"Where's Riley?"

"She's taking a shower."

"I don't hear water running." Tautness spiked his tone.

"She's probably soaking in the tub."

The sound of a kiss carried past the bedroom door. Riley felt like a voyeur. She should've shut the bedroom door when she had a chance.

"I have a meeting. Remember, it's our little secret, wear this at the gala."

"My lips are sealed." Frénie tittered like a little girl. "I love secrets."

As she'd done so often in Romania, Frénie had probably zipped her tiny fingers across her lips.

The door to the suite clicked shut. Now what? Riley sank on

the bed. She couldn't exactly turn herself into a fly and hide in the curtains. Even though she was dying to know what Armand had given Frénie.

The door to the suite clicked again.

Rats. Now she'd have to wait to find out.

HOW COULD Jacob nail the people who'd fled in the van when the magistrate denied them a search warrant for the orphanage? Insufficient evidence. No proof of drugs or illegals, per se, in the van. The police questioned the staff at the orphanage, and no one admitted having driven the vans.

Jacob threw the rest of his coffee down the sink drain. Raked a hand through his hair. At least CT and Interpol's background checks had uncovered suspicious financial dealings among quite a few names on Armand's guest list for the gala.

Laptops open, he joined Ian on the couch, handed him a steaming mug of tea. Outside, the sounds of traffic hummed like bees on a rampage. What he needed was soothing praise and worship music. If he were alone, he'd pull up his playlist. "Any leads on who sabotaged Frénie's brakes?"

"Nothing concrete." Setting aside his computer, Ian upended a plastic baggie on the coffee table. Labeled slips of white paper spilled across the surface.

"What's this?"

"A wee bit of Where's Waldo." Ian reached for his mug of tea.

"You're a jigsaw fan?"

"My kids love the books. In the UK, we call them *Where's Wally.*" Ian spread the slips of paper in a circle. "Puzzles and games make great family time."

"Yeah." Jacob's jaw muscle twitched. Family time he ought to be creating with Noel's son. And Tracy. But how could he do that and his job?

"Perhaps we'll spot connections we hadn't considered." Ian

pushed Mandouri and Gorilla Guy's names to the center of the table. Whistling between his teeth, he moved Tommy the mechanic, Armand, two Russian oligarchs, and twenty-five patrons of Armand's gala to the uppermost part of the circle. He tapped the gala guests' names. "Any one of them could be the Priest. Our preliminary digging shows they all have a connection to Mandouri. Business transactions of some sort."

"What about the mechanic?"

"The police called him in for questioning, but he swears the brakes on the Lambo were fine, that he always does an under-the-hood precheck on Découvrir's cars." Ian slurped a sip of tea. "I could retire tomorrow on what he's paid for that little service."

"Okay." Jacob arched his back and flexed the kinks from his muscles. "Armand knows how to buy loyalty. Maybe our focus needs to be on someone who works for him and feels Frénie's become a liability to Armand, someone willing to take matters into his own hands. Or a gala patron who's jealous of our Frenchman's success."

"Definitely worth consideration." Ian set his mug on the coffee table.

Jacob spread out the remaining paper scraps. Most of them names of guests at the gala. "Maybe Frénie saw this guy, doesn't realize she could identify him as a criminal. Ergo, he decides to have her eliminated, hires someone to sneak in and sabotage the brake lines. Drains off most of the brake fluid when the mechanic is busy with another car."

"What about Mandouri?" Ian tapped the man's name. "There doesn't seem to be any love lost between him and Découvrir."

"Yes, that's plausible."

"With you attending the gala tomorrow night, we have a man on the inside," Ian said with a grin. "Marcus and I tried to insert two of our undercover agents on the hotel staff, but Découvrir's office nixed them. Maybe they do their own background checks."

"Or maybe he's extra cautious." Jacob sipped his lukewarm tea.

"Any financial warning bells on your investigation of Découvrir's business ventures and the charity?"

"None." Jacob clunked the mug on the table. "The man's cleaner than a newly washed penny whistle."

"Exactly. Newly washed." Ian dragged Armand's name from the top of the circle to a space above Mandouri and Gorilla Guy.

"Nothing in his records suggests he's the Priest or involved in anything criminal." All he had to go on was a personal dislike of the man.

"My gut tells me we're close to uncovering the Priest's identity." Ian leaned back, laced his fingers behind his neck. "What if he's one of Découvrir's friends, or works for him? Someone using Découvrir as his saintly cover?"

"That's logical. Especially since we're out of dead bodies with silver cross necklaces." Jacob rubbed a hand over his chin. "Money launderers use innocent fronts all the time."

"Why not a wealthy, above-reproach man who supports a charity for orphans? A charity gala charging ten thousand pounds per ticket." Ian stifled a yawn. "The Priest might be on tomorrow night's guest list."

"It's possible." Jacob stifled his own yawn. If he didn't get a good night's rest soon …

"If this gala goes south, you may need backup." Fingers racing across his keyboard, Ian whistled through his teeth. "Seriously, think about transferring to the UK. We need you here."

"It's a great place to live." But not without Riles. And she had no other gigs in England. "Can we photograph the guests as they arrive and run them through our facial-recognition databases, check for criminal activity and connections that haven't surfaced?"

"Yes. I'll notify Marcus." Ian typed up another email. "And ask my chief for permission to book a guest room, set up my team in there."

"Current room rates are over a thousand per night."

"Ah ..." Ian gave him a wicked grin. "Anything for King and country."

"Or commandeer one of the vacant residential flats." Those were on higher floors than the hotel. If anything happened, Ian's men would be racing to reach the Ren Room.

"I'm sure our chaps would enjoy the view." Ian carried his mug to the kitchenette and rinsed it out.

Jacob shifted on the cushion. Hopefully the view would be the most excitement they'd experience. But twenty-five guests with suspicious connections ... "Could you loan me a military-grade body wire?"

Ian's grin faded. "No problem."

If only Ian could loan him a gun, anything to protect Riles and Frénie. After that sabotaged Lamborghini ... Jacob's cell buzzed in his pocket. He answered the call on the second ring. "Coulter here."

"PC Jenkins. From the Canada Square murders. We've identified the female victim."

"Yes?" Jacob grabbed a pencil from the table, pulled a notepad to him.

"The victim was a voice student at the Royal Conservatory in London. Maria Salciu. From Bucharest, Romania."

Jacob's chest tightened. "Any idea what voice type, soprano, mezzo ..."

"A coloratura soprano. She was working on *The Magic Flute* in her lessons."

"The music found pinned to her chest." Riles' role.

31

London, Day 17

Evening gown lifted above her ankles, Riley stepped off the Shangri-La Hotel elevator, Jacob at her side. Willing away the nausea from the ten-second blast-off, she braced her hand against the wall. Eighteen floors of hotel, starting at level thirty-four, where she'd be singing.

At least Armand hadn't rented the top of the Shard for his gala. No. She released her hand from the wall. This fainting and puking had to stop. Mind over matter, right?

"You okay, hon?" Her music tote bag in one hand, Jacob cupped her elbow, his palm warming her skin.

"Never better." She resisted the urge to straighten his bow tie. "Always did love a man in a tux."

"Savile Row's finest rental." At his lopsided grin, heat spread through her chest, and the knots in her stomach loosened.

When he'd called for her at the Savoy, he'd been a soldier on point in enemy territory. Eyes scanning the hall, the lobby, roving the traffic as he drove to the Shard.

Inside the Ren Room, the sounds of clattering glassware and chairs thunked into neat rows echoed off the floor-to-ceiling windows. City lights winked below the night sky, the perfect backdrop for the grand piano on the dais. White-coated staff scurried into the room, trays of canapés and champagne flutes in hand.

Although the event room accommodated only 140 people, for a singing engagement, this was an intimate gathering. Intimate enough for the front row guests to count her fillings.

"We're awfully early." Jacob shifted her music tote to his other hand. His gaze had that on-point alertness again.

"Wasn't sure how the elevator ride would affect my body."

As his eyes searched hers, she tried for a reassuring smile. "I've never sung for such a posh crowd."

"Sorry you declined his designer evening gown?"

"Nope." Riley smoothed the folds of her turquoise chiffon skirt, tugged the pearl-encrusted bodice up an inch. "His offer made me feel like a kept woman. So did his fee."

"I'm proud of you, Riles."

Staring into his blue eyes, she longed to spend the evening drowning in them. Instead, she drew tiny circles on his sleeve. "Do you think the Priest will be here?"

"Your sleuthing proved useful. Half the guests have made our wanted lists." His cell pinged from his trousers. Jacob pulled out the phone, frowned at the screen. He held it toward her to read. "It's from Ian."

FYI, someone paid mega-pounds to have the observation deck closed to visitors tonight. Hosting a private party there after the gala.

Have a couple agents surveilling the area now.

"If Armand's hosting the party, you'd probably have been invited. Maybe it's Mandouri's shindig."

"Darling." She let her fingers wander over Jacob's jaw and below his ear. "I hope you catch him and these other criminals,

216

but after this is over, I want to go home to Brussels and be with you."

A smile quirked his lips. "You don't like living the high life?"

"It's been an adventure, but it's not for me. More than anything, I want us to be together."

"You got it, babe." He nuzzled her earlobe, sending a trail of shivers down her neck.

"You know, some day you may not be able to protect me. You need to learn to live with that."

The slump in his shoulders tugged at her heart. "I know." His voice guttered to a whisper. "But I can't help trying."

At the tenderness in his words, a lump lodged in her throat. "It's one of the many things I love about you, but we can't continue to live our lives in fear, not trusting God to protect us." Hypocrite. She'd pleaded with Jacob to be with her in Antwerp, certain she couldn't survive without him.

With every crisis, she'd made Jacob and chocolate her crutch. Instead of running open-armed to her heavenly Father. She pressed her fingers between her eyes, but the tears welled anyway. *Dear God, please forgive me. I've made everything except You my God. No more. The next crisis, I'm turning to You first.*

"You okay?"

Unable to trust her voice, she nodded.

The elevator doors opened, and Frénie swept out. The formfitting skirt of her red silk gown swished as she sashayed into the hall. Peaked flanges jutted above the right side of the strapless bodice, accentuating her delicate shoulders. Her well-muscled biceps and triceps.

The purple bruise on her forehead had vanished beneath her exquisite makeup job. But if the diamond studs in her ears sparkled any brighter, the Ren Room could turn off the lights.

"*Ma chérie*, look." Frénie wiggled her arm, jiggling a double-rowed diamond bracelet looped around her wrist.

A low whistle escaped Jacob's mouth. "That's a bucket load of carats."

"I know." Frénie giggled like the irrepressible child she must've been. "But I'm worth every euro."

Maybe her charm was part of her appeal to Armand. "The bracelet's the gift he gave you yesterday?"

Frénie gasped, pressed her freshly manicured nails to the base of her throat. "I forgot. Thank you for reminding me."

"So, what about the estate?" Jacob smiled at her.

"Oh, that." Frénie's shoulders hiccupped. "It was nothing. Armand didn't want me to spoil his surprise." Her eyes shone like a kid on Christmas Eve. "Last night he told me he wants to show me the estate himself."

"Uh-huh." With everything in her, Riley wanted to believe in Armand, for Frénie's sake. "The same estate we tried to visit?"

"He won't tell me where this one is."

"What about the severed brake lines?" Jacob's mouth hardened.

"His mechanic swears the brakes were fine." Sparks flashed from Frénie's eyes. "Tommy wouldn't lie."

"Well, someone cut the brake lines." Riley gave her a pointed look. "They didn't sever themselves."

"Excuse me." Frost dripped from Frénie's voice. "I have things to attend to." Flicking her skirt with one hand, she swung her back to them and jabbed the elevator button. The doors glided open. Guests flooded the hall, and she stepped inside, eyes frigid.

As the doors closed, Riley fought the urge follow her. "There goes a beautiful friendship."

"Give her time." Arm around her shoulder, Jacob squeezed her to him. "When you're in love, it's hard to recognize what others see in your wannabe mate."

"You aren't referring to me, are you?" Riley elbowed his ribs.

"Naw. Anyone can see you're absolutely perfect. And I'm unbiased."

"Uh-uh." But every woman needed a starry-eyed male in her court.

A bell dinged, and Armand stepped from the second elevator. "Ah, our lovely prima donna." Eyes sweeping her, he bent over her hand. His lips brushed her skin. "I'm looking forward to your performance."

"You're too kind."

Armand clapped Jacob's shoulder. "Glad you could come. Allow me to introduce you to the other guests."

"Great." Jacob set her music bag beside the table in the corner.

Cupping Jacob's elbow, Armand walked him toward a bevy of bejeweled women and men in tuxes milling in the back of the Ren Room.

The ripple of muted conversations and soft laughter washed over Riley as she stashed her purse inside the music tote. Tonight's performance should be fun. If she could forget that the Priest, and whoever hired the thug to push her in front of the bus, might be in the audience. Skirt lifted in one hand, she mounted the step to the dais.

Pulling deep breaths to rewarm her vocal folds, she set the scores on the piano, ready for her accompanist, Felix. With glass walls and wood flooring, the acoustics would be kind to her voice. Cell muted, she laid the phone inside the bowels of the grand piano, its lid arching behind her like a black-winged butterfly. Never in her life had she carried her phone onstage. But after the attacks on her life, she wanted the cell nearby.

In the back of the room, Yousef Mandouri seemed to be holding court. A man sidled next to him, their fists touching. Mandouri slipped his hand in his pocket. Another man took his place, brushed his fist against Mandouri's. Face devoid of expression, Mandouri thrust his hand in his pocket, then joined Jacob and Armand chatting near the windows. Had she just witnessed a business transaction? Had Jacob seen any of it?

Two of the men who dined with Mandouri at La Gavroche took aisle seats on the last row. She squelched the niggle in her gut. From here, she felt like a pawn on a chess board, faced with the opposing team's master chessman.

Had Mandouri ordered one of his henchmen to push her under the bus?

At the doorway, Frénie swept past Felix and flounced toward Armand. She snatched a champagne flute from a waiter's tray, keeping her back to Riley as she chatted with guests.

Riley ran her fingers over the rim of the open piano. *Oh Lord, don't let this visit end with Frénie not speaking to me.*

Tux tails flipped behind him, Felix sat on the piano bench. He flicked her a smile as he opened her book of Schubert Lieder and propped it in place with *The Magic Flute* score.

Seconds later Armand turned toward the dais and raised his champagne flute. "Ladies and gentlemen, may I present our performer this evening, opera star Riley Williams. I assure you, her singing is worth every pound you paid for the privilege of being here tonight."

Chuckles tittered across the room. Conversations dimmed as the guests chose seats in front of her. Her fingers chilled on the rim of the piano. Was she really singing for a room full of terrorist financiers?

One hand on Jacob's shoulder as if he owned him, Armand gave her a regal nod. The classic you-may-begin sign.

Waiting for the audience to settle, Riley stepped to the edge of the dais. "Good evening. My superb pianist, Felix Comer, and I would like to offer you a selection of Schubert Lieder. And of course, the evil Queen of the Night's tour de force, 'Der Hölle Rache,' from Mozart's *The Magic Flute*." Why had she picked an aria advocating murder when there'd been three attempts on her life in two weeks? If the Priest was here, she didn't want to give him any ideas.

As she stepped back into the bend of the piano, Mandouri walked away from Jacob, pinpointed her with his laser gaze. Jacob flexed his shoulders, glanced at Mandouri. At least Interpol was on to the guy.

The opening bars of the cheerful song, "Die Forelle," rippled from Felix's fingers. In the last verse of "The Trout," the fisherman caught the unsuspecting fish. Had all of Armand's gifts been hooks into Frénie?

Four songs later, Riley reached for Felix's hand and bowed, acknowledging the applause.

Armand slipped from the room.

Smiling, she bowed once more. Odd, an opera lover leaving before the aria. Especially Armand.

Frénie sidestepped the man who'd blocked her from Riley's view while she sang. Frowning, her friend stared after Armand. Beneath the pot lights, a diamond-encrusted cross necklace glinted at the base of Frénie's throat.

32

London, Day 17

Riley's heart shot into overdrive. Was the necklace the gift Armand had told Frénie to wear tonight? What was so significant about tonight? Head bowed as applause swelled across the room, Riley gripped the inside of the grand piano. It could be a coincidence. The necklace didn't match Jacob's description of those left with the Priest's victims. And Armand's little sister had worn a cross necklace. But someone had sabotaged the brakes on the Lamborghini.

Gathering her silk skirt, Frénie darted from the room.

Brows pinched, Felix stared at Riley. She should be shifting her posture into the evil Queen. Proud. Dominating. Deadly. *God, help me. What should I do?* She glanced toward the back of the room where Mandouri chatted with Jacob. In the hall, an elevator dinged.

Hands hovering over the keyboard, Felix cleared his throat. She needed to alert Jacob. Find Frénie. *Now.* Not ten minutes later. In less than four minutes the aria would be over. There'd be applause. Possibly requests for an encore. Her fingers iced on the rim of the piano. By then, Frénie could be dead.

People in the front rows grew restless, and Felix launched into the thunderous introduction to her aria. She raised her head and shifted into the Queen's persona. The words and melody poured from her mouth on autopilot. *Dear God, lead me. Don't let me fail my friend.*

Fingers scrabbling inside the piano, she palmed her phone. Stepped off the dais, other arm outstretched, the evil Queen rendering a deadly decree. The audience ate it up as she walked down the aisle, aiming her roulades and vocal pyrotechnics inches from their faces.

Mandouri riveted his eyes on her, hands fisted, legs poised to pounce. A silly grin widened Jacob's cheeks, his gaze besotted.

What was wrong with him, didn't he realize she'd sing her program from the dais? Readying her body for her high *Fs*, she aimed the tones at him.

Five steps before she reached the last row, Mandouri's goons rose and blocked her path.

No, this couldn't be happening. Jacob's face riddled with alarm. He darted toward the two men but they closed off his access to the aisle. Jabbing her index finger like a javelin toward the ceiling, she retreated up the aisle, praying she wouldn't trip on the hem of her gown.

As the last note poured from her throat, she fled the room while Felix played the postlude. The applause rolled over her in waves as she punched the service elevator button. Red numbers gleamed above the metal doors. Floor sixty-eight. The entrance to the observation deck. Had Frénie gotten off there?

Pulse pounding, Riley punched the elevator button again. The red number didn't disappear. She moved to the other bank of elevators, stabbed the button. Texted Jacob while she waited for the doors to open.

> Headed after Frénie to observation deck via service elevator. She's wearing a diamond cross necklace.

The elevator whisked her toward the sixty-eighth floor. Pressure squeezed her skull like a vise. Bile spurted on her tongue. She swallowed the sourness as black dots swirled in her eyes. *Dear God, don't let me be too late.*

The last ounce of strength in her leg muscles unraveled, and she collapsed on the floor. *Oh God, help me.* She couldn't faint, not tonight.

Somewhere in her subconscious, a bell dinged. The doors glided open. Head swimming, Riley crawled from the elevator, the wood floor chilling her palms. How could she make it any higher? Frénie's brochures had mentioned two flights of stairs to the uppermost observation level. City lights twinkled miles beyond the windows surrounding the deck.

What was taking Jacob so long? Surely he'd read her text message by now. She clutched the garbage tin and staggered to her feet. Tottered toward the other open elevator. Why hadn't its doors closed by now?

As she peered inside the elevator, the contents of her stomach lurched. Frénie lay sprawled on the floor. Dark lashes brushed her ashen face. Crimson welts splotched her forehead and one cheek. Heat surged through Riley's chest. Who'd done this to her friend?

Thunks and *scritching* and *thuds* came from the roof of the elevator. She glanced at a large opening in the ceiling, and a man in a tux dropped to the floor. She stared at his Neanderthal jaw, and her lungs seized. Her feet rooted to the ground. Gorilla Guy.

"Good. Saves me the trouble of hunting you down." He grabbed her arms and tossed her into the back corner.

Her head struck the wall, and fiery shards lanced her skull. Body throbbing, she slumped on the floor.

Stale breath hot on her cheek, he wrenched her cell from her fingers, threw it outside the elevator, turned a key in the wall pad, darted into the hall.

Nausea rose in her throat, threatened to erupt. Must—get—out— Black dots swam in her eyes as she crawled toward the doors, but they whooshed shut. As the elevator hurtled toward the ground floor, bile spurted on her tongue.

Her heart slammed her chest. Had Gorilla Guy tinkered with the elevator to crash on the ground floor? She wobbled to her knees, scrabbled for the control panel, shoved in the red emergency stop button. The elevator jerked to a halt, slapped her spine into the side wall.

Groans escaped her lips as she collapsed on the floor. Focus. Focus. How many seconds had they been moving before she pressed the knob? If the elevator traveled sixty-eight floors in sixty seconds, where were they now? Trapped between floors?

"Frénie." Riley hauled herself to her feet and tottered over to her friend. Tapped her face. "Frénie, wake up."

Frénie's eyelashes fluttered open. Eyes wide, she gaped at the ceiling. Sobs shook her chest. "Bobby set a bomb on top of the elevator."

33

London, Day 17

Jacob scanned the Ren Room for Riles. Where'd she gone? Mandouri's goons blocked the aisle, applauding, while Mandouri strode to the front of the room, yelling "Brava, brava. Encore, encore." Jacob checked his text messages. Riles' text sucker-punched his gut.

What an idiot he'd been. Riles had tried to snag his attention with her antics. But he'd been so captivated by the beauty of her voice, the magic of her singing. Until Mandouri's goons had blocked his path. Racing from the room, Jacob forwarded the text to Ian and Marcus, added his own message.

> Send backup.

> Heading to floor sixty-eight. Praying I'm not too late. Arrest Mandouri and his henchmen.

If he could believe Armand's not-so-subtle hints, Mandouri was the Priest. A sick feeling wormed through Jacob. Despite Riley's fear of heights, she'd try to rescue her friend. She'd be no match for whoever was behind this.

Precious seconds later the service elevator sped him toward floor sixty-eight.

As the doors glided open, he almost collided with Gorilla Guy, dressed in a tux, a small carry-on case hanging from his shoulder.

Pulse ratcheting, Jacob blocked the door open with his fist. Waited for his adversary to make a move, his own feet urging him to dance like a boxer.

The man startled. "The observation deck is closed to visitors tonight."

"Oh. Thanks for telling me." The bell dinged. The door pushed against Jacob's fist. Unarmed, he'd lost the element of surprise. And Gorilla Guy was likely packing and definitely dangerous. Sweat pricked the back of Jacob's neck. Should he focus on Riles and Frénie, or try to take down Gorilla Guy?

Most likely the police would arrive too late. He'd have no backup. "Going down?" Jacob smiled at him.

Something glimmered in Gorilla Guy's eyes. Recognition?

If this worked, he'd have only one chance. Gut and legs taut, Jacob gestured toward the back of the elevator. "Be my guest."

Gorilla Guy nodded and stepped over the threshold. Lightning-fast, Jacob released the door, karate chopped the man's neck, aimed for his carotid artery. The side of his palm connected with steel-like flesh. Fire spiraled through his hand and wrist.

As Gorilla Guy went for the gun bulging inside his cummerbund, Jacob rammed his foot in the guy's groin, aimed a second kick to his liver, another chop at his carotid artery. The gun discharged, thudded on the floor.

Moaning, Gorilla Guy toppled to the ground, head lodged over the threshold between the closing doors. His fingers uncurled, and a small round-holed key skittered across the floor. As the doors reopened, his eyes rolled back in his head. Jacob snatched the gun, the key, and Gorilla Guy's phone from his trousers and pocketed them, then unzipped the carry-on.

A small out-of-order sandwich-board sign. A long, cylindrical elevator key firemen used to free passengers trapped inside elevators in the States. Duct tape, shears, wire cutters, bits of color-coated wire, a pair of needle-nose pliers.

Ice slewed through his veins. Bomb-making tools.

"Ian." Jacob yelled toward his body mic as he duct-taped Gorilla Guy's wrists, ankles, mouth, and eyes. "Possible bomb in the Shard. Evacuate the building now. And get a bomb squad up to the observation deck. Suspected perpetrator, Gorilla Guy, trussed in the entrance to a service elevator on floor sixty-eight."

"Any idea where the bomb is located?"

The calm in Ian's voice did nothing to lessen the pounding in Jacob's chest. "No. Possibly on this floor." He grabbed the carry-on. Eased out between the elevator doors. "Riles!" The deck was eerily silent. Darting between the banks of service elevators, he jabbed the call buttons. Two of them dinged. The third one didn't light up. Adrenaline thrummed through his veins. Where would a bomb cause the most damage?

INSIDE THE ELEVATOR, Riley staggered to her feet. Pressed the door open button. Nothing happened. "We have to get out of here."

"How?" Frénie flicked a lock of hair from her forehead as she sat up.

"Climb out. There should be steps built into the exterior elevator wall that houses the cage and run the height of the shaft. It's a safety feature on all newer elevators." Not that she'd ever elevator surfed, but there was supposed to be enough room to climb to other floors without being crushed by the elevator cage. Riley grabbed Frénie's hands, yanked her upright. "Probably not much time before the bomb explodes."

"But you don't like heights."

"I don't like getting blown to bits either. Here's the plan. One of us crawls through that hole. Then pulls the other one up and out." Never mind how they'd manage that with one of them still inside the elevator. In heels, she was close to six feet tall. She fluttered her fingers above her head. Not enough to clear the opening. "You're the bench-press queen. Give me a boost."

"*D'accord.* Okay." Frénie's red silk gown crumpled as she squatted and cupped her palms. Riley hoisted her bare foot into Frénie's waiting hands. Grunting, Frénie inched upward from her squat. Arms and ribs stretched until her muscles screamed, Riley flailed her fingers toward the opening, black as outer space. She reached again. Not close enough. Icy tentacles wrapped around her heart. *Dear God, help.* How much longer before the bomb detonated?

THE CARRY-ON BAG thumping his hip, Jacob dashed around the deck, jiggling the door handles. Chances were, this was a traction elevator. The machine room would be housed at the top of the elevator shaft. He slipped inside a room with electrical control panels on the wall. Bypassing the smaller boxes with red levers, he flipped the main power switches for service elevators three and four. Now he wouldn't be electrocuted. Guests trying to escape the hotel could still use all the other elevators.

The fact that Gorilla Guy had elevator keys suggested he'd planted the bomb in an elevator or in the shaft. Jacob sprinted back to the third elevator, breaths heaving his chest. How much longer before the bomb detonated?

Steadying his hand, he inserted the long cylindrical elevator drop key into the half-inch hole on the steel door. The end piece dropped ninety degrees inside the shaft. Metal clinked on the lock mechanism. He flexed his wrist left, right. Four tries later, the lock disengaged. *Thank You, God.* Key laid on the floor, he opened the outer door and peered inside the cavernous shaft.

Metal tracks lined the cement walls as far as his light penetrated the darkness. Where was the elevator?

He shucked off his tux jacket. Slung the carry-on bag over his shoulder. A pro would wear protective gear, carry a flashlight, and a rope. Have a backup team. No time. He'd have to do the job himself.

"Bomb Disposal Unit chopper en route." Ian's voice was terse in Jacob's earpiece. "Building evacuation underway."

"Great." His experience with bombs was nil. Would the bomb unit make it up here in time?

────────

As FRÉNIE SAGGED toward the elevator floor, Riley hopped off her friend's hands. *God, help us. Please don't let these evil plans succeed.*

Weeping, Frénie sank to the floor. "I haven't been very nice to you. You warned me, and I treated you terribly. Can you forgive me?"

"I've already forgiven you." Riley pressed her cheek against Frénie's. "You're the best friend ever. Now come on." She yanked Frénie to her feet. "Hoist me up again. We were close to making this work."

Frénie positioned herself, and Riley stepped up on her friend's cupped palms. Grunting. Shoving. Grunting and shoving again, Frénie inched Riley past the upper edge of the elevator wall. She thrust her arms through the open edge of the ceiling. Cool air swept her skin. "Two. More. Inches."

Groaning as if she were lifting Atlas, Frénie jerked her upward. Riley grasped a metal bar on top of the roof and wiggled her torso outside the elevator. Arm muscles nearly popping from their sockets, she worked her thighs, calves out of the cage.

Breaths heaving her chest, she stared at the bomb. Wires protruded from a square device. Threaded into two bricks of C-

4 still encased in plastic wrappers. The seconds ticked with frightening speed on the bomb's red timer dial.

Six minutes and counting.

She whipped off her evening gown, laid down in her bustier and full-length slip on the cold metal roof. "Quick, grab the bodice and I'll pull you up." Chilly air pimpled her skin as she dropped most of the dress through the hole.

Grunting and groaning, Frénie crab-walked her legs up the elevator wall while Riley tugged on the skirt. *Sckwuck, schwuck.* The chiffon tore from the back of the bodice. *Dear God, no.* Let the stitching hold.

Frénie's head and elbow popped through the hole, and Riley yanked Frénie's arm onto the elevator deck. A dangerous hold, but no time for a second attempt.

Grunting, Frénie clawed her way through the hole. "*Merci.*" Breaths heaving her chest, she huddled across from Riles. Glanced toward the bomb. Her eyes widened. "Now what?"

"We climb out of here." *Don't look down. Don't look down.* She could do this. She *had* to do this. Palms and soles of her feet slippery with sweat, she forced her trembling legs up the wall ladder's icy rungs. Frénie followed close behind.

The number sixty-four was painted over the next elevator shaft door. *Thank You, God.* They'd traveled down only five floors. A faint light bled into the shaft above her. Not that reaching the observation deck would be safe.

34

London, Day 17

"Riles!" Thank God she was alive. Jacob scrambled down the last rungs on the elevator shaft ladder to reach her. She shivered as she clung to the ladder wearing only her longline bra and slip. If only he still had on his tux jacket.

Sobs punctuated her words as she gripped the rung below his shoes. "There's a bomb on top of the elevator. Two bricks of C-4."

His gut seized. "That's enough C-4 to do massive damage to the building and everything in the area. Including the train and tube station below the structure. You and Frénie squeeze past me on the ladder. The shaft is open at the top floor. Grab my jacket upstairs and take another elevator. Evacuate the building ASAP, get as far away from the Shard as you can. Help is on the way."

"No. I'm not leaving you." Easing around him, she climbed level with him, her tears moistening his cheek.

With everything in him he wanted to take her in his arms. But one of them had to remain strong. "As an Interpol agent, I'm ordering you two to vacate the premises now." Inwardly, he cringed at the harshness in his tone, but she'd never leave otherwise.

"For Tracy's sake, please go now." His voice cracked as he cupped her chin, memorized the flecks of green and gray in her eyes. "She'll need someone there for her, to help her grow into a woman like you. Please. For my sake, do this. You can't save me. But you can bless my sister."

"I promise." Riley pressed her lips to his then hurried up the ladder.

Arm looped around the railing, Jacob clung to one side of the ladder as Frénie shimmied past him up the stairs. "Frénie, can you identify the man who did this to you?"

"Bobby. He works for Armand, lives next door, but I don't know what he does." She yelled down the shaft as she scurried toward the top floor. "Once I saw him inside Armand's study, then he disappeared."

"I saw him, Jacob," Riley said. "After Gorilla Guy set the bomb, he threw us in the elevator."

No way was Gorilla Guy walking away from a criminal conviction for this.

Dreading what he'd find, Jacob clambered down the remaining steps and squatted on top of the elevator car. The seconds ticked down on the timer's red-digital dial attached to two bricks of C-4. Heart slamming his chest, he spoke into his body mic. "Ian. Gorilla Guy planted two bricks of C-4 on top of one of the service elevators." His armpits glued to his shirt.

"ETA on that chopper, eight minutes. How many minutes left on the timer?"

"Less than three. In case this doesn't end well, Armand left the Ren Room before Riles started her aria. Mandouri was leading the bravas."

"Any experience with C4 and timers?" Ian's tone was as casual as NASA guiding in a damaged space capsule.

"Nope."

"Well, there's a first time for everything."

This was one first he'd happily forgo.

"Nothing to it, I hear."

"Right." Ian's subtle way of telling him he'd have to defuse the bomb himself. Jacob wiped his palms on his trousers. "Like performing brain surgery from a med-school textbook."

"Unfortunately, protocol requires us to break off all communication. Mobile phones, radios. Your earpiece. They could detonate the bomb." A few moments silence at Ian's end. "Good luck."

Luck? No, he needed God. "Thanks, Ian. Be seein' ya."

Horror stories he'd read of experts severing the wrong lead swirled in his mind. More than anything he wanted to live. To spend his life with Riles at his side. Be there for his sister. But maybe that wasn't God's plan. And if it wasn't, he'd have to accept that. Jacob ripped out his earpiece, powered off his phone.

The faint shrill of police and ambulance sirens echoed in the shaft.

Two minutes and ticking. Sweaty rivers coursed down his chest.

Thank you, God. Now I need Your wisdom, Your holy angels to help with this midair tutorial. And most of all, fill me with Your peace. And please get Riles and Frénie out of danger before this thing blows.

The seconds on the dial rolled to one minute. He grabbed the wire cutters. Leaned in close to the bomb.

Fifty seconds left.

Against the timer's *tick, tick, tick*, he steadied the blades with his other hand.

Forty seconds.

Thirty seconds.

If this failed ... At least he was certain where he'd spend eternity. Perspiration streamed into his eyes, burning, blurred his vision. He locked the jittering wire cutters around the first two wires. Holding his breath, he snipped the wires.

Without waiting, he rammed the wire cutters around the

next pair. Nipped them in two. Severed the final four wires. The held breath fled his mouth. He was still alive. *Thank You, God.*

He tossed aside the wire cutters and pulled out the timer, the detonator. The clock had stopped at two seconds. Thank God Gorilla Guy was no bomb expert.

Adrenaline seeped from his muscles. His limbs leaden, he climbed the steps to the open elevator doorway and shoved in his earpiece. Static crackled in his ear. He drew a breath, faked a calm in his voice. "Bomb defused."

Cheers rose in the background. "Good show," Ian said. "The Army Bomb Disposal Unit is two minutes out. They'll want the bomb intact for fingerprinting and analysis, and check for secondary devices hidden elsewhere up there."

Secondary devices. Sounded like something Gorilla Guy would do. If he'd had the time.

Thank You God, thank You for giving us another chance.

35

London, Day 17

Head reeling, Riley clutched Jacob's tux jacket around her chest. *Jacob, oh Jacob, be safe.* Would she ever see him again?

The elevator doors glided open on the first floor of the Shangri-La Hotel.

"Come." Frénie grasped Riley's arm, and they rushed through the hotel lobby, took the escalator to the street level over the London train and tube station.

Grim-faced, Ian met them at the base of the escalator. "You made it. Come along." He gripped Riley's free arm, hustled them away from the building and to the back of an ambulance waiting across the street. "Jacob defused the bomb, but we're not certain there weren't other explosives planted in the building."

A female ambulance tech helped Riley onto the back lip of the vehicle and wrapped a blanket over her lap. Teeth chattering, Riley nodded her thanks. Who'd have thought an evening gown could be a lifesaving device?

If only Jacob would come out of the building.

Dark splotches stained Frénie's scarlet evening gown. *"Chérie*

..." Her friend's voice cracked, hoarse. The tech handed her a blanket, and Frénie cowered beside her, cocooned in the cover.

Rack lights on police cars flashed, and a bevy of ambulances lined the crowded street. Hotel guests and uniformed staff clustered across the street from the Shard. Laden with equipment, an Army Bomb Disposal Unit jumped from the back of a truck and sprinted toward the entrances, their boots heavy on the pavement.

A few yards down the street, six PCs guarded Mandouri and his goons, their hands cuffed behind them. Another group of PCs herded cuffed guests from the gala into a waiting paddy wagon. The knots in Riley's shoulders loosened. Thank God the evening had reaped a haul for Interpol. Maybe the Priest was among those arrested.

Riley's pulse surged as Jacob emerged from the hotel entrance, took the escalator steps two at a time, and darted over to their ambulance. A pallor clung to his skin, but the haunted look in his eyes shredded her heart. He'd been through so much, risked everything to save them.

Clutching the blanket around her for modesty's sake, she scooted off the lip of the ambulance, and let him fold her in his arms. Tears clogged her throat as she pressed her cheek to his sweat-soaked shirt.

"Hey, hon." His voice caught. "Quite an exit you made tonight."

A giggle erupted between her sobs. Cutting the tension with humor had been her forte. Maybe she was rubbing off on him.

Ian crossed over to them. He tapped his fingers to his forehead, palm facing out on his right hand, and released a salute. "Well done, Special Agent. Looks like you found Waldo."

"Thanks." Jacob clapped him on the shoulder. "I'm not sure Gorilla Guy or Mandouri is the Priest. The Priest's top henchman, maybe."

"While you were playing the hero, we uncovered enough evidence to arrest and charge Mandouri. It seems he has business dealings with a British couple awaiting trial. They decided to implicate Mandouri as the financier behind their terrorist activities."

A sigh escaped Riley's mouth. Thank heavens. One more nail in Mandouri's professional coffin.

"His movements in Paris and Vienna match the dates of the silver cross murders," Jacob said as he tightened his arm around her shoulders.

Riley edged against his side. If Jacob's suspicions were accurate, this nightmare was far from over.

"Maybe Gorilla Guy will talk," Ian said. "The police have him in custody."

A uniformed PC walked over to her and Frénie.

"PC Watkins, Miss Frénau. I'd like to ask you a few questions. Interpol may have some of their own as well."

"*Oui*, yes."

While Watkins activated his recorder and pulled out a notebook and pen, Riley returned to the back of the ambulance.

Given the grayed hair at his temples, the grooves in his forehead, Watkins was no newcomer to the force. "If you'd please start at the beginning."

"At the gala, I was standing next to Armand." Frénie reached for Riley's hand, her death grip pulverizing Riley's knuckles. She tried not to wince. "When he left the room before Riley's aria, I followed him to the sixty-eighth floor. He was talking with Bobby, a man who works for him."

PC Watkins scribbled more notes. "Can you describe him for us?"

"A giant. Massive build, brush-cut hair, wearing a tuxedo tonight."

"Did he say why he was doing this?" PC Watkins asked.

Shoulders slumped, Frénie pressed a hand to her chest.

"I need a verbal answer for the recording, miss."

"Before they spotted me, I overheard Armand tell Bobby to shorten the timer on the bomb to make sure everyone in the Shard was blown up." Sobs hiccupped in her throat. "But–but Armand saw me and told Bobby to throw me into the elevator with the bomb."

Gasping, Riley clasped her friend's hand. If Jacob hadn't defused the bomb, hundreds of people might have died.

"You're saying Mr. Découvrir ordered him to kill you."

"Yes."

"Découvrir appears to have fled. He managed to leave the Shard before my team could seal off the exits," Ian said. "He filed a flight plan with London City Airport which he failed to honor. Would you have any idea where he might head?"

"*Non*. I know he does business in Vienna and Paris, sometimes in Germany, but he never talked to me about these things."

"What if Armand hasn't left the country?" Riley gripped the blanket. "Filing a flight plan could be a ruse, a sleight of hand to misdirect your focus."

"He may be responsible for the severed brakes on your car," Jacob said.

Frénie's face blanched.

Lips clamped against the words she wanted to hurl at Armand, Riley wrapped her arm around her friend's shoulder. How long had Armand been planning this dreadful finale?

"The damage from two C-4 bricks could've rivaled America's nine eleven, had they detonated." Ian scratched his cheek.

"Did Armand give you the cross necklace yesterday in the suite?" Riley asked.

"Yes." Frénie's chin drooped to her neck, voice hushed to a whisper. "He said it was to be our secret."

"We haven't made this common knowledge," Ian said. "But the person we think is responsible for a string of murders leaves a silver cross necklace on his victims."

"Oh!" Frénie's fingers flew to Armand's necklace at her throat. "How could he do this to me?" Tears muffled her voice. "I loved him."

"I suspect your friendship with Riles convinced him you'd become a liability," Jacob said. "She was probing too deeply in his affairs."

"You mean when I took her to his townhouse, and she searched his desk?"

"In part, yes," Jacob said. "Bobby or the maid probably told him about the visit."

"All those nights and afternoons you left me to be with Armand ..." Riley patted Frénie's hand. "Did he ever ask you about me, what I was doing, where I planned to go?"

"Oh yes, all the time. He was so concerned for your safety. And he wanted you to have enough money so he had me slip some pounds in your wallet."

Her skin crawled. Armand's money tainting her purse. Where had she spent it? "By any chance did you remove an Interpol photograph from my purse?"

"Yes. The paper was bulky, so I set it on the table when I put the money in your wallet. I guess I forgot to put the picture back."

"Armand may have taken it when you weren't looking. The picture wasn't there when I needed it." Riley cleared her throat. "So, he might've ordered his henchman to throw me in front of the bus."

Frénie gasped. "How could I have been so deceived?"

"We both were." It didn't solve who ordered the attack on the hydraulic lift, but she might never know that.

"Can you recall anything else that might help our investigation?" PC Watkins flipped to a clean page in his notebook, jotted a few more notes.

"*Non.*"

"If Découvrir tries to contact you, it's imperative you inform us at once." The constable's steely eyes glinted at her.

"*Bien sûr*, of course." Frénie kneaded her hands in her lap.

Recorder deactivated, PC Watkins tucked his pen and

notebook in his pocket. "We'll provide a police escort to your hotel, check the rooms before you enter."

"Thank you," Riley said. Then she and Frénie would be on their own. Jacob and Ian would probably work on the case through the night. Her fingers chilled. But Gorilla Guy's arrest didn't mean Armand lacked the resources to finish the job.

36

London, Day 17

I f he never had to defuse another bomb, he'd be a happy guy. Arm around Riles' waist, Jacob walked her away from Frénie. "We'll have to move fast if we hope to catch Armand." It'd be another all-nighter, applying for search warrants to Armand and Gorilla Guy's houses. The orphanage, again, in case Armand was hiding there. "And then interview Bobby."

"I understand. Wish I could help."

"I'd like you to come to the boarding school tomorrow. I need to talk to his daughter. You can ease the way for me." If Armand was smart, she'd be as clueless as Frénie. But Amira might know places her father liked to stay, cities he visited.

"Of course." Taut lines etched the corners of Riles' mouth. Bits of mascara and eyeliner crusted her cheeks. If only they could spend time together and process the horrendous events. But Riles wouldn't leave Frénie alone in the suite, and he needed to find Armand.

"Hon." He turned Riles to face him and rested his hands on her shoulders. "I appreciate you trying to save Frénie, but I want your word of honor next time you will leave the heroics to

Interpol. I can't do my job worrying about your safety and Tracy's."

Nibbling her lipstick, Riley stared toward the ground.

The seconds stretched so long his fingers tightened on her shoulder. No. She couldn't do this to him. He had to have her word.

Finally, she nodded.

"Thanks." Letting his hand wander to the small of her back, he circled the knotted muscles and pressed his lips to hers in an all-too-short kiss. *Thank God, it wouldn't be their last one.*

As she broke the embrace, tears spilled onto her cheeks. "I love you, Jacob Coulter. You're the bravest man I've ever known."

Heat exploded across his chest. He couldn't restrain the grin pushing toward his ears. "Anything else you like?"

Eyebrow cocked, she traced her fingernail along his chest, her touch rocketing his pulse into orbit. "How much time do you have?"

"A lifetime, I hope." One hand around her waist, he inhaled the faded scent of her Chanel No. 5.

"Excuse me." A female constable handed him Riley's music tote. "I believe this is yours, Miss Williams."

"Thank you." Riley brushed the moisture from her cheeks.

As the PC left them, he snugged Riles to him. "Your singing was sensational. A couple more performances, and the goosebumps on my arms will be permanent."

Chin dug into his sternum, she gazed up at him. "Better watch out, or I'll make you the lifetime president of my fan club."

"Are you accepting applications?" More than anything, he wanted to make her dreams come true.

"I might be."

LONDON, Day 18

After hours of night terrors, their cries and moans waking each other up, she and Frénie would be mainlining caffeine today. Riley peeked out the blackout drapes, let her eyes adjust to the sunlight and traffic flooding the street below. *Thank You, God. It's wonderful to be alive.*

Bare feet sinking into the carpet, she carried a steaming mug of *café au lait* to Frénie.

"*Merci.*" Dwarfed by a plethora of pillows and the duvet, Frénie slurped the hotel-room brew.

"How are you feeling?" Riley sat on the side of the bed.

"*Comme-ci, comme ça,* so-so." Shoulders hiked to her ears, Frénie sighed. "All those nightmares last night. But grateful to be alive." With her free hand she squeezed Riley's fingers. "Grateful to *mon Dieu,* my God, and to you and Jacob."

"I'm so thankful he was able to defuse the bomb."

Fingers curled around the mug, Frénie sank against the pillows. "You were right about Armand. I should've listened to you."

"There's no denying he's drop-dead gorgeous."

Shudders trembled Frénie's shoulders. "Oh, don't use that word. We speak no more of death. But *oui,* he's handsome, charismatic, does—did everything with panache."

"True." He'd snowed her too.

"And you, my friend, have captured the heart of a true prince. All the jewels in the world pale next to Jacob."

Curls fell around her cheeks as Riley picked at a slub in the hotel bathrobe.

"I tell you my friend, do not let this man get away from you. Why have you not set a wedding date?"

"It's complicated. We need time to build our relationship."

"*Pah!* What more is there to know? He loves you, he risks his life for you over and over. I tell you he's a good man. Honest. Trustworthy. Don't be a fool. If you keep him dangling, he may look elsewhere."

"I know." Riley knotted her hands, fingers digging her knuckles. Why couldn't she commit? Was it because Jacob's protectiveness might grow into Dad's controlling spirit? Part of the reason she'd come to Europe to study and perform was to escape home.

The hotel phone buzzed on the nightstand. Frénie reached for the receiver. "*'Allo?*"

Frowning, she held the receiver away from her ear and Riley leaned in. "The hotel manager?"

"I don't know how to say this, but there seems to have been a misunderstanding." He cleared his throat. "May I come to your suite and discuss this matter with you?"

"*Bien sûr.*"

"I'll be there directly." The call disconnected.

"*Vite, vite.* Hurry." Frénie whipped off the duvet and thrust her feet in her slippers, shrugged on a hotel bathrobe.

Riley yanked navy slacks from the wardrobe and slipped them on beneath her robe. A knock sounded at the door. "He must've called you from the hall." If he'd been skulking outside the door, the matter must be serious.

Still tweaking her pixie haircut into shape, Frénie opened the door. "*Bon jour, monsieur.*"

"Good afternoon, ladies." As he ducked to clear the doorway, his balding pate gleamed beneath their living room chandelier. Adam's apple bobbling, he tugged at the vest of his gray three-piece suit. Hand-tailored by the looks of it.

"Well, what is it? That you disturb us so early in the morning." Frénie tightened the knot in her bathrobe sash.

"Mademoiselle, it's noon." He consulted his watch. "Actually, it's fifteen minutes past the hour."

Frénie shrugged. "And why is that important?"

"Because checkout time is at noon."

"Why would we want to check out today?"

"Because, *mademoiselle* ..." He cleared his throat. "Yesterday morning Monsieur Découvrir paid the bill through this morning."

"*Non.*" Frénie's hand fluttered to her throat. She sank onto the nearest armchair. "I—I didn't know."

The rat. Riley dug her fists in the robe's pockets. Armand was cutting ties, making sure his movements couldn't be traced. But then, he'd expected them to perish at the Shard.

A flush mottled the manager's face. "Normally, the late check-out fee is fifty percent of the room charge."

"Oh." Jaw gaping, Frénie stared at Riley. "What should I do? I can't pay ..."

"Sir, as you can see, Miss Frénau had no idea. Nor did I. We can vacate in thirty minutes. Please forgive the misunderstanding."

"Very well." He dabbed a silk hanky to his brow, then shut the door behind him.

"Come on." Riley darted to the bedroom and threw open the suitcases. "Start packing."

"But where will we go?"

"Haven't a clue, but we can't afford a thousand-dollar tab."

37

London, Day 18

A chill pervaded the interview room in the Paddington Police Station as Jacob stared across the table at Gorilla Guy, now dressed in jail-issued gray sweats and slip-on paper shoes.

Prisoners in the UK usually wore their own clothes to the interview, but the forensics team had found bombmaking residue on his tux, now evidence for the court. At least the custody sergeant had deemed the suspect sufficient risk to have Bobby handcuffed.

Seated between Ian and Marcus, Jacob stifled a yawn. He'd have preferred a dehumanizing orange jumpsuit. Samson-proof shackles around the guy's wrists and ankles, tethering him to the table and floor. But the British were known for civility and good manners, even toward dangerous criminals. Gorilla Guy didn't know how good he had it.

The police constable who'd delivered Gorilla Guy stepped outside. He'd wait in the hall in case their suspect grew violent. It had taken four PCs to subdue Gorilla Guy as they loaded him in the police van at the Shard.

Jacob leaned toward Ian. "Any word from the magistrate?" They needed a search warrant for the orphanage ASAP. In the middle of the night, they'd been given warrants for Armand and Bobby's townhouses and told to return later for the third warrant. No call to disturb the children in the middle of the night, the officer on duty had said. And nothing they'd uncovered in the townhouses supported a search of the orphanage.

Ian checked his phone, shook his head.

"Thanks." Jacob shifted on the chair. If von Bingen hadn't insisted he hear Bobby's interview firsthand, he'd have headed to the girls' school with Riles. Instead, he was holed up in an interview room with a hostile suspect.

In the corner, a red light flickered on the CCTV camera. The room even had a panic alarm in case Gorilla Guy leapt at them.

Eyelids puffy from lack of sleep, Ian popped a CD into the three recorder trays, and flicked on the DVD camera linked to the recording system. One copy of each would be sealed and opened only by the authority of the court. The custody staff would store the two working DVD/CD copies in the disk library until transcription was needed for the trial. Safe from Armand's prying hands.

The fluorescent lights overhead hummed and buzzed. "For the record, this interview is being taped and filmed." Ian intoned the lengthy British version of mirandizing the guy, informing him of his rights and entitlements, legal counsel of his choosing, or the duty solicitor, which Gorilla Guy declined.

Maybe he'd decided to talk, give them what they needed to arrest Armand. As soon as they found him. Jacob laid his copy of their questions for Gorilla Guy on his lap, adjusted his Personal Protective Equipment, the sergeant had urged them to wear. Like all interrogation rooms, the air reeked of foul-smelling socks, burnt coffee, and overworked sweat glands. Jacob rubbed his nose. Not even industrial disinfectant and floor cleaner masked the odors.

Ian settled in his chair. "The purpose of this interview is to discuss your involvement in money laundering for a terrorist financier, confirmed by your lunch contact in Vienna, rigging an IED in the Shard in an attempted mass murder confirmed by two rescued victims, and evidence supporting your presence at a murder in Vienna and Paris. Do you have anything to say about this?"

Gorilla Guy chewed his cheeks, eyed the wall behind them.

"For the recording, no response from the suspect." Ian held up six passports they'd found in Gorilla Guy's wall safe at three this morning. "Our search warrants proved most helpful. Would you care to explain these passports, the six different identities bearing your photograph?"

Again, Gorilla Guy studied the wall, mouth tight. But a muscle ticked the corner of his left eye.

"For the record, the suspect has chosen not to respond. However, your physical description and the French passport issued in the name of Roman Lachalle matches one used to leave Vienna fifteen days ago. Verified by the airline agent and Austrian security."

"As well as this one—" Ian held up another passport. "A Bulgarian passport used to enter Austria the day before the murder at Stefansdom, the cathedral in Vienna." He slid a third passport forward on the table. "And this Romanian passport for Mihai Popescu, is on record for entering and leaving Paris, fourteen days ago."

But none of their databases had turned up Gorilla Guy's real name. Frénie knew him only as Bobby. Jacob checked his watch. Where was that search warrant?

Digging inside the large manila envelope, Ian pulled out receipts and hotel register verifications of multiple stays in Paris and Vienna. Courtesy of Jean-Pierre and Margot's teams. "You seem to be quite the traveler. Would you care to explain these trips to Paris and Vienna?"

Jacob bounced his heel on the floor. This was going nowhere.

He didn't envy Ian having to build the case against Gorilla Guy, necessary for the Crown Prosecution Service, who'd review the paperwork and determine the charges against Gorilla Guy. And whether or not he'd be released on bail.

Scrabbling inside a large manila envelope, Ian held up a dozen silver cross necklaces. "For the record, these cross necklaces found at the suspect's home are identical to those left on the murder victims in Vienna, Paris, and London."

Moisture beaded Gorilla Guy's upper lip.

"Going into the jewelry business?" Ian asked.

"I'm a religious man."

"I'll bet. And what faith is that?" Marcus asked.

"Faith in myself."

"How's that working for you?" Jacob leaned back in his chair, nodded toward the handcuffs on Gorilla Guy's wrists.

Fists straining at the metal bands, Gorilla Guy's glare read *you're-dead-meat*. Flamethrowers in his eyes. The energy of a pit bull terrier pulsated across the table.

"We found the secret passage from your home to Armand Découvrir's." Ian laid the necklaces on the table. "Clever, hiding it behind that Flemish tapestry."

"Must've been a lot of work, building that. Your idea or his?" Jacob asked.

"Great minds think alike, they say."

"What firm did you hire to do the work?" Ian asked.

"You'd have to ask Armand."

"Right." Jacob stifled a yawn behind his hand. "About those corpses our cadaver dog and the specialist forensic team located behind the walls in your townhome early this morning ... Are those the workmen's bodies?"

Gorilla Guy stiffened. Blinked a couple of times.

Hacking through the sheetrock and processing the four men's remains had taken hours. Jacob drummed his fingers on the table. "Where's your pal Armand?"

"He's a busy man. Many business interests." Gorilla Guy snickered. "Has an orphanage to run."

"Yes, we'd like to ask him about those business interests." Ian cleared his throat. "Where might he be? He filed a flight plan to Aruba, but his plane never flew remotely near the island."

Cheeks clenched between his teeth, Gorilla Guy flexed his fists in the cuffs.

"Look, pal. Armand's not coming to your rescue." Jacob slapped his palm on the table. "He set you up as his patsy months ago. Left you to take the blame for those murders at Stefansdom, the Eiffel Tower. Didn't even hire you a smooth-talking solicitor."

Fuming, Gorilla Guy squirmed as if fire ants had invaded his sweatpants.

"Face it, man." Ian folded his arms. "Your only chance of survival is to talk, cooperate with us. Especially since we now have a DNA match for you at the scene of those crimes."

Jacob stifled a grin. Courtesy of an unwashed drinking glass in Bobby's home.

"Are you crazy?" Chest ballooning his shirt, nostrils flaring, Gorilla Guy glared at Ian. "And risk having my tongue cut out?"

"Actually..." Ian picked at his fingernail. "Your tongue will be the least of your worries when Découvrir sends his men after you."

Sweat dribbled through Gorilla Guy's brush cut, beaded his brow. A muscle tic pulsed his jaw.

"I can't promise." Ian scratched his cheek. "But turn crown's evidence ..."

In the tiny room, Gorilla Guy's gaze ping-ponged from corner to corner. His shirt heaved and lowered like a threatening volcanic eruption. "Armand does not leave loose ends."

"True." Jacob shifted on his chair. The near disaster at the Shard proved that.

Lunging across the table, Gorilla Guy gave Jacob a pointed look. "And *you* are a loose end!"

38

London, Day 18

This might be his worst idea yet. Jacob unlocked his flat and motioned Frénie and Riley inside the pencil-thin foyer.

Bags stacked, he rolled their suitcases and evening gown bags inside and double locked the door. With Gorilla Guy in jail, how many of Armand's associates still roamed the streets? Faces he didn't know. Agendas he could only guess at. And if one of Armand's henchmen showed up at the apartment door, what then? Bobby's threat hadn't been idle bluster.

"Bedroom and loo are to your left. Kitchenette and living area are off the end of the hall." As a bachelor pad, the space worked. Ian had insisted on sleeping on the couch. But until Armand was caught, the women would need bodyguards. Armed bodyguards. And neither he nor Ian were allowed to carry weapons. Nor did British policemen.

"Not exactly the Savoy." Or even a bare-bones Motel 6.

"It's fine, Jacob." Squeezing around the luggage, Riley stroked his cheek. Touched her lips to his.

Jolts of electricity radiated through his face. How he wanted to take her in his arms and smother her with kisses. They needed time together. Alone.

Sighing, she slid her hand to his chest. "Thank you for picking us up."

"Hey ..." His voice went husky. "Couldn't leave you stranded outside the Savoy." He hefted his chin and mimicked a British accent. "It wouldn't be proper."

Riles stood aside while he pushed their luggage into the bedroom and laid their evening gown bags across the queen-sized bed. He walked her down the hall, his hand at the small of her back.

At the kitchenette, Frénie shot him a halfhearted smile. "I'd better see if the cruise line will rehire me."

"Not yet. Please, have a seat." While Riles and Frénie sat on the sofa, he peered out the windows and shut the drapes. Eight stories, his flat on the second floor. "Here are the house rules. No opening the door to anyone other than a bona fide police officer, Ian, Marcus, or myself. No leaving the apartment without a police escort, understand?"

White-knuckled grips on each other's hand, they nodded, faces drawn and pale.

"And absolutely no texting, phoning, or trying to reach Armand or anyone connected to him." His gut told him to ask for Frénie's phone. Even if she didn't contact him, Armand might try to reach her and lure her outside. And Riles was sure to follow.

But leaving them without a way to reach him or the police ... "If Armand calls or texts you, do not respond. It's a trap."

"But—" Frénie squirmed on the couch. "Ian said he left the country."

"Not his henchmen. This morning we received a warning. Anyone involved with Armand is in danger. Ian's trying to find us a safehouse off Armand's radar. In the meantime, he's setting up a roster of off-duty policewomen to stay with you. As soon as the first PC arrives, I need Riles to come with me." He glanced at her taut face, waited for her nod.

"We'll be back after dark, so don't wait up for us. Food's in the fridge, and the officer will bring more when she arrives." He glanced at his watch. Every minute they delayed, he risked losing his last connection to Armand's trail.

SEATED beside Riles in his car, Jacob scanned the grounds of the Saint Aminta Orphanage, the search warrant on the console. Stating what they expected to find at the orphanage had been pure guesswork. Drugs. Evidence of a money laundering op. The man himself?

Apart from three police vans, four cars were parked in the lot. No white vans. No Range Rover. The place was as deserted as the last time he and Riles visited. "Hate to leave you alone in the car." He wrapped his hand around hers. "But we can't make two round trips from London in a day." And he needed her to help him talk to Tracy and her BFF, his last possible connection to Armand.

"I understand." At her smile, warmth oozed through his chest. "We'll stop and picnic after we visit her school."

"Sounds good." He touched his lips to hers, not wanting to pull away.

Outside the car, he straightened his Interpol jacket over his loaner stab-proof vest, then joined Ian and PC Finkhorst waiting by the third police van. If they found people today whose DNA matched the food wrappers and drink cans in the wrecked van, Interpol would've chinked another notch in Armand's airtight armor.

Paired off, the constables dashed toward the back of the building. Four more positioned themselves at the sides of the orphanage.

The faster they finished here, the sooner he could talk to Tracy.

As Ian reached for the doorbell, the front door opened.

Blinking like a semaphore, Ms. Martin slicked her lips. Today she'd dressed in mousy gray. "Yes?"

"We have a search warrant for the premises." Jacob handed her the document.

Face ashen, her gaze swept over his jacket. Crushing the warrant to her chest, she stepped back from the door.

"Where can we chat?" PC Finkhorst kept his voice casual.

"This way." She pointed to the parlor.

Jacob and Ian joined PC Finkhorst on the couch. Ms. Martin sat in the armchair she'd chosen last time.

"Miss." PC Finkhorst cleared his throat. "We have reason to believe one of your vans picked up a driver and passengers after a Road Traffic Collision, the day before yesterday."

Her fingers skittered over the warrant in her lap.

"Without summoning help for the injured. Or reporting the incident to the police. A matter two PCs discussed with you the day after the accident."

She clamped her lips between her teeth.

"According to their report, you denied any knowledge of the incident. Fleeing the scene of an injury accident carries a serious charge."

"I—I don't know anything about this." The pitch of her voice rose like one of Riles' scales. "I told the constables that."

Leaning forward, Jacob elbowed his knees. "Do you live on the premises, Ms. Martin?"

"Yes. I have a room upstairs."

"We'll need to see it," PC Finkhorst said. "The warrant authorizes a search of all rooms and buildings on the property."

"I have nothing to hide." She squared her shoulders. Shallow breaths pulsed her gray sweater.

"Ms. Martin, when was Mr. Découvrir last here?" Jacob asked.

"I—I think..." A flush crept up her neck. "I-I don't recall."

"I see." He'd take that as confirmation Armand had been here after the van's passengers arrived.

Upstairs, doors squeaked open and slammed shut.

"They'll wake the babies." The woman leapt from her chair and scurried upstairs.

Jacob took the steps two at a time, memories of cradling Peter in his arms washing over him. Inside the nursery, Ms. Martin picked up a squalling baby from a crib along the wall. No nanny on duty. He scooped Peter from his crib and snugged the mewing infant to his chest. Stroking circles on Peter's back, Jacob drank in the scent of talcum powder and the baby's skin, as he shushed his cries.

The tightness in his chest loosened. Thank God, Armand hadn't harmed Peter. After last night's bomb attempt at the Shard, he hadn't been certain Armand would spare the children. When the baby calmed, Jacob laid him in the crib and tucked the blanket around his tiny body. "Take care, little buddy."

Footsteps clattered in the hallway.

"You'll need to return downstairs, Ms. Martin." For the babies' sake, he'd like to leave her with them. But she was a part of Armand's schemes.

Face taut, Ms. Martin settled the baby in the crib and left the nursery.

Jacob stepped into the hall, closed the nursery door behind him. Four girls with matted hair and rail-thin arms, dressed in dirt-stained T-shirts and jeans, cowered between two PCs. Wincing, he jammed his fists in his trouser pockets. The girls looked like malnourished teens.

"We couldn't get anything out of them," the constable on his left said. "Not even a name."

"Probably terrified." Jacob let his eyes soften and smiled at the girls. *"Parlez-vous français? Sprechen Sie Deutsch? Habla español?"* If they didn't speak French, German, or Spanish, he was out of luck. He'd aced those Interpol language tests.

The first girl shook her head. Dark hair and eyes, olive-toned skin. That could cover a lot of territory, languages he didn't speak or recognize. He tapped his chest. "Jacob. Coulter." Palm out, smile in place, he gestured to the girl who'd shaken her head.

"Ilinca Comenici."

"Romanian?"

Hope flickering in her eyes, she nodded.

Thank. You. God. With her years living in Bucharest, Riles was fluent in the language. And Romania was notorious for male and female human trafficking, smuggling illegals into other countries. Especially to the UK. Cell out, he texted Riles.

> May have four Romanian illegals in here.
> Please come to parlor to translate.

Three bouncing dots flicked across his screen.

> On my way.

"Where did you find the girls?" Jacob asked, as they led them downstairs.

"Hiding in the corner of the attic," the taller constable said. "As well as a stash of weapons, cash, phones, ID documents. This place must be an op center for money laundering and labor trafficking."

Jacob's gut clenched. Typical ops with ties to Romania. Participants and their families were threatened with bodily harm by the criminal network if they didn't cooperate or wanted out. "Any other children here?"

"Two toddlers and signs of children who occupy the dorm rooms. The worker said they were at school. And there were other cots in the attic that seemed recently used."

"Any workers who don't look as though they're on staff?"

"Possibly, yes."

"Once the girls are settled with my translator, let's check out the staff."

39

London, Day 18

W hile Ian and PC Finkhorst activated voice recordings on their phones and laid them on the coffee table, Riley waited at the door for Jacob and the girls. Ms. Martin sat in her armchair, hands tucked beneath her thighs, her face a mask. "Anything in particular you wish me to ask them?"

"We'd like as much detailed information as possible, how they reached the UK. Who transported them here and how. A thorough report on their stay here," PC Finkhorst said. "And if others came with them."

Blanching, Ms. Martin rammed her shoulders against her chair.

As Jacob motioned the girls inside the salon, they shuffled into the parlor, their steps hesitant.

"*Buna ziua*, good day." Riley introduced herself in Romanian and shook the girls' clammy hands.

Lips taut, they glanced toward Ms. Martin, the whites of their eyes wide.

"*Te rog*, please." Fighting tears, Riley motioned them to the couch. Minors, every one of them. "Could we interview them without staff members present?"

"Right. Come along, Ms. Martin." PC Finkhorst motioned one of the constables to escort her from the room.

The men moved to the windows, and the girls huddled on the couch, knees and thighs locked, twisting their hands in their laps. Riley pulled a chair close enough to smell their rank bodies. The grooves in their cracked lips suggested dehydration. Bruises discolored their cheeks and foreheads. A fireball pitted her stomach. How dare the staff deny the girls proper food and hygiene? Had they been beaten, or violated?

Longing to ask Jacob what they'd found out, she glanced at him, but he left the room with a constable. She spoke to the girls in Romanian, then translated her questions and their responses into English for the recordings. "What are your names? And where are you from?"

The one closest to her said, "Ilinca Comenici. I am from Cluj-Napoca."

"I know your city. I studied singing in Bucharest."

"Really?" Whispering to each other, they cast glances her way.

The girl next to Ilinca held up one finger. "I am Elena Dumitru, from Sibiu." She pointed to the two girls beside her. "This is Zandra from Oradea, and Viorica from Bucharest."

"Have you eaten since you arrived here?" Tea and sandwiches for the girls would be nice, but if they'd been mistreated here, Ms. Martin might poison them.

The girls exchanged frightened looks. Viorica shook her head.

"Have you been given water to drink?"

Rolling her eyes, Viorica shrugged. "One bottle."

"Ian, would you please bring the picnic basket from Jacob's car?" She'd packed the lunch herself. Enough for two, but it should help.

"When did you arrive here?" Riley pointed to the floor.

"Two nights ago?" Ilinca fingered her lips. "They locked us in the attic. We slept on army cots. The last time they fed us was in the back of the van."

A moment later, Ian returned and set the zippered lunch box on the coffee table. "Here you go."

Riley handed the girls the sandwich halves, set out apple slices and carrot sticks, the bag with four Burie's chocolates. "Were you in the van hit by a car?"

The girls nodded, dove into the sandwiches and fruit.

If only she and Frénie hadn't been knocked unconscious, the girls might've been rescued sooner. "Were there other girls or boys brought here with you?"

The girls tensed, exchanged looks. Trembling, Ilinca whispered, "Yes. There were twenty of us in the back of the van. They took the others somewhere after the first night here. Six of them were teenaged boys."

"Was everyone from Romania?"

Ilinca nodded.

"How old are you?"

"Fourteen." Ilinca answered around the apple bulge in her mouth. "We came because they promised us good-paying jobs."

"What kind of jobs?" Riley held her breath, afraid of their answer.

"As housemaids, *au pairs*." Ilinca twisted her index finger. "Our families need the money."

Maybe this was how Armand had hired his maid. "Do they know where you are and why you came here?"

"Viorica's older brother sold her to the man who helped us get here."

Blinking hard, Riley swallowed over the lump in her throat. Even when she'd studied in Romania, exploitation of innocent young women had been a serious business. One of their major exports. But this was her first exposure to its victims.

"My mother knows why I left Romania. Zandra and Viorica

signed a contract with a man in their town, and he paid their way here."

"Do you know the names of the people who transported you to the UK, and once you reached England?"

"No. They spoke very little, gave us no names." Elena flicked her greasy bangs to the side.

"Could you identify pictures of them, their faces?"

"I don't know. We were so scared." Ilinca slumped over her knees. "What will happen to us now?"

"One thing is certain, you'll be fed and given good care." Riley looked at PC Finkhorst.

"Quite right." The flint in his eyes looked dangerously close to sparking. "I have daughters myself. You'll be placed in foster care until you can be returned to your parents in Romania." He paused, motioned Riley to translate into Romanian.

But the alarm in the girls' eyes told a different story. They didn't want to go home. Life in the UK would've provided means to help support their families. An ache settled in Riley's chest. There was nothing she could do to help them.

"Until then, your case will be handled by specially trained immigration officers and Social Services Child Protection," he said. "Not the police."

With everything in her, Riley wanted to launch into "Der Hölle Rache," vent her rage on Armand, order him stabbed to death with the evil queen's dagger. She hated it all—being duped by him, lending her reputation to his phony orphanage, the cruelty he'd allowed inflicted on these girls and probably others like them. An unquenchable fire burned inside her. More than anything, she wanted justice for these precious teens and every other exploited child.

Two men sat at the long metal table in the kitchen, one blond, the other as redheaded as Ian. To Jacob, they looked well fed and well-muscled in their jeans and long-sleeved T-shirts. He needed to wrap up his visit to the orphanage, drive to Tracy's school. Now. Before they lost more time locating Armand.

"What's the scoop on these two?"

The constable closest to him paged through his notebook. "They claim they pick up the children at school, take care of the lawn."

"And what about their employer?"

"They said they haven't seen Mr. Découvrir in days, that he's seldom at the orphanage."

The men's faces flushed, their vice-like fists flexing on the table. Not a pair he'd like to meet in a dark alley.

"Will they be taken into custody?"

"Yes, for the time being."

Moving swiftly, Jacob opened the cabinets and drawers. Not enough place settings to feed more than thirty people. Upstairs, he'd counted fifty beds in the rooms. Two highchairs and four toddlers' seats. A pity he couldn't meet the orphans supposedly at school right now.

He checked the fridge, the massive freezer in the walk-in pantry. Well stocked with frozen and canned goods. But not enough to keep thirty or fifty well fed. He clenched the loose coins in his trousers pocket. The police had arrested twenty-five men at the gala with ties to terrorist cells and illegal financial operations.

A couple of them owned car washes, typical fronts for illegal workers. Illegals forced to work for little or no wages sixteen hours a day, seven days a week. Poorly fed and poorly housed. Were all the orphanage's patrons in on this sham? Or were he and Riles the sole patsies at the gala?

Now they had proof Armand was involved in human trafficking and an attempt to bomb the Shard. Today, they'd started to unravel his financial empire. But nothing uncovered today implicated him as the Priest. And finding the Priest was Jacob's assignment.

40

Near Brighton, Day 18

The side trip to the orphanage had taken way too much time. At least it had been profitable. Jacob parked in the Chumley Girls' School car park and opened Riley's door. "Think Tracy and Armand's daughter will give us a lead on him?"

"I don't know. Last visit Tracy seemed rather bitter. I wish we could take her out of boarding school. She needs to experience family life. Love and acceptance."

"Something we can't give her." He wove his fingers in Riley's, savoring the feel of her palm. "Yet."

"Jacob, I love you. But I'm still not ready to set a wedding date."

When would that be? The last thing he wanted was to push her away. But sometimes she seemed like a skittish colt. "Take your time, Riles. I'm here for you." But his love for her was so intense he could scarcely breathe.

Shafts of late afternoon sun turned the skimpy foliage on the trees into a gleaming gold and amber. The tangy scent of molting leaves bit his nose as he walked her across the parking lot, the

SARA L. JAMESON

dead leaves crunching beneath his loafers. Inside the building, a school bell shrilled. "Bet that brings back childhood memories."

Riley's girlish laugh was music to his ears. Twenty-four hours ago, he thought he'd never hear it again, this side of heaven. *Thank You, God.*

"You bet. Locker doors banging, shared don't-tell-him-I-said-so secrets, early morning choir practice. When Lacy and I were six, the principal asked us to sing duets while the choir sang Christmas carols in the halls. We were too young to join the choir, we could hardly read. Boy, we thought we were special."

"You were. You still are." Inhaling her familiar perfume, he planted a kiss on her cheek. With her hand still clasped in his, he walked her up the steps to the main entrance, her hip grazing his.

"Mr. Coulter." Mrs. Foster met him inside the entrance hall. Her navy cardigan and white blouse tucked into a gray skirt fit his image of a headmistress. "This is highly irregular, visiting during school hours." She shook his hand. "I haven't told Tracy you were coming."

Hating to do it, he pulled his Interpol ID from his coat pocket. "Actually, it's Special Agent Coulter. I'm here on official business." He cupped Riley's elbow. "Miss Williams, my fiancée, is assisting me with a case in the UK." TMI in his opinion, but the woman might grill Tracy after they left. Their stories needed to match.

Shoulders bristling, she acknowledged Riley with a nod. "I see. Please come with me." She motioned them into a salon, its décor meant to impress parents. Silk drapes. Photographs of past head mistresses dominating the white paneled walls behind plush settees and antique tables.

"I trust your business isn't connected to the school. We run a dignified establishment for the finest girls and faculty with a reputation for academic excellence. One I intend to maintain."

"That's comforting to hear." Riley flashed her a smile. "I

hope it's not a problem for us to speak privately with Tracy. It's quite important."

A layer of frost thawed from the woman's face. "I'll have her summoned. Please make yourselves comfortable."

The double doors clicked behind her.

"Thanks, hon. Needed your special touch to soften her." He activated the recorder on his cell and laid the phone on the mahogany table in front of the couch.

The door opened, and Tracy shuffled in, clutching a wad of tissues in her fist. The yellow cardigan, white shirt, short navy skirt, knee socks and clunky black shoes whisked him to his own boarding school days in France. He'd hated wearing a uniform, feeling like one of the impersonal masses.

Judging from Tracy's glum expression, neither did she. Last visit she'd radiated an energy, a young woman-kid, eager to burst forth into who she really was. Today her nose and eyes were red-rimmed.

"Hey, sis." He rose and kissed her forehead. "You remember Riles."

"Hi." She flicked her palm up at Riley.

Arm around her shoulders, he led her to the couch, and seated her between him and Riles. "How's it going?"

"Okay." She gave him a one-shoulder shrug. "I guess."

"Doesn't look like it's okay."

Head down, she fingered the tissue.

"Want to talk about it?"

"No. Why are you here? Mrs. Foster never lets us have visitors during school hours."

"We have something we need to talk to you about."

Head bolting upright, she glared at him. "You're leaving the UK, getting married. You won't be back, right? Just like Mum and Dad."

Mum. Not Mother. Tracy had been overseas so long she even sounded British.

"When we set a wedding date, you can be certain you'll be a

part of it," Riley said. "In fact, I'd love for you to be my bridesmaid."

Tracy's jaw dropped. "You would? Honest?"

"Yes, of course. And we want you to become part of our lives."

"You mean I can leave this place and come live with you?"

"Well ..." Riles swallowed, licked her lips. "Given your brother's career and mine, that's not possible right now. I rent a room from an elderly woman."

"Oh." Shoulders slumped, Tracy picked at her skirt.

"But we'd love for you to spend school vacations with us." Tears pooled at Riles' lashes.

"Might as well. Haven't got anywhere else to go now."

A question in her lifted brow, Riles glanced at him. He nodded. She had the golden touch with Tracy.

"Last week I saw a framed picture in Armand Découvrir's home, the same photo you showed me of your best friend."

"So? Amira's his daughter. He keeps the picture in his study."

"You've visited the house?"

"Lots of times."

Pulse pounding his veins, Jacob gripped the armrest. His kid sister, cozying up with a terrorist financier, a human trafficker.

"Since Mum and Dad and Jacob don't want me."

"That's not true, sis. I'd love to spend time with you. But my job ..." He raked a hand through his hair. Somehow, he had to make time to invest in Tracy.

"Amira's dad gives her lots of cool presents, lets us do really neat things."

"Sounds like fun." Jacob could barely contain the undercurrent thrumming in his voice. "What sort of things, where do you go?"

"We've flown in his private jet to Paris. Vienna."

His eyes bulged at Riley, and she directed Tracy's focus away from him.

"Wow. When do you take these trips?"

"Over school holidays. Sometimes over a weekend."

"A weekend?" Jacob jolted forward on the couch. "Mrs. Foster lets you leave school without parental permission, or mine?" All he had was medical power of attorney, not guardianship.

Eyes venomous, Tracy whipped toward him. "You aren't around to do the job now, are you."

"I'm as close as a phone call." His voice shook.

"Tell me about the weekend trips." Riley angled toward Tracy. "They sound exciting. Do you stay in hotels?"

"Sometimes. Really posh places. But mostly in villas. You wouldn't believe the things we get to do. The worst part is having to come back here. But Papa Armand makes the flight so much fun."

Jacob nearly bolted off the couch. Papa Armand—she called him Papa?

"You mean like drinking champagne?" Riles cleared her throat.

"Oh, no. He'd never let us do that."

"That's one point in his favor," Jacob muttered into his fist.

"On the trips he gives us tons of money to spend. Even when we stay in London."

Internally, Jacob's hair stood on end. "What's a lot of money?"

"Oh." She shrugged. "Sometimes thousands of euros a day. Each. If we want more, all we do is ask. Neat, huh?"

"Yeah, cool." He rubbed his fingers over his brow. That's how Tracy could afford to pay their entry to the Royal Pavilion. Was Armand using his own daughter and Tracy to disperse illegal funds, using them to launder money? If so, he and Riles had aided a money laundering op. Fists clenched, he rammed them in his trouser pockets. Right now, he'd like to bash the guy's face.

"He's been like a father to me."

"I'll bet." Jacob jammed his fists into the seat cushion. If he could yank her out of this school today, he'd do it. At Riles' warning look, he nodded, dug an elbow into the armrest, knuckles tapping his mouth.

"Sounds like you've had some neat adventures." Riles snuggled next to Tracy on the couch, flashed her a thousand-volt smile, eyes dancing. "Where do you go, what do you do?"

Go for it, Riles. All he'd done was alienate Tracy with his ranting and raving.

"We don't go to casinos, or anything like that."

"That's a relief," Jacob muttered into his palm.

"We buy fancy dresses, fur hats. I'm not really into art, but Amira is. And jewelry. When he gives us lots of thousand-note euros, or pounds."

Jacob clawed his forehead. The recorder better be getting every word of this.

"Last time I was at his house, Papa Armand gave me this." Tracy reached inside her shirt. She looped her finger beneath a diamond-encrusted necklace around her neck, a bronze key behind it.

Ashen faced, Riles stared at the necklace. "A cross, with real diamonds, huh?"

"When was that?" Jacob's voice cracked. He stared at the necklace glinting at the base of her neck.

"Last weekend."

Ice coursed through his veins. While he and Riles were in London, not ten miles away. "Does his daughter have a cross necklace?"

"Oh no. She's Muslim. Like Papa Armand."

That wasn't the only reason she didn't have a matching necklace. Jacob's breaths came so fast he could barely suppress them. Every instinct told him he'd found the Priest.

And he'd marked his next victim.

His kid sister.

41

Near Brighton, Day 18

A cross necklace. Bile rose in Riley's throat. Swallowing the bitter acid, she gripped her fingers in her lap. How could Armand be so cruel? Tracy was probably no older than his kid sister when she died. His daughter's best friend. Think. Think. There had to be a way to outsmart Armand. Everyone had vulnerabilities, didn't they? Amira.

"I'm sorry we didn't get to meet Amira last time. Do you think she'd like to join us for dinner?"

"Sure." Chin sunk to her chest, Tracy fiddled with her wad of tissue. "If she were here."

Riley's stomach sank. "She's—not here?"

"No, she was gone when I woke up yesterday morning. Her bed was made up."

Clutching his forehead in his hand, Jacob shook his head, his eyes bleak.

"Made up?" Riley refocused on Tracy. "Did she call you or text you about where they were going?"

"You mean Papa Armand is gone too?" Tracy bolted upright on the cushion. "Like, for good?"

"It looks that way."

"No." Rivers rolling down her cheeks, Tracy drooped against the back cushions. "Amira wasn't in school yesterday. This morning all her stuff was gone from our room." Sniffling, she dabbed a tissue at the wetness. "We didn't even get to say goodbye."

"Goodbyes hurt." Riley slid her arm around Tracy's shoulders. "Losing a best friend is as bad as losing a sister." Tears clogged her throat.

"You have a sister?"

"Did. A twin. And last night my best friend nearly died."

"I'm sorry." Tracy offered her a wrinkled tissue. "At least Amira is alive. Even if I can't visit her anymore."

"Did Amira text you and say that?"

Tracy stared toward the floor, the seconds stretched. Finally, she nodded.

Electricity prickled Riley's arms. "Could we see her message?"

"My cell is in my desk. We're not allowed to carry our phones to class."

"Any idea where Armand might've taken her?"

Another unhelpful shrug. "He can fly anywhere, anytime. There's his yacht, the Aminta. That's his dead sister's name. He owns houses all over Europe. Maybe elsewhere, but I've only been to the ones in Paris and Vienna."

Unable to restrain herself, Riley's hand fluttered to her temple. Hardly surprising Armand had kept Frénie out of the big picture. He probably used his trips to meet with terrorists, collect laundered funds, authorize murders. Riley wadded the used tissue in her fingers. If Frénie had traveled with him or their relationship didn't work out, she could identify his business associates. Sooner or later, she'd sense he was up to something shady. Much simpler to send Tracy and Amira shopping on those trips while he took care of deadly business at all hours of the day. Or night.

Tremors rippled across Riley's shoulders. No wonder Tracy had been marked with the silver cross necklace. Even in her ignorance, she knew enough to dismantle multiple tentacles in Armand's empire.

BREATHS ROILING IN HIS CHEST, Jacob pulled Gorilla Guy's snapshot from his breast pocket and showed the picture to his sister. "Ever seen this guy before?"

"Sure. That's Uncle Bobby."

Uncle Bobby—she called that murderer her uncle? Jacob twisted the edge of the snapshot in his fingers.

"He works for Armand, takes trips with us, hangs around to make sure Amira and I are safe. Gives us money to spend."

Bingo. If Tracy would testify, they'd have Gorilla Guy on additional charges of money laundering and using minors as cleaners. Jacob tucked the photo in his shirt pocket. That day at the Royal Pavilion, Gorilla Guy could've been checking up on Tracy or there to give her spending money.

"Yeah, he's a real MacGyver."

"Who's that?"

"A TV show before your time. The man could do anything, get out of any scrape."

For the first time, Tracy laughed. "That's Bobby all right."

"You suppose we could see your room?"

"I—I don't know. I'll have to ask Mrs. Foster."

"Why don't I take care of that?" Jacob rose from the couch. "You wait with Riles." He shut the door behind him and knocked on the headmistress's office door.

Heavy steps sounded on the floor. Mrs. Foster opened the door and smoothed her skirt. "Yes?"

"I'd like to speak with you, please."

"I'm rather busy at the moment."

"Well, we could do this at police headquarters." He kept his tone casual. "If you'd prefer."

Nostrils flaring, she motioned him inside and closed the door.

Three large suitcases were tucked in the corner. Steam heat whispered in the radiator beneath the windows. He scanned the booklined walls, the broad desk that looked as if fifty predecessors had used it. A green banker's light lit the scarred surface. He sat facing her desk, tried to get a handle on her attitude.

"I understand Amira Découvrir is missing."

"Not missing. Withdrawn from school." Mrs. Foster shuffled the quiz papers on her desk. "Two nights ago, Mr. Découvrir showed up after lights out."

Which meant Armand had seen his arrest coming. Acid burned a hole in Jacob's gut. How long had Armand been playing him—since the day he arrived in London? "What time was that?"

"Midnight to be precise. He demanded I wake Amira, tell her to dress, and bring her downstairs." Sniffing, she fiddled with a red grading pencil. "Without waking Tracy."

So, Armand did care about his daughter. They never should've assumed he'd leave her in boarding school, abandon her there like Tracy. "Didn't that seem odd, leaving Amira's possessions here, if she was withdrawing from school?"

"A wealthy man like Mr. Découvrir ... well, these things happen."

"Often, at your school?"

"No." She slapped the pencil on the desk. "Of course not."

"Were you aware of the money-laundering operation running through your school?"

"A money—" She slumped in the chair. "No, that's impossible."

"Unfortunately, it's true. And the proof lies upstairs."

"You must be mistaken." She rose and paced the room, hand

fluttering to her forehead. "We keep a close watch over our girls, we'd know if something illegal were taking place."

"Your Wednesday afternoon shopping trips to town were a front for money laundering." The part of it he was willing to divulge. If he could keep Tracy out of this, he would. "And if we can't break this case and arrest the man behind this operation, he's likely to recruit more of your students. The temptation of a free wad of euros and pounds is more than some people, children included, can withstand." Particularly if they weren't being taught strong moral values.

"How would you describe Amira?"

"She and Tracy are—were bosom buddies, soulmates. Amira is self-assured, Tracy is not. Coming from such an affluent home, Amira was accustomed to having whatever she wanted. For some reason she doted on Tracy. However, in Tracy's defense, I must say she's loyal, and keeps a confidence."

No doubt Mrs. Foster could've added moody and insolent. Unless those were qualities Tracy had reserved for him.

"Who were Amira's other girlfriends?"

"No one in particular. She and Tracy were friendly with their classmates but tended to pair off by themselves."

"Thank you. You've been most helpful." He rose. "I'd like your permission to search Amira's things and see Tracy's room."

"Do you have a search warrant?"

"Not yet. But if you prefer, I'll have the police search."

Her lips thinned. "I suppose it can't hurt." She gestured toward the suitcases. "While Tracy was in class, I packed Amira's things."

Squatting beside the bags, Jacob opened the first one. Riffled through the spare school uniforms, nightclothes, swimwear, slacks and sweaters, underwear, and socks. A zippered bag filled with expensive-looking makeup. *Vogue* and *Marie Claire* magazines. Thirteen years old, reading this stuff.

Inside the second suitcase, he leafed through the stack of

spiral notebooks, quiz papers, and books. A bright girl. He turned toward Mrs. Foster. "Did you check under the bed?"

"Oh yes. The desk and the wardrobe."

He unzipped the third bag. Empty. Running his hands along the interior walls, he felt for keys, slips of paper, pieces of jewelry. Then searched the linings of the other two suitcases. Where had her stash gone? He swiveled toward Mrs. Foster, her lips pursed, fists flexing on her desk. "You're certain she left nothing else here?"

"Quite. She must've taken things home on her weekend trips and left them there."

A sick feeling wormed through him. Once again, Armand was three steps ahead of him. He'd made sure Tracy was left holding the goods. Her sicko Papa had set her up to take the blame.

42

Near Brighton, Day 18

Tracy's dorm room looked typical for teenaged girls. Apart from the motheaten teddy bear his parents had given her when she was two and a poster of a rockstar heartthrob, her side of the room was as devoid of personality as von Bingen's office. Jacob scrubbed his chin. Where had his sister hidden her ill-gotten purchases?

Riles perched on the end of Amira's bed. Cutouts of glamorous models from *Vogue* and *Marie-Claire* magazines were stuck to the wall. Each of them a bejeweled woman in an exquisite evening gown or a skimpy swimsuit.

Did Armand care he'd polluted his daughter's mind, her desires? "How about letting us read Amira's message? Maybe I can track her down for you."

"Really?" Tracy slipped her cell from her desk drawer, keyed in her password and showed him the message.

> Goodbye, my friend. I won't be seeing you again. Papa says it's not safe. xoxox

"How about I buy you a new phone, and you let me keep this one to get a trace on her?"

Tracy's eyes lit. "You can do that?"

"I have friends who can help." An encrypted phone with a few hidden apps, courtesy of Interpol. If Armand or Amira contacted Tracy, he'd know about it. He yanked at the knot in his tie. He was leading her on, not telling her why he was here, and what Armand was.

Seated on Amira's bed, he elbowed his thighs. No way could he protect Tracy at school. If he kept her in the flat with Riles and Frénie, he'd have to tell her the truth about Armand. Jacob loosened his tie another notch. Maybe Armand assumed he'd move everyone into the flat. Easy targets to take out at will.

By surprise.

He rubbed his palms on his thighs. Flexed his fists. As soon as he was out of Tracy's sight, he'd text Ian to find them an Interpol safe house. Riles scooted beside him and massaged the back of his neck. He ignored the tingles her stroking fingertips sent down his spine. Somehow, he had to take down Armand. ASAP.

"Did you tell Amira about the afternoon Riles and I spent with you?"

"Sure. We tell—told—each other everything."

Jacob tried to squelch a twitch in his jaw muscle. Armand hadn't needed tracking devices. Thanks to Tracy and Frénie, he'd had 24/7 access to Riley's whereabouts. "And Armand gave you that cross necklace after we visited."

"Yeah, I guess so." Tracy studied him. "You don't like Papa Armand, do you?"

"He's a generous man, been your surrogate father." The tic in Jacob's jaw muscle double-timed. "Shown you a lifestyle you'd never dreamed of."

"You're jealous." Palms out, she gaped at him. "My big brother is spit-eyed jealous of how God's provided for me."

"I'm not sure God was behind this."

"Oh puh—lease." She flounced off her bed and paced the room. "Grow up, bro. If you want more money, get a better job."

He clasped his hands in his lap. Had he been this difficult as a teenager? "I'm not interested in more money. I'd like to make a difference in this world, help others in need." Whether they recognized their need for help or not. "The pleasures of wealth are fleeting."

She harrumphed. "How would you know."

"Because I have what really matters." He pointed to his heart. "And this—" Chest tight, he pulled out his Interpol ID, "is who I work for."

"You—you're with the police?" Her eyes bulged at him.

"I work in tandem with them. I was sent to London to uncover international terrorist financiers. Help the police arrest them and confiscate illegally purchased goods funded through their money-laundering ops." Gripping Riley's hand, he drew a breath. "Ops which often include using others to spend cash on expensive goods."

As Tracy slicked her lips, wheels turned beneath her knit brows. The lightbulb clicked in her startled eyes. "You think Papa Armand is a financier?"

"Every piece of evidence we've collected supports that conclusion."

"You fink. You deceived me." She stomped between the beds, flailing her arms. "You didn't come because you care about me." Hand fisted, she slugged him in the chest. "You used me."

The force of her words stabbed far worse than the flames searing his sternum. He captured her hand in his. "Until a few days ago, I had no idea you were connected to Armand."

"Why should I believe you?" She wrenched her wrist in his grasp.

"It's the truth." Riley touched Tracy's arm. "We came to visit you last week because Jacob wanted to see you and spend time with you. He was worried about you. If his boss had found out, she'd have been furious." She took Tracy's hand in hers. "Your brother loves you far more than you know. He agonizes over not being here for you. But his job is saving lives, and that means those of us who love him make sacrifices for his service to Europe."

Sniffling, Tracy brushed her free hand over her nose. Jacob released her wrist and handed her a tissue from his shirt pocket. Turning away from him, she blew her nose and lobbed the tissue into the waste basket.

Wisps of blonde hair escaping her ponytail, she knelt beside her bed and slid out a metal box the size of a blanket storage container. She lifted her arms toward her neck like a slow-motion film, unfastened the necklace, then inserted the bronze key on the chain into the container's lock. She drew a long breath, blew out her air. Opened the lid.

Jacob stifled a gasp. A matching mink jacket and hat lay in the bottom. Sapphires, diamonds, rubies, and emeralds set in bracelets, delicate chain necklaces, rings, and ear studs winked beneath the overhead light. No wonder his little necklace had seemed paltry.

"This is all of it. Everything I purchased. Except for some dresses I left at Papa Armand's townhouse."

Tears spilling from her lashes, she laid the cross necklace on Jacob's palm. She plopped beside her bed pillow and slid the teddy bear onto her lap, fingers picking at its fur.

Aching to comfort her, Jacob slid his arm around her shoulders and pulled her to his side. "I'm proud of you, sis."

"Am I going to jail?" She huddled over the stuffed animal, her voice muffled into its fur.

"No. You're a minor and a victim of child criminal exploitation. You had no idea why he was giving you the money."

Sobbing, she threw her arms around his chest.

Swallowing the lump in his throat, he kissed her head, inhaled the scent of her strawberry shampoo. *Thank You, God.* Maybe it's not too late to reach her.

JACOB GLANCED at Tracy in the back seat of his car, then slammed the trunk lid over her suitcases and container of booty. He'd have Marcus turn in the contraband for Counter Terrorism processing, along with her taped interview. He turned to Riles waiting beside him. "What are they teaching them in that school?"

"Mrs. Foster probably didn't know she had a crime ring operating under her nose." Riles stroked his arm, but he was too worked up for her touch to calm him. "Armand offered the girls glamour and unlimited money. Freedoms no child should have."

His toes cramped inside his shoes. "Yeah."

"How did Mrs. Foster take the news about Tracy leaving with us?"

"Shocked, until I said Tracy's life is in danger, and her presence might endanger other students and staff. Then she seemed relieved."

"You were wonderful." Riles leaned in and kissed his cheek. "And I love you all the more for it."

What would he do without her? He pulled her into a tight embrace, kissed her long and hard. Breathless, he pulled back a few inches. "For now, she'll have to stay with you and Frénie in the safe house. I'm moving her to Brussels, pulling her out of this environment before it's too late."

43

London, Day 18

Jacob stepped from the elevator and rapped on the safehouse door, Tracy and Riles trailing behind him. On Ian's advice, he'd parked on the street behind the building and entered through a back entrance. Even in the dark, the flat's brick exterior appeared relatively new. The second-floor hall smelled of fresh paint, waxed floors, and stale coffee. At least they were miles from his own apartment. Stifling a yawn, he wiped the grit from his eyes.

The drive from Chumley had been the longest two hours of his life, the atmosphere in the car so heavy he could scarcely breathe. Tracy's quiet sobs and sniffling. Pulling off the road so Riles could move to the back seat to comfort his sister.

Footsteps sounded behind the apartment door. He stepped back so the policewoman could ID him through the peephole. Clutching her suitcase, Tracy cowered next to Riles.

If they didn't get a good night's rest, none of them would be worth much tomorrow. At ten in the morning a specialist officer would interview Tracy and piece together as many details of her trips with Armand and Gorilla Guy as possible.

Ian had assured him the Achieving Best Evidence interview would take place in a room with child-friendly furnishings and toys. Too childish for Tracy, but it was better than questioning her in a regular interrogation room. An officer would record the interview from outside the room, where he, Ian, and Marcus could observe and take notes.

Bolts shot back, and the door opened. The muscled policewoman was still dressed in her black uniform, her black protective vest over her shirt, police insignia embroidered on her shirt sleeve, her police number on her shoulder. Her bowler with its black-and-white band hung on a coatrack in the corner of the hall.

Clipped to her vest were her body cam and radio. A can of pepper spray, her collapsible baton and a pair of handcuffs hung from her equipment belt. No gun. How could she protect them against a weapon-carrying assassin?

Scoping the exterior hall like a soldier on point, the policewoman motioned them inside, then bolted the door. The narrow hall didn't look much different than his flat. "PC Marlow." Ruffling her short-cropped hair, she smiled at Tracy.

Tracy's lips flickered upward, but the fear in her eyes ripped at his heart. If only he hadn't had to destroy the last vestiges of her innocence, her sense of safety.

"Come along." PC Marlow gestured toward the light filtering from the living room. "You're safe now."

"Yes." He'd feel safer if British police officers were armed. Even a Taser. But British philosophy had long believed defusing a situation without force was ultimately lifesaving. Still, hiring these officers was worth every euro he'd drained from his honeymoon account. He was on foreign soil. British police were well trained. "Everything quiet?"

"Miss Frénau slept all afternoon." PC Marlow pointed to the closed door to her left. She picked a few breadcrumbs from her black trousers. "We finished supper a while ago. Have you eaten?"

"No." Not since two canapés in the Ren Room last night. Right now, he needed to figure out the sleeping arrangements.

"If you're wondering about beds, your sister can sleep on the couch. There's a second bedroom here." She gestured to the second closed door on her left. "We're using our four days off our normal duty shifts to cover you. The next officer will come at seven in the morning."

"Thanks for your help."

"And for yours." Her blue eyes bored into him. "Wrapping up a terrorist op."

"We're not there yet." But would they ever wrap this one up? He nudged Riles and Tracy past the wall-unit kitchenette and inside the living room. Two armchairs in front of the double windows faced a coffee table and sofa. Against the opposite wall were four metal chairs clustered around a wood dining table. Ultra-modern sleek.

Drifting away from Riles, Tracy sidled behind the armchair and peeked between the closed drapes.

As streetlight pierced the room, Riles darted toward her. "No —don't."

"Sis, stay away from the windows."

Pfft. Pfft. Pfft. Shards of glass sprayed the air, tinkled to the floor.

Tracy shrieked, threw her arm over her face.

"Get down." Arms wide, Jacob lunged for his sister and Riles. Shoved them to the floor, pushed them toward the couch. Sobbing, Tracy huddled beneath him, her body quivering against his. "Shh. Stay here with Riles."

"You're okay, Tracy." Riles scooted toward her, smoothed her hair.

Face taut, PC Marlow radioed for a response officer and a specialist firearms team. "Armed attack in progress. Multiple shooters possible."

How had Armand's men found them? Crouching low, Jacob scrabbled toward the kitchenette, the knife block on the counter. With everything in him, he wanted to violate Interpol policy and grab the butcher knife.

Thud. Thud. Thud. Wood cracked and splintered through the apartment door.

His heart slammed his chest. Help had better come fast or they'd never survive the attack.

Kaazzing, kaazzing. Bullets pinged on metal. Probably the doorknob, the locks. Bits of metal ricocheted at the end of the hall, struck the fridge door. Shielding his head with one hand, Jacob dove for the dining table.

Baton extended full length in her hand, PC Marlow crept along the living room wall, legs bent, ready to strike.

Had Armand's men tailed his car, hidden a tracking device on it? Jacob grabbed the kitchen chair. He aimed the seat like a lion tamer, the metal chilling his hands. Keeping a few feet between them, he followed PC Marlow to the edge of the hall.

Out on the street, more gunfire erupted. Another window shattered. Tracy's screams and sobs tore through his chest. *Dear God, help.* If He didn't, they'd never survive.

The faint sounds of police and ambulance sirens echoed on the street.

The first bedroom door clicked open.

PC Marlow whipped into the hall. Darted for the gunman as he stepped into the doorway and fired into the darkened room. Hugging the wall, Jacob dashed toward the assassin. But the gunman whirled toward PC Marlow and fired twice. One bullet *thunked* into her metal baton. The stick spun out of her hands and skittered toward him.

Jacob dropped the chair, leapt for the baton. He flicked it like a boomerang at the ski-masked man. The baton struck the gunman's forehead with a *thwack*. The man slithered to the ground.

Fist jammed to her mouth, Frénie wobbled to the bedroom doorway, sobbing.

Rivulets of blood trickled from PC Marlow's upper arm as

she headed for the gunman and checked his pulse. "Unconscious." She grabbed his wrists and clicked her cuffs around them.

Thank You, God. Another suspect in custody linked to Armand. "Thank you, Constable. You saved our lives."

"All in a day's work." Wrapping her uninjured arm around Frénie's heaving shoulders, a grin spread across PC Marlow's face. "Bet you didn't think a baton could fell an armed gunman."

"You're right."

The elevator doors dinged open, and Ian and three armed officers burst into the flat. "Thought something like this might happen." The bluish shadows beneath Ian's eyes had purpled. Red stubble covered his cheeks and chin. Neither he nor Ian had slept in almost thirty-six hours.

"Glad you're on it. But PC Marlow's wounded."

"Just a flesh wound." PC Marlow grimaced. "I think."

This time. Jacob snugged Riles to his chest, her heartbeat pulsing against his. "Hey, sis." She darted to him and let him fold her into a three-way embrace. Moisture pooled in his eyes as he planted kisses on Tracy's head, Riles' forehead, then her mouth. *Thank You, God.* Once again, He'd delivered them and protected them.

Every inch of his skull throbbed. How long would he and Riles and Tracy have to live like this, looking over their shoulders, avoiding windows, changing safe houses? Armand wouldn't give up until he'd achieved his goals.

"I know what you're thinking." Riles pushed back from him and stared into his eyes. "Don't go there. Every time Armand lashes out, he's risking exposure and his own capture."

Swallowing hard, Jacob nodded.

Paramedics wearing green uniforms and waterproof jackets over their vests crowded into the flat. While two of them tended PC Marlow's wound, another two loaded the gunman on a second gurney and wheeled him from the flat, still unconscious.

"Oh, Jacob." Frénie stumbled over to him. A paramedic

dogged her heels, a blanket and blood pressure cuff in his hands. "What's to keep Armand from disappearing on a desert isle? I want him brought to justice."

"A desert island's not his style. He's über-confident, likes to manipulate things front and center. And that's his weak spot. We'll catch him. You'll see."

Fingers pressed to his earpiece, Ian crossed the room, flashed Jacob a grim smile. "It was a coordinated attack. The gunman in the hall and another one on the street out front, whom the firearms team took down."

"How'd you get here so fast?"

Grinning like a Cheshire cat, Ian blushed. "Never left. I've been hanging out at the café across the street since you toddled off to Chumley. Now let's pack everyone out of here pronto. We have a new safehouse waiting for you."

Lead weighted every limb and muscle in Jacob's body. How long would they be on the run? "Thanks, partner."

"Any time." Ian offered him a fist bump.

44

London, Day 19

If he had to listen to any more details of Tracy's trips and stays with Armand and Amira, shopping excursions with Uncle Bobby, he'd go nuts. Jacob clutched his head in his hands. Tracy running to Gorilla Guy and Armand for approval on her purchases, slipping extra cash into her hand, pats on her head, claiming the role of a parent.

The PC shut off the camera.

The specially trained constable had handled the interview well, offering acceptance, sympathy, and hugs when Tracy's sobs had become unbearable. Good thing he hadn't been in the room. He'd have wanted to punch out Armand's lights while he needed to comfort his sister.

"I know how you must feel." Ian squeezed Jacob's shoulder. "With every tale, Tracy was destroying a dream life, an innocence lost—"

"Severing herself from the only father figure she's known." Jacob choked out the words. "Our maternal grandparents provided funding for her schooling, and our parents shipped her off to boarding school in first grade, followed their call to a foreign mission field." Places too dangerous to take a young child. The same excuses they'd used with him.

"Look at it this way," Ian said. "Thanks to Tracy's honesty, Interpol and CT now have credible details and insight into Armand's psyche."

"Yeah. Using children to launder funds." Jacob yanked his water bottle from the table. "The guy's a souped-up Fagin out of *Oliver Twist*."

The police artist entered and handed Jacob the sketches she'd created with Tracy's help.

"Thanks." Jacob glanced at the two men's likenesses Tracy had seen with Armand in Austria and Paris. "Now we have new locations to stake out, new faces on our radar." He forwarded copies of the sketches to the team.

As soon as possible, he'd liaise with Margot onsite to expose Armand's businesses in Austria. Ian and Marcus's phones pinged with the photos while Jacob texted the team.

> Leak word ASAP to your national press and expose the suspected terrorist plots against the EU meetings.

Meetings seven days from now. Typically, once terrorists lost the advantage of surprise, they behaved like rats. Turn the light on and they fled. Waited for a more opportune time to strike.

If only this strategy would work now. The EU had beefed up security but publicly revealing the plots could make the difference. He uncapped his water bottle and took a sip.

"Money laundering using innocent children and unsuspecting adults like Frénie is despicable." Jacob shoved his notebook in his computer case. In less than two months of dating the guy, Frénie had been the unwitting conduit of an estimated billion-pound money-laundering scheme. He slung the strap over his shoulder. "Wonder how widespread Armand's operations are ..."

"Right. A Lambo, a designer wardrobe, and more jewels than most crown heads possess." Ian whistled through his teeth. "And a seaside-cliff estate on Guernsey, purchased in her name. A Crown Protectorate Island, no less."

"Wouldn't mind a place like that." The last drops of water swigged, Jacob capped the bottle. A cash sale two days ago in the town of St. Peter Port, for ten-million-plus pounds. Secret sales typical of wealthy purchasers in the UK seeking anonymity through discrete estate agents. He grinned. Information he and his team now had thanks to Marcus and Ian's all-nighters of research.

"You think Armand expected to hide out on Guernsey?" Ian shoved his phone in his pants pocket.

"The guy's an enigma. Loves children but exploits them." Wooed a woman who could pass for his dead sister. Jacob lumbered to his feet, tossed the water bottle in the waste basket. "We might not have the Priest in hand, but we will, given time. We've uncovered Armand's base in London, arrested his top henchman."

"Tracy's taped interview and Frénie's willingness to testify against him in court are death blows against him." Marcus's phone pinged. "The terrorist financiers who attended the gala, and Mandouri and his goons are in custody."

A hand clapped Jacob's shoulder.

"You all right?" Concern wreathed Marcus's face.

"Yes." Jacob swiped a hand over his jaw. He probably looked as haggard as Ian and Marcus.

"Just received a text. Someone attempted to kill Gorilla Guy last night. He's willing to talk." A slow grin lifted Marcus's cheeks.

A burst of energy jolted through Jacob's body. "What are we waiting for?"

Paper slippers scuffing on the floor, Gorilla Guy entered the police interview room uncuffed. His gray sweats reeked of perspiration and excrement. A far cry from his hand-tailored gray suit and patent leather shoes in Vienna. Red welts encircled his neck from the ligature marks. How his attacker had managed to subdue him long enough to nearly strangle him was a puzzle.

Cement encased Jacob's half-smile. Armand had done the Crown a favor by trying to have his righthand man murdered. "Thank you for speaking with us today."

Taking his seat, Gorilla Guy nodded. Ian started the recordings, informed him of his rights, announced for the CD and DVD the interview was being filmed. Pen in hand, Marcus readied his notebook. Once again, Gorilla Guy declined the offer of legal counsel.

"Will you start by telling us your real name?" Marcus asked.

His voice raspy, Gorilla Guy responded, "John Robert Beecham, born in Liverpool, ninth of April, nineteen eighty."

None of the passports Ian had found matched the information. "What duties did you perform for Armand Découvrir?" Jacob asked.

"For the past twenty years I have been his top lieutenant, fixer, and facilitator."

"For the record, would you please define those duties," Ian said.

"I arranged or carried out executions of non-compliant employees, collected funds from wealthy clients. Set up new operations. Resolved disputes between businesses."

"You mean money laundering clients?" Marcus asked.

"Yes. And other projects. I was the liaison between Armand's ops and Yousef Mandouri's. They occasionally collaborated on certain ventures."

"Such as ..." Marcus said.

"Trafficking illegals."

"Minors?" Icicles fringed Jacob's tone.

"Sometimes." Sweat slicked Bobby's forehead. "And gambling."

"Why were you at the Royal Pavilion a few weeks ago?" Jacob asked.

Smirking, Bobby stared at him so long Jacob thought he wouldn't answer the question.

"To give your sister spending money. I left when I saw you and your girlfriend."

His guess had been right, but hearing the man admit it still wrenched Jacob's gut. "Whose idea was it to plant a cross necklace on the recent victims?"

Bobby's grin widened over a sea of gleaming teeth.

"Were those murders sanctioned by Armand?" Jacob asked.

"Yes. But he didn't know about the cross necklaces or the way I positioned the bodies."

"You were sending us a message, weren't you? Leading us to Armand. Why?" Jacob shifted on his chair.

"Aren't you the bright one?" Bobby said.

"Clue us in," Ian said.

"I wanted a bigger piece of Armand's action, the proceeds." He spread his palms like St. Francis of Assisi. "You know how important it is to feel appreciated. Once he met Frénie, a lot of the—shall we say—rewards I used to receive were going to her."

"Did you sabotage the brakes on her Lamborghini?" Jacob asked.

"All in a morning's work, as they say."

"Was that your idea or Armand's?" Marcus asked.

"I always say, never lose the ability to think for yourself."

"Which means what, precisely?" Ian asked.

"It was my idea. After the wreck, Armand was furious, but I convinced him the job had to be done."

"Did Armand sanction Rat Eyes—Jacques Ibert's, murder?" Jacob asked.

"Armand didn't know a thing about it. Ibert was in the way, tailing the women, wanting money to wipe them out. He'd outlived his usefulness. Run out of the euros a terrorist group paid him to monkey with the hydraulic lift."

"Really?" Hand fisting at his side, Jacob leaned forward. "You seem to know a lot about him. I think you murdered him. And the woman."

"Look at it this way." Bobby shifted on the chair. "His was a life well lived, sacrificing himself and that bimbo to send you a warning. Wasn't sure you caught the significance of planting the bodies at Canary Wharf."

"You mean, placing Ibert's body facing the Shard?" Jacob asked.

"You're smarter than you look." Eyes lasering him, Bobby grinned, lips stretched back over his cavernous-shaped mouth. "But this time you're pinning it on the wrong guy. Like I said, I'm just an enforcer."

Jacob thrust his hand in his pocket. Smart wasn't how he'd describe himself the past three weeks. More like a toddler trying to keep up with a street-smart adult. But something didn't add up. If Bobby was telling the truth, and Armand didn't know about Rat Eyes' death, then who ordered the murder? He motioned Marcus and Ian out of the room.

As they left, the PC on guard duty in the hall stepped inside the interview room and closed the door. Jacob walked them down the hall, kept his voice low. "If Armand didn't know about Ibert's death, what if Bobby committed the murder, or knows who did? He admitted working primarily for Armand but occasionally liaising with Mandouri."

"You're suggesting Mandouri ordered Riley's attempted murder in Antwerp?" Ian asked.

"It's possible. Several terrorists we arrested in June bragged they represented the largest cells in the UK. We now know they worked for Mandouri. They would've been in contact with him during the cruise. And Riles and I were on their radar." Jacob texted Inspector Vlincken and Brussels Interpol.

Will be sending photos of terrorist suspects to
trace on CCTV in relationship to Jacques
Ibert's movements in Antwerp and Brussels.

"And Mandouri and three of his goons were at the same restaurant the night you and Riley dined with Armand." Stifling a yawn, Ian leaned against the wall. "Maybe you disrupted a turf war between Armand and Mandouri. Bobby could've alerted Mandouri you'd be present."

"I suspect Armand is the Priest and the attack on the Shard was in part, a personal vendetta against Interpol and perhaps Riles and myself. Via the gala, he saw a chance to remove his key competitor—Mandouri—and small fry competitors in the local terrorist-financier pool."

"And in the process..." Ian chuckled. "Armand handed us quite a coup."

"I'm on it." Marcus sent several text messages then pocketed his cell. "I requested names and photos of Mandouri's known associates. If we can trace them to Antwerp or Brussels, we'll have additional proof and more groups on our radar." He led the way back to the interview room.

As they took their seats, Marcus said, "We'd like a complete list and details of all Armand's operations and connections to terrorist groups."

"Don't have that. Armand played his cards close to the vest." Bobby scratched his temple. "What's that saying—no honor among thieves?"

"But you ran his ops in Paris and Vienna," Ian said.

Bobby folded his arms across his chest. "What's in it for me?"

"You can hope the Crown Prosecution looks favorably on your help. After all, your boss tried to have you killed last night. Fortunately for you, the prison guards responded swiftly to your defense," Marcus said.

Sucking a breath, Bobby chewed his lips. As the seconds

ticked, he stared toward the wall, then eyed them. "I'll give you what I have."

Inwardly, Jacob heaved a sigh. The info would be a start, but they'd need to move fast on it. "Who's the man known as the Priest?"

A slow grin spread across Bobby's face. "The Priest. Who's that?"

"Are you the Priest?" Jacob asked.

"Define 'priest' for me."

"Not a man ordained to serve in the church. We want the man known as the Priest on the street," Jacob said. "A terrorist group financier."

"Well ... I'd like to say you're talking to him, but in the interest of fair play, being honest and all, it's Armand. He's the Priest. Known for his kindness to others. Always reminding me to make the sign of the cross over somebody before I killed them." Bobby's teeth-baring grin sent shivers down Jacob's spine. "That's what gave me the idea of leaving the necklace on his latest victims. Once he met Frénie."

"Back to the diamond cross necklaces Armand gave Frénie and Tracy." Jacob shifted on his chair. "Were those necklaces given to sanction their deaths?"

Fingers tapping his thighs, Bobby eyed the table so long Jacob's heart sank. He wasn't going to tell them. He'd drag this out into an eternity of worry, uncertainty.

Finally, Bobby locked eyes with him. "Yes. Armand enjoyed toying with you. You not knowing he was grooming your kid sister. Hitting at the heart of what you believe. The people you love."

Blood pounded in Jacob's skull. He fought to slow his breaths. Whatever it took, he had to bring down Armand and his ops. "Tell me. Why would a man who lost his mother and sister to an act of violence become a terrorist financier?"

Bobby shrugged. "He blamed the United States for the bombing. Destroying his country. He vowed to do everything he could to ruin pro-west nations who didn't protect his family. You made him into the terrorist and highly successful financier he became."

Scary what greed and bitterness could do to a person. Jacob crossed his arms over his chest. "Who pushed Riley in front of the bus?"

"Mack Pardy. One of Mandouri's men."

Jacob uncurled his fist in his pocket. *Thank You Lord for exposing one of them.*

"Tell us about the terrorist groups Armand funds," Marcus said.

"For me, it was just a job, moving money around, making sure things ran smoothly. Armand's pet charities meant nothing to me."

"Pet charities?" Jacob asked.

"Terrorist groups. Helping those poor, unfortunate girls at the orphanage find a better life."

"You're a real philanthropist." Jacob pushed back his chair. He ought to feel elated with their breakthrough. Instead, he'd vomit if he had to listen to more of Bobby's depraved mindset. A mindset Bobby had inculcated in Tracy. A child.

45

Ghent, Belgium, Day 20

Breathing in the smell of freshly cut wood, wet paint, and dust motes, Riley crossed the stage of the Ghent Opera House. How good to be back in an opera house. Even for a confrontation.

Annie Verhalen stood centerstage, arms crossed over her sweater, legs braced in her black jeggings like a tiger about to pounce. She shot Riley a sullen-mouthed I-dare-you look. "I suppose you're going to press charges."

What—no admission what she'd planned was wrong? Maybe Jacob and Inspector Vlincken were right. Some people refused to learn their lessons outside prison. Riley stopped three feet from her. "Give me a good reason why I shouldn't."

The young woman slicked her lips. Shifted her weight to the other foot.

"How old are you?"

"Eighteen." The hike of Annie's chin matched her defiant gaze.

"Wow." Riley gentled her tone. "A child prodigy. That's awesome." The kid's life, her whole career lay in front of her. A career she held the power to destroy. If she pressed charges. "Belgian law considers intent to cause bodily harm or death a serious crime."

Not a whit of fear flickered in Annie's face.

"Or don't you see it that way?" What was she dealing with here—a sociopath, a latent psychopath? *God, help me make the right choice.* "I'm disappointed in you. I'd hoped to see remorse. Hear a heartfelt apology."

Annie stared beyond Riley, mouth hardened to stone.

"Very well." Riley crossed her arms. "Maybe the police are right. You're a danger to society. Not just Americans. You deserve to go to prison."

Blanching, Annie stepped back, her face crumpling.

Riley shifted the strap on her shoulder bag. Nothing had gone the way she had hoped. She'd forgiven Annie, but whether she'd learned her lesson and could be trusted not to harm anyone else, was as predictable as a winning lotto ticket.

"Okay then." Riley turned and walked toward Jacob in the wings. Did she have a moral right to see Annie incarcerated? The Bible meted out an ultimate punishment for unrepentant wrongdoers. Her steps faltered. But Jesus pardoned those who'd crucified him.

Maybe Annie's attitude was a typical teenage façade because she expected to be punished. Like Tracy. Riley glanced over her shoulder.

Chin quivering, Annie swiped the tears tracking through her makeup.

Opening her purse, Riley walked over to her and handed her a tissue. "I forgive you for what you tried to do to me."

Frowning, Annie dabbed the bleeding makeup. "I—I don't understand."

"I'm a Christian. My faith requires me to forgive those who hurt me. But forgiveness isn't a few glib words, it must come from the heart." Riley touched Annie's arm. "Despite what you did, Jesus loves you. He always will. And I do forgive you. I'd like us to be friends."

Fist on her hip, Annie snorted. "Friends?"

"Next week Dortmund Opera House is holding auditions for a Queen of the Night." Riley handed Annie a business card. "I wrote the information on the back."

"So?" Annie rolled her eyes and snatched the card.

"I'll look for you at the cattle call."

"But—" Annie blinked, stepped back. "How can I—the trial—"

"I've decided not to press charges. But I want your word of honor you'll never harm anyone again or treat a colleague the way you treated me."

"I promise." Annie's shoulders sagged. "Thank you. And I am sorry I tried to hurt you. I was so jealous."

"Singing is a tough profession and full of uncertainties." Riley squeezed Annie's arm. "Learn to look for the good in other people." Smiling, she pulled Annie into a hug. "Now go wow the world with your stunning voice and sweet spirit."

Sweet spirit? Wow, that was a new one. Standing in the offstage wing, Jacob glanced up from his phone screen. At least Annie hadn't clawed out Riley's eyes. Hopefully not because of his presence.

He reviewed the transaction on his phone, then punched purchase. Done. Two weeks from now he and Riles could soak up the rays in Wörthersee, Austria, their first vacation. Alone. Time to talk about them. Their future. By then, he should have finalized new school arrangements for Tracy.

A text pinged his cell. Marcus.

> Interpol confirmation: two of Mandouri's men were captured on Brussels and London CCTV, meeting with Ibert.

Chances were, Mandouri hired Ibert to sabotage Riley's hydraulic lift, then ordered his killing. Which meant Mandouri was aware of Riles' career, given the female victim at the double murder site. The back of Jacob's neck prickled. Thank God, Mandouri and his henchmen were behind bars.

Another text message pinged his phone. HQ. Von Bingen.

> Yes, take the weekend off. You've earned it.
> Job well done, Coulter.

Great. He and Tracy could stay in Ghent for Riles' final performance as the Queen of the Night. With Mandouri's arrest and the Belgian saboteur dead, he and Vlincken had convinced the *Vlaamse Oper's* general manager to restore Riles' final performance of her contract, provided there were undercover police in the house.

Even without the hydraulic lift shtick, why Riles wanted to sing the role again, he'd never understand. Maybe it was her finish-the-job streak, a need to hoist the flag atop the hill. Whatever the reason, he loved her for it.

He texted von Bingen.

> Thanks.

But three dots bounced on his screen.

> I'll expect you in the office Monday morning, thorough report in hand. Your strategy for catching the Priest.

> Already on it.

Armand would be sorry he'd ever messed with him, Tracy, Riles. The man might fancy himself a Goliath, but David and his God had toppled him and the Philistines. History had a way of repeating itself.

Another text message pinged. He scrolled to Frénie's latest communique.

> Merci, my dear Jacob. I had no problem passing through British immigration. Managing my luggage on the train to Paris was a nightmare. But nothing like nearly being bombed to death. After that, I think I can cope with anything. Well ... maybe not everything.

Not arresting her for the car collision was up to the Brits. But then, she'd promised to testify against Armand once he was caught and went to trial. Her police interview had yielded little of interest, other than using her, unwittingly, to disperse funds and order her death.

Riley walked toward him, eyes glistening.

Closing the distance between them, he slid his arm around her shoulders. "Sure you made the right decision?"

"I think Annie needs a second chance."

"Don't let the Armands of this world hear you."

"Far as I'm concerned, he's used up his chances."

Sighing, Jacob drank in her auburn curls, the spunk in her eyes. "When's the last time I told you this?" He swung her to him, savoring the scent of her Chanel No. 5. "You're an amazing woman, Riles."

She tilted her face up to him, her smile saucy. "I try to be."

Chuckling, he snuggled her to his chest, then pressed his mouth to hers and kissed her, tasting strawberries in her lip gloss. Adam's apple working, his voice went hoarse. "I'm glad you're mine."

"Hmm ..." She held up her left hand and rocked her fingers.

The diamond's facets glittered beneath the stage lights. "As long as you don't ask me to return your engagement ring."

The knots in his chest released in a flood. *Thank You, God.* She wasn't ready to ditch him. He still had a chance.

"I'm not ready to commit to a wedding date. There are things we need to talk through first." She trailed her fingers over his cheek. "But I love you, and with all my heart I want to marry you."

"Fair enough." He longed to wake up beside her every morning, discover new facets of her personality, her likes and dislikes and little quirks. He shoved his hand in his pocket. With terrorists, she'd plunge headlong into danger, but with relationships, she inched forward with caution. Somehow, he had to get to the bottom of that. *God, help me become what she needs, wants in a husband.*

"See that seven-foot ramp over there, the Harley beside it?" She pointed upstage.

He eyed the metal scaffolding, the wicked-looking chute aimed at the edge of the stage. The silver-and-black Harley. His heart skidded a beat. "Yes?"

"Today I have to master cycling down the slope without spinning into the orchestra pit."

"Oh, Riles." He laughed. No doubt, she'd ace it. "What am I going to do with you?"

Eyes twinkling, she jabbed his ribs. "Rescue me, of course."

AUTHOR NOTES

I am deeply indebted to the many people who played a part in the crafting and publication of *Death in High Places*. Many thanks to fellow Scrivenings Press author, Delores Topliff, for suggesting the series title, *Troubled Waters*. Without the brainstorming input of my sister, Susan B. Pearcy, this story would be languishing on the computer. Many thanks also to Steve Ringenbach, a US Marine, for guidance on bombmaking, and story input from Robert C. Goodwin and Sandra Goodwin.

Huge kudos and gratitude are due Robin Larin of robineditorial.com, for her insightful developmental edits on this manuscript. The book is a far better story because of her suggestions.

Without the assistance of Lynne Wilson, a lifelong friend in the UK, the London/UK portion of the story would have been seriously flawed. Little did I realize our daytrips in 2019 would surface in a novel. I am indebted to Lynne for verifying things at the Royal Pavilion and for contacting relatives and friends to help me with this book: Sue Osbourne for questions about the Shard and Helen Bryan, a former PC with the Metropolitan Police, who kindly typed seven, single-spaced pages of details on every aspect of British police procedures and issues addressed in this novel. Any errors in the police procedures and locales in this book are solely those of the author.

Because this is a work of fiction, liberties were taken with elevators and avant-garde opera staging at the *Vlaamse Oper* in Antwerp and the fictional directors of Regent's Opera in London. The *Vlaamse Oper* is a great place to perform, and I wanted to feature Antwerp in another novel. And of course, our family's favorite Belgian chocolate shop had to appear, too: Burie's Chocolatier at Nationalstraat, 4.

As a Christian, I believe every aspect of writing a novel requires prayer. Without the faithful prayers of Peggy A. Bell, Susan B. Pearcy, Amy Amenu-Zotter, authors Delores Topliff and Patricia Bradley, the manuscript would not have met the Scrivenings Press deadline. Many, many thanks, my dear friends.

And to my Lord and Savior, Jesus Christ, thank You for fulfilling a little girl's dream of one day becoming a published novelist.

BOOK CLUB DISCUSSION QUESTIONS

1. Have you ever been in Jacob's shoes, torn between important commitments in your job and family obligations? How did this affect you emotionally? What solutions helped you balance the demands?

2. Have you ever lived in Europe or a foreign country? Was that a difficult adjustment? Did the experience change your perspective of your native culture and homeland? What did you enjoy most about your time abroad?

3. Riley is terrified of heights but determined to fulfill her contract. Have you lived through traumatic events? How did you deal with the aftereffects?

4. She turns to emotional eating as a coping mechanism. Have you ever used eating or a specific activity to relieve pressure?

5. Jacob fears he'll lose Riley; that she'll call off their engagement, or that terrorists will kill her. Do you feel his upbringing in boarding schools contributed to his fears?

6. Riley appreciates his protectiveness but worries it could grow into the overbearing control her father exerted over her. Is she right to be concerned?

ABOUT THE AUTHOR

Author Sara L. Jameson makes her home in the desert southwest. When Sara isn't working on a novel, she loves dog sitting, reading, cooking, and gardening. In addition to romantic suspense, she also writes historical novels often set in WWII. She loves to write about women facing challenging situations who display heroism and courage and grow in their Christian faith. Her sense of humor has been known to creep into her books.

As a child she dreamed of becoming a singer and a writer. Having done the singing bit, she is thrilled to pursue a career in writing. She enjoys editing and helping writers develop their skills.

ALSO BY SARA L. JAMESON

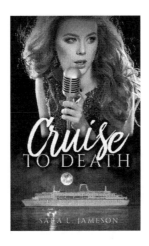

Cruise to Death

Troubled Waters - Book One

Winner of the 2020 Scrivenings Press

Get Pubbed Contest!

When opera singer Riley Williams agrees to sub as a musical-theater performer on a luxury Rhine/Moselle River boat cruise, she gets more than she bargained for. Not only does she have to come up with 250 Broadway songs, she must dance with the male passengers. Dance—the subject she nearly failed in her conservatory courses, and the cause of her recent flop in an opera house. To make matters worse, she overhears two terrorists at a café in Antwerp, Belgium, discussing the transfer of deadly Agent X to the highest bioterrorist bidders.

Interpol Agent Jacob Coulter, an anti-terrorism desk analyst in Brussels, Belgium, insists on serving as an undercover agent after his best friend Noel is murdered by terrorists from the cell he infiltrated in Brussels. Shortly before Noel dies, he manages to tell Jacob snippets of the terrorists' plans. Plans that seem to involve the same river boat cruise Riley is on.

When Interpol learns of Riley's encounter with terrorists at the café, Jacob's supervisor insists he work with her to identify the terrorists and retrieve Agent X. But their relationship is fraught with distrust because of Riley's suspicious past and a romantic attraction neither of them wants.

MORE ROMANTIC SUSPENSE FROM SCRIVENINGS PRESS

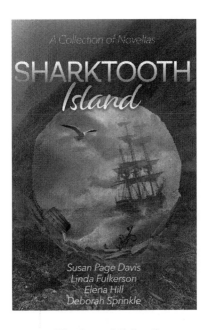

Sharktooth Island

A fabled island that no one dares to tame.

This collection contains four novellas:

***Book 1 - Out of the Storm** (1830)* by Susan Page Davis

Laura Bryant sails with her father and his three-man crew on his small coastal trading schooner. After a short stay in Jamaica, where she meets Alex Dryden, an officer on another ship, the Bryants set out for their home in New England.

In a storm, they are blown off course east of Savannah, Georgia, to a foreboding island. Captain Bryant tells his daughter he's heard tales of that isle. It's impossible to land on, though it looks green and inviting from a distance. It has no harbor but is surrounded by dangerous rocks and cliffs.

Pirates outrun the storm and decide to bury a cache of treasure on this island and return for it later. On board is Alex, whom the cutthroats captured in Jamaica and forced to work for them. Alex risks his own life to escape the pirates and tries to help Laura and Captain Bryant outwit them. Beneath the deadly struggle, romance blossoms for Laura.

Book 2 - *A Passage of Chance* (*1893*) by Linda Fulkerson

Orphaned at a young age, Melody Lampert longs to escape the loveless home of the grandmother who begrudgingly raised her. Stripped of her inheritance due to her grandmother's resentments, Melody discovers her name remains on the deed of one property—an obscure island off the Georgia coast that she shares with her cousin. But when he learns the island may contain a hidden pirate treasure, he's determined to cheat her out of her share.

Ship's mechanic Padric Murphy made a vow to his dying father—break the curse that has plagued their family for generations. To do so, he must return what was taken from Sharktooth Island decades earlier—a pair of rare gold pieces. His opportunity to right the wrong arrives when his new employer sets sail to explore the island.

After a series of unexplainable mishaps occur, endangering Padric and his boss's beautiful cousin Melody, he fears his chance of breaking the curse may be ruined. But is the island's greed thwarting his plans? Or the greed of someone else?

Book 3 - *Island Mayhem* (*1937*) by Elena Hill

Louise Krause stopped piloting to pursue nursing, but when money got too tight she was forced to give up her dreams and start ferrying around a playboy who managed to excel during the Great Depression. When a routine aerial tour turns south, Louise is unable to save the plane.

After crash landing, the cocky pilot is stranded. She longs to escape the uninhabited island, but her makeshift raft sinks, and she and her companions are in even worse trouble. Can Louise learn to trust the others in order to survive, or will the island's curse and potential sabotage lead to her demise?

Book 4 - *After the Storm* (*present day*) by Deborah Sprinkle

Mercedes Baxter inherited two passions from her father—a love for Sharktooth Island, a spit of land in the middle of the ocean left to her in his will, and a dedication to the study of the flora and fauna on and around its rocky landscape.

For the last five years, since graduating from college, Mercy led a peaceful, simple life on the island with only her cat, Hawkeye, for company. Through grant money she obtained from a conservancy in Savannah, she could live on her island while studying and writing about the plants and animals there. Life was perfect.

But when a hurricane hits the island, Mercy's life changes for good. Her high school sweetheart, Liam Stewart, shows up to help her with repairs, and ignites the flame that has never quite died away. And if that's not enough, while assessing the damage to the island, they make a discovery that puts both their lives in danger.

Get your copy here:

https://scrivenings.link/sharktoothisland

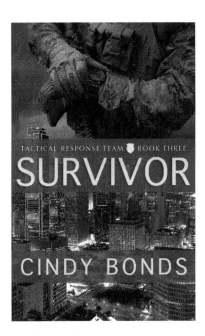

Survivor

Book Three of the Tactical Response Team series

As the TRT reels from past attacks, Jeff Powers is determined to figure out who wants them gone. But on the job, he becomes distracted by a beautiful doctor dealing with a stalker. While helping Dr. Shelby During, Jeff falls deeper and deeper into a strange plot that puts both in grave danger.

Will Shelby's secret finally reveal who wants the TRT gone and why?

Get your copy here:

https://scrivenings.link/survivor

Scrivenings
PRESS
Quench your thirst for story.
www.ScriveningsPress.com

Stay up-to-date on your favorite books and authors with our free e-newsletters.

ScriveningsPress.com

Made in the USA
Columbia, SC
19 February 2023